SPELLBOUND

FANTASY STORIES
CHOSEN BY
DIANA WYNNE JONES

KINGFISHER

CONTENTS

THE PEASANT AND THE DEVIL

THE BROTHERS GRIMM

THERE WAS ONCE upon a time a peasant who had been working in his field, and as twilight had set in, he was making ready for the journey home, when he saw a heap of burning coals in the middle of his field, and when, full of astonishment, he went up to it, a little black devil was sitting on the live coals.

"Do you sit upon a treasure?" inquired the peasant.

"Yes, in trust," replied the Devil, "on a treasure which contains more gold and silver than you have ever seen in your life!"

"The treasure lies in my field and belongs to me," said the peasant.

"It is yours," answered the Devil, "if you will for two years give me the half of everything your field produces. Money I have enough of, but I have a desire for the fruits of the earth."

The peasant agreed to the bargain.

"In order, however, that no dispute may arise about the division," said he, "everything that is above ground shall belong to you, and what is under the earth to me."

The Devil was quite satisfied with that, but the cunning peasant had sown turnips. Now when the time for harvest came, the Devil appeared and wanted to take away his crop; but he found nothing but the yellow withered leaves, while the peasant, quite pleased, was digging up his turnips.

"You have had the best of it for once," said the Devil, "but the next time that won't do. What grows above ground shall be yours, and what is under it, mine."

"I am willing," replied the peasant.

When, however, the time came to sow, the peasant did not again sow turnips, but wheat.

The grain became ripe, and the peasant went into the field and cut the full stalks down to the ground. When the Devil came, he found nothing but the stubble, and went away in a fury down into a cleft in the rocks.

"That is the way to cheat the Devil," said the peasant, and went and fetched away the treasure.

BORIS CHERNEVSKY'S HANDS

JANE YOLEN

BORIS CHERNEVSKY, son of the Famous Flying Chernevskys and nephew to the galaxy's second greatest juggler, woke up unevenly. That is to say, his left foot and right hand lagged behind in the morning rituals.

Feet over the side of the bed, wiggling the recalcitrant left toes and moving the sluggish right shoulder, Boris thought about his previous night's performance.

"Inept" had been Uncle Misha's kindest criticism. In fact, most of what he had yelled was untranslatable, and Boris was glad that his own Russian was as fumbling as his fingers. It had not been a happy evening. He ran his slow hands through his thick blond hair and sighed, wondering – and not for the first time – if he had been adopted as an infant or exchanged *in utero* for a scholar's clone. How else to explain his general awkwardness?

He stood slowly, balancing gingerly because his left foot was now asleep, and practised a few passes with imaginary *na* clubs. He had made his way to eight in the air and was starting an over-the-shoulder pass, when the clubs slipped and clattered to the floor. Even in his imagination he was a klutz.

His uncle Misha said it was eye-and-ear co-ordination, that the sound of the clubs and the rhythm of their passing were what made the fine juggler. And his father said the same about flying: that one had to hear the trapeze and calculate its swing by both eye and ear. But Boris was not convinced.

"It's in the hands," he said disgustedly, looking down at his five-fingered disasters. They were big-knuckled and grained like wood. He flexed them and could feel the right moving just a fraction slower than the left. "It's all in the hands. What I wouldn't give for a better pair."

"And what *would* you give, Boris Chernevsky?" The accent was Russian, or rather Georgian. Boris looked up, expecting to see his uncle.

There was no one in the trailer.

Boris turned around twice and looked under the bed. Sometimes the circus little people played tricks, hiding in closets and making sounds like old clothes singing. Their minds moved in strange ways, and Boris was one of their favourite gulls. He was so easily fooled.

"Would you, for example, give your soul?" The voice was less Georgian, more Siberian now. A touch of Tartar, but low and musical.

"What's a soul?" Boris asked, thinking that adopted children or clones probably weren't allowed any anyway. "Two centuries ago," the voice said, and sighed with what sounded like a Muscovite gurgle, "everyone had a soul and no one wanted to sell. Today everyone is willing to sell, only no one seems to have one."

By this time, Boris had walked completely around the inside of the trailer, examining the underside of chairs, lifting the samovar lid. He was convinced he was beginning to go crazy. "From dropping so many imaginary *na* clubs on my head," he told himself out loud. He sat down on one of the chairs and breathed heavily, his chin resting on his left hand. He didn't yet completely trust his right. After all, he had only been awake and moving for ten minutes.

Something materialized across the table from him. It was a tall, gaunt old woman whose hair looked as if birds might be nesting in it. Nasty birds. With razored talons and beaks permanently stained with blood. He thought he spotted guano in her bushy eyebrows.

"So," the apparition said to him, "*hands* are the topic of our discussion." Her voice, now that she was visible, was no longer melodic but grating, on the edge of a scold.

"Aren't you a bit old for such tricks, Baba?" asked Boris, trying to be both polite and steady at once. His grandmother, may she rest in pieces on the meteorite that had broken up her circus flight to a rim world, had taught him to address old women with respect. "After all, a grandmother should be . . ."

"Home tending the fire and the children, I suppose." The old woman spat into the corner, raising dust devils. "The centuries roll on and on, but the Russian remains the same. The Soviets did wonders to free women as long as they were young. Old women, we still have the fire and the grandchildren." Her voice began to get louder and higher. *Peh*, she spat again. "Well, I for one have solved the grandchildren problem."

Boris hastened to reach out and soothe her. All he needed now, on top of last evening's disastrous performance, was to have a screaming battle with some crazy old lady when Uncle Misha and his parents, the Famous Flying Chernevesky Family, were asleep in the small rooms on either side of the trailer. "Shh, shh," he cautioned her.

She grabbed at his reaching right hand and held it in an incredibly strong grip. Viced between her two claws, his hand could not move at all. "This, then," she asked rhetorically, "is the offending member?"

He pulled back with all his strength, embarrassment lending him muscles, and managed to snatch the hand back. He held it under the table and tried to knead feeling back into the fingers. When he looked up at her, she was smiling at him. It was not a pretty smile.

"Yes," he admitted.

She scraped at a wen on her chin with a long, dirty fingernail. "It *seems* an ordinary-enough hand," she said. "Large knuckles. Strong veins. I've known peasants and tsars that would have envied you that hand."

"*Ordinary*," Boris began in a hoarse whisper and stopped. Then, forcing himself to speak, he began again. "Ordinary is the trouble. A juggler has to have *extraordinary* hands. A juggler's hands must be spider-web strong, bird's-wing quick." He smiled at his metaphors. Perhaps he was a poet-clone.

The old woman leaned back in her chair and stared

at a spot somewhat over Boris's head. Her watery blue eyes never wavered. She mumbled something under her breath, then sat forward again. "Come," she said. "I have a closetful. All you have to do is choose."

"Choose what?" asked Boris.

"*Hands!*" screeched the old woman. "Hands, you idiot. Isn't that what you want?"

"*Boris*," came his uncle's familiar voice through the thin walls. "*Boris*, I need my sleep."

"I'll come. I'll come," whispered Boris, just to get rid of the hag. He shooed her out the door with a movement of his hands. As usual, the right was a beat behind the left, even after half a morning.

He hadn't actually meant to go anywhere with her, just manoeuvre her out of the trailer, but when she leaped down the steps with surprising speed and climbed into a vehicle that looked like a mug with a large china steering rudder sticking out of the middle, his feet stepped forward of their own accord.

He fell down the stairs.

"Perhaps you could use a new pair of feet, too," said the old woman.

Boris stood up and automatically brushed off his clothes, a gesture his hands knew without prompting.

The old woman touched the rudder, and the mug moved closer to Boris.

He looked on both sides and under the mug for evidence of its motor. It moved away from him as soundlessly as a hovercraft, but when he stuck his foot under it cautiously, he could feel no telltale movement of the air.

"How do you *do* that?" he asked.

"Do what?"

"The mug," he said.

"Magic." She made a strange gesture with her hands. "After all, I am Baba Yaga."

The name did not seem to impress Boris, who was now on his hands and knees peering under the vehicle.

"Baba *Yaga*," the old woman repeated as if the name itself were a charm. "How do you do," Boris murmured, more to the ground than to her.

"You know . . . the witch . . . Russia . . . magic . . ." Her voice trailed off. When Boris made no response, she made another motion with her hands, but this time it was an Italian gesture, and not at all nice.

Boris saw the gesture and stood up. After all, the circus was his life. He knew that magic was not real, only a matter of quick hands. "Sure," he said, imitating her last gesture. His right hand clipped his left bicep. He winced.

"*Get in!*" the old woman shouted.

Boris shrugged. But his politeness was complicated by curiosity. He wanted to see the inside anyway. There had to be an engine somewhere. He hoped she would let him look at it. He was good with circuitry and microchips. In a free world, he could have chosen his occupation. Perhaps he might even have been a computer programmer. But as he was a member of the Famous Flying Chernevsky family, he had no choice. He climbed over the lip of the mug and, to his chagrin, got stuck. The old woman had to pull him the rest of the way.

"You really are a klutz," she said. "Are you sure all you want is hands?"

But Boris was not listening. He was searching the inside of the giant mug. He had just made his third trip around when it took off into the air. In less than a minute, the circus and its ring of bright trailers were only a squiggle on the horizon.

They passed quickly over the metroplexes that jigsawed across the continent and hovered over one of the twenty forest preserves. Baba Yaga pulled on the china rudder, and the mug dropped straight down. Boris fell sideways and clung desperately to the mug's rim. Only a foot above the treetops the mug slowed, wove its way through a complicated pattern of branches, and finally landed in a small clearing.

The old woman hopped nimbly from the flier. Boris followed more slowly.

A large presence loomed to one side of the forest clearing. It seemed to be moving towards them. An enormous bird, Boris thought. He had the impression of talons. Then he looked again. It was not a bird, but a hut, and it was walking.

Boris pointed at it. "Magic?" he asked, his mouth barely shaping the syllables.

"Feet," she answered.

"Feet?" He looked down at his feet, properly encased in Naugahyde. He looked at hers, in pointed lizard leather. Then he looked again at the house. It was lumbering towards him on two scaly legs that ended in claws. They looked like giant replicas of the chicken feet that always floated nails-up in his mother's chicken soup. When she wasn't practising being a Famous Flying Chernevsky, she made her great-great-grandmother's recipes. He preferred her in the air.

"Feet," Boris said again, this time feeling slightly sick.

"But the subject is hands," Baba Yaga said. Then she turned from him and strolled over to the hut. They met halfway across the clearing. She greeted it, and it gave a half-bob, as if curtseying, then squatted down. The old woman opened the door and went in.

Boris followed. One part of him was impressed with the special effects, the slow part of him. The fast part was already convinced it was magic.

The house inside was even more unusual than the house outside. It was one big cupboard. Doors and shelves lined every inch of wall space. And each door and cupboard carried a hand-lettered sign. The calligraphy differed from door to door, drawer to drawer, and it took a few minutes before Boris could make out the pattern. But he recognized the lettering from the days when he had helped his uncle Misha script broadsides for their act. There was irony in the fact that he had always had a good calligraphic hand.

In Roman Bold were **Newt, eye of; Adder, tongue of;** and similar biological ingredients. Then there were botanical drawers in Carolingian Italic: **Thornapple juice, Amanita,** and the like. Along one wall, however, in basic Foundational Bold were five large cupboards labelled simply: **Heads, Hands, Feet, Ears, Eyes.**

The old woman walked up to that wall and threw open the door marked **Hands.**

"There," she said.

Inside, on small wooden stands, were hundreds of pairs of hands. When the light fell on them, they waved dead-white fingers as supple and mindless as worms.

"Which pair do you want to try?" Baba Yaga asked.

Boris stared. "But . . ." he managed at last, "they're miniatures."

"One size fits all," Baba Yaga said. "That's something I learned in the twentieth century." She dragged a pair out of the closet on the tiny stand. Plucking the hands from the stand, she held them in her palm. The hands began to stretch and grow, inching their way to normal size. They remained the colour of custard scum.

Boris read the script on the stand to himself. **Lover's Hands.** He hesitated.

"Try them," the old woman said again, thrusting them at him. Her voice was compelling.

Boris took the left hand between his thumb and forefinger. The hand was as slippery as rubber, and wrinkled as a prune. He pulled it on his left hand, repelled at the feel. Slowly the hand moulded itself to his, rearranging its skin over his bones. As Boris watched, the left hand took on the colour of new cream, then quickly tanned to a fine, overall, healthy-looking beige. He flexed the fingers, and the left hand reached over and stroked his right. At the touch, he felt a stirring of desire that seemed to move sluggishly up his arm, across his shoulder, down his back, and grip his loins. Then the left hand reached over and picked up its mate. Without waiting for a signal from him, it lovingly pulled the right hand on, fitting each finger with infinite care.

As soon as both hands were the same tanned tone, the strong, tapered, polished nails with the quarter-moons winking up at him, Boris looked over at the witch.

He was surprised to see that she was no longer old but, in fact, only slightly mature, with fine bones under a translucent skin. Her blue eyes seemed to appraise him, then offer an invitation. She smiled, her mouth thinned down with desire. His hands preceded him to her side, and then she was in his arms. The hands stroked her windtossed hair.

"You have," she breathed into his ear, "a lover's hands."

"Hands!" He suddenly remembered, and with his teeth ripped the right hand off. Underneath were his own remembered big knuckles. He flexed them experimentally. They were wonderfully slow in responding.

The old woman in his arms cackled and repeated, "A lover's hands."

His slow right hand fought with the left, but managed at last to scratch off the outer layer. His left hand felt raw, dry, but comfortingly familiar.

The old woman was still smiling an invitation. She had crooked teeth and large pores. There was a dark moustache on her upper lip.

Boris picked up the discarded hands by the tips of the fingers and held them up before the witch's watery blue eyes.

"Not *these* hands," he said.

She was already reaching into the closet for another pair.

Boris pulled the hands on quickly, glancing only briefly at the label. **Surgeon's Hands.** They were supple-fingered and moved nervously in the air as if searching for something to do.

Finally they hovered over Baba Yaga's forehead. Boris felt as if he had eyes in his fingertips, and suddenly saw the old woman's skin as a map stretched taut across a landscape of muscle and bone. He could sense the subtle traceries of veins and read the directions of the bloodlines. His right hand moved down the bridge of her nose, turned left at the cheek, and descended to her chin. The second finger tapped her wen, and he could hear the faint echo of his knock.

"I could remove that easily," he found himself saying.

The witch pulled the surgeon's hands from him herself. "Leave me my wen. Leave me my own face," she said angrily. "It is the stage setting for my magic. Surgeon's hands indeed."

Remembering the clowns in their makeup, the wire-walkers in their sequined leotards, the ringmaster in his tie and tails – costumes that had not changed over the centuries of circus – Boris had to agree. He looked down again at his own hands. He moved the fingers. The right were still laggards. But for the first time he heard and saw how they moved. He dropped his hands to his sides and beat a tattoo on his outer thighs. Three against two went the rhythm, the left hitting the faster beat. He increased it to seven against five, and smiled. The right would always be slower, he knew that now.

"It's not in the hands," he said.

Baba Yaga looked at him quizzically. Running a hand through her bird's-nest hair and fluffing up her eyebrows, she spoke. But it was Uncle Misha's voice that emerged between her crooked teeth. "Hands are the daughters of the eye and ear."

"How do you *do* that?" Boris asked.

"Magic," she answered, smiling. She moved her fingers mysteriously, then turned and closed the cupboard doors.

Boris smiled at her back, and moved his own fingers in imitation. Then he went out the door of the house and fell down the steps.

"Maybe you'd like a new pair of feet," the witch called after him. "I have Fred Astaire's. I have John Travolta's. I have Mohammed Ali's." She came out of the house, caught up with Boris, and pulled him to a standing position.

"Were they jugglers?" asked Boris.

"No," Baba Yaga said, shaking her head. "No. But they had soul."

Boris didn't answer. Instead he climbed into the mug and gazed fondly at his hands as the mug took off and headed towards the horizon and home.

THE HOBGOBLIN'S HAT

TOVE JANSSON
from Finn Family Moomintroll

The Moomins are a family of daylight-loving Finnish trolls who live in a tall, round house in a remote valley by the sea. In winter they hibernate. When spring comes they wake and so do the other folk in the house: the two Snorks, who look rather like the Moomins, a Hemulen (who wears a dress and collects stamps), a grumpy Muskrat, small Sniff and the strange, wandering Snufkin. On their first walk after waking, Moomintroll, Sniff and Snufkin find a shiny top hat.

Very rashly, they bring it home.

In which Moomintroll suffers an uncomfortable change and takes his revenge on the Ant-lion.*

ONE WARM SUMMER DAY it was raining softly in the Valley of the Moomins, so they all decided to play hide-and-seek indoors. Sniff stood in the corner with

* In case you don't know, an Ant-lion is a crafty insect who digs himself down into the sand leaving a small, round hole above him. Into this hole unsuspecting little animals fall and then get caught by the Ant-lion, who pops up from the bottom of the hole and devours them.

You can read all about this in the Encyclopaedia if you don't believe me – Translator's note.

his nose in his paws and counted up to ten before he turned round and began hunting – first in the ordinary hiding-places and then in the extraordinary ones.

Moomintroll lay under the veranda table feeling rather worried – it wasn't a good place. Sniff would be sure to lift the tablecloth, and there he would be, stuck. He looked about, and then caught sight of the tall, black hat which stood in a corner. That would be a brilliant idea! Sniff would never think of looking under the hat. Moomintroll stole quietly to the corner and pulled the hat over his head. It didn't reach further than his middle, but if he made himself very small and tucked in his tail he would be quite invisible. He giggled to himself when he heard all the others being found, one after another. The Hemulen had obviously hidden himself under the sofa again – he could never find a better place. And now they were all running about searching for Moomintroll.

He waited until he was afraid they would get bored with the search, and then he crept out of the hat, stuck his head through the door and said, "Look at me!" Sniff stared at him for a long time, then he said, rather unkindly, "Look at yourself!"

"Who's that?" whispered the Snork, but the others only shook their heads and continued to stare at Moomintroll.

Poor little chap! He had been turned into a very strange animal indeed under the Hobgoblin's hat. All his fat parts had become thin, and everything that was small had grown big. And the strangest thing about it was that he himself didn't realize what was the matter.

"I thought I'd surprise you all," he said taking an

uncertain step forward on his long, spindly legs. "You've no idea where I've been!"

"It doesn't interest us," said the Snork, "but you're certainly ugly enough to surprise anybody."

"You are unkind," said Moomintroll sadly. "I suppose you got tired of hunting. What shall we do now?"

"First of all perhaps you should introduce yourself," said the Snork Maiden, stiffly. "We don't know who you are, do we?"

Moomintroll looked at her incredulously, but then it dawned on him that perhaps this was a new game. He laughed delightedly and said, "I'm the king of California!"

"And I'm the Snork Maiden," said the Snork Maiden. "This is my brother."

"I'm called Sniff," said Sniff.

"I'm Snufkin," said Snufkin.

"Oh, dear! How boring you all are," said Moomintroll. "Couldn't you have thought of something more original! Now let's go out – I think the weather's clearing." And he went down the steps into the garden, followed by a rather surprised and suspicious little trio.

"Who's that?" asked the Hemulen, who was sitting in front of the house counting the stamens of a sunflower.

"It's the king of California, I think," said the Snork Maiden.

"Is he going to live here?" asked the Hemulen.

"That's for Moomintroll to decide," said Sniff. "I wonder where he's got to."

Moomintroll laughed. "You really are quite funny at times," he said. "Shall we go and look for Moomintroll?"

"Do you know him?" asked Snufkin.

"Ye-es," said Moomintroll. "Rather well as a matter of fact." He was thoroughly enjoying the new game and thought he was doing rather well at it.

"How did you come to know him?" asked the Snork Maiden.

"We were born at the same time," said Moomintroll, still bursting with laughter. "But he's an impossible fellow, you know! You simply can't have him in the house!"

"How dare you talk about Moomintroll like that!" said the Snork Maiden, fiercely. "He's the best Moomin in the world, and we think a great deal of him."

This was almost too much for Moomintroll.

"Really?" he said. "Personally I think he's an absolute pest."

Then the Snork Maiden began to cry.

"Go away!" said the Snork to Moomintroll. "Otherwise we shall have to sit on your head."

"All right, all right," Moomintroll said, soothingly. "It's only a game, isn't it? I'm awfully glad you think so much of me."

"But we *don't*," screamed Sniff, shrilly. "Take away this ugly king who runs down our Moomintroll."

And they threw themselves on to poor Moomintroll. He was much too surprised to defend himself, and when he began to get angry it was too late. So when Moominmamma came out on the steps he was lying underneath a large pile of flailing paws and tails.

"What are you doing there, children?" she cried. "Stop fighting at once!"

"They're walloping the king of California," sniffed the Snork Maiden. "And it serves him right."

Moomintroll crawled out of the scrum, tired out and angry.

"Mother," he cried. "They started it. Three against one! It's not fair!"

"I quite agree," said the Moominmamma seriously. "However, I expect you had teased them. But who are you, my little beast?"

"Oh, please stop this awful game," wailed Moomintroll. "It isn't funny any more. I am Moomintroll, and you are my mother. And that's that!"

"*You* aren't Moomintroll," said the Snork Maiden, scornfully. "He has beautiful little ears, but yours look like kettle holders!"

Moomintroll felt quite confused and took hold of a pair of enormous crinkly ears. "But I *am* Moomintroll!" he burst out in despair. "Don't you believe me?"

"Moomintroll has a nice little tail, just about the right size, but yours is like a chimney sweep's brush," said the Snork.

And, oh dear, it was true! Moomintroll felt behind him with a trembling paw.

"Your eyes are like soup plates," said Sniff. "Moomintroll's are small and kind!"

"Yes, exactly," Snufkin agreed.

"You are an impostor!" decided the Hemulen.

"Isn't there anyone who believes me?" Moomintroll

pleaded. "Look carefully at me, Mother. You must know your own Moomintroll."

Moominmamma looked carefully. She looked into his frightened eyes for a very long time, and then she said quietly, "Yes, you are my Moomintroll." And at the same moment he began to change. His ears, eyes, and tail began to shrink, and his nose and tummy grew, until at last he was his old self again.

"It's all right now, my dear," said Moominmamma. "You see, I shall always know you whatever happens." A little later on, Moomintroll and the Snork were sitting in one of their secret hiding-places – the one under the jasmine bush which was hidden by a curtain of green leaves.

"Yes, but you *must* have done something to change you," the Snork was saying.

Moomintroll shook his head. "I didn't notice anything unusual," he said. "And I didn't say any dangerous words either."

"But perhaps you stepped into a fairy ring," suggested the Snork.

"Not that I know of," said Moomintroll. "I sat the whole time under that black hat that we use as a wastepaper basket."

"In the *hat*?" asked the Snork, suspiciously.

Moomintroll nodded, and they both thought for a long time. Then suddenly they burst out together, "It must be . . . !" and stared at each other.

"Come on!" said the Snork.

They went on to the veranda and crept up to the hat very cautiously.

"It looks rather ordinary," said the Snork. "Unless

you consider that a top hat is always somewhat extraordinary, of course."

"But how can we find out if it *was* that?" asked Moomintroll. "*I'm* not going to get into it again!"

"Perhaps we could lure somebody else into it," suggested the Snork.

"But that would be a low-down trick," said Moomintroll. "How should we know that he would be all right again?"

"What about an enemy?" suggested the Snork.

"Hm," said the Moomintroll. "Do you know of one?"

"The Pig-Swine," said the Snork.

Moomintroll shook his head. "He's too big."

"Well, the Ant-lion, then?" the Snork suggested.

"That's a good idea," Moomintroll agreed. "He once pulled my mother down into a hole and sprayed sand into her eyes."

So they set out to look for the Ant-lion, and took a big jar with them. You should look for ant-lions' holes in a sandy place, so they wandered down to the beach, and it wasn't long before the Snork discovered a big, round hole and signalled eagerly to Moomintroll.

"Here he is!" whispered the Snork. "But how shall we lure him into the jar?"

"Leave it to me," whispered Moomintroll. He took the jar and buried it in the sand a little distance away with the opening on top. Then he said loudly, "They are very weak creatures, these ant-lions!" He signed to the Snork and they both looked expectantly down at the hole, but although the sand moved a bit, nothing was to be seen.

"*Very* weak," repeated Moomintroll. "It takes several hours for them to dig themselves down into the sand, you know!"

"Yes, but—" said the Snork, doubtfully.

"It does, I tell you," said Moomintroll, making frantic signs with his ears. "Several hours!"

At that moment a threatening head with staring eyes popped up from the hole in the sand.

"Did you say weak?" hissed the Ant-lion. "I can dig myself down in exactly three seconds!"

"You should really show us how it's done, so that we can believe such a wonderful feat is possible," said Moomintroll, persuasively.

"I shall spray sand on you," replied the Ant-lion very crossly, "and when I have sprayed you down into my hole I shall gobble you up!"

"Oh, no," pleaded the Snork. "Couldn't you show us how to dig down backwards in three seconds instead?"

"Do it up here so that we can see better how it's done," said Moomintroll, and pointed to the spot where the jar was buried.

"Do you think I am going to bother myself with showing tricks to babies?" said the Ant-lion, huffily. But all the same he simply could not resist the temptation to show them how strong and quick he was, so, with scornful sniffings, he scrambled up out of his hole and asked haughtily, "Now, where shall I dig myself in?"

"Here," said Moomintroll, pointing.

The Ant-lion drew up his shoulders and raised his mane in a terrifying manner.

"Out of my way!" he cried. "Now I'm going

underground, but when I come back I shall gobble you up! One, two, three!" And he backed down into the sand like a whirling propeller, right into the jar which was hidden under him. It certainly did only take three seconds, or perhaps two and a half, because he was so awfully angry.

"Quick with the lid," cried Moomintroll, and scraping away the sand they screwed it on very tightly. Then they both heaved up the jar and began to roll it home, with the Ant-lion inside screaming and cursing and choking with sand.

"It's frightful how angry he is," said the Snork. "I daren't think what will happen when he comes out!"

"He won't come out now," said Moomintroll, quietly, "and when he does I hope he will be changed into something horrible."

When they arrived at Moominhouse, Moomintroll summoned everyone with three long whistles. (Which means: Something quite extraordinary has happened.)

The others arrived from all directions and collected round the jar with the screw-top.

"What have you got there?" asked Sniff.

"An ant-lion," said Moomintroll, proudly. "A genuine furiously angry ant-lion that we have taken prisoner!"

"Fancy you daring!" said the Snork Maiden, admiringly.

"And now I think we'll pour him into the hat," said the Snork.

"So that he will be changed like I was," said Moomintroll.

"Would somebody please tell me what all this is

about?" the Hemulen asked plaintively.

"It was because I hid in that hat that I was changed," explained Moomintroll. "We've worked it out. And now we're going to make sure by seeing if the Ant-lion will turn into something else as well."

"B-but he could turn into absolutely anything!" squeaked Sniff. "He could turn into something still more dangerous than an ant-lion and gobble us all up in a minute." They stood in terrified silence looking at the pot and listening to the muffled sounds coming from inside.

"Oh!" said the Snork Maiden, turning rather pale*, but Snufkin suggested they should all hide under the table while the change took place, and put a big book on top of the hat. "You must always take risks when experimenting," he said. "Tip him in now at once."

Sniff scrambled under the table while Moomintroll, Snufkin, and the Hemulen held the jar over the Hobgoblin's hat, and the Snork gingerly unscrewed the lid. In a cloud of sand the Ant-lion tumbled out, and, quick as lightning, the Snork popped a Dictionary of Outlandish Words on top. Then they all dived under the table and waited.

At first nothing happened.

They peeped out from under the tablecloth, getting more and more agitated. Still there was no change.

"It was all rot," said Sniff, but at that moment the big dictionary began to crinkle up, and in his excitement, Sniff bit the Hemulen's thumb thinking it was his own.

* Snorks often turn pale when emotionally upset – Author's note.

Now the dictionary was curling up more and more. The pages began to look like withered leaves, and between them the Outlandish Words came out and began crawling around on the floor.

"Goodness, gracious me," said Moomintroll.

But there was more to come. Water began to drip from the brim of the hat and then to overflow and to splash down onto the carpet so that the Words had to climb up the walls to save themselves.

"The Ant-lion has only turned into water," said Snufkin in disappointment.

"I think it's the sand," whispered the Snork. "The Ant-lion is sure to come soon."

They waited again for an unbearably long time. The Snork Maiden hid her face in Moomintroll's lap, and Sniff whimpered with fright. Then suddenly, on the edge of the hat, appeared the world's smallest hedgehog. He sniffed the air and blinked, and he was very tangled and wet.

There was dead silence for a couple of seconds. Then Snufkin began to laugh, and in a very short time they were all howling and rolling about under the table in pure delight. All, that is, except the Hemulen who did not join in the fun. He looked in surprise at his friends and said, "Well, we expected the Ant-lion to change, didn't we? If only I could understand why you always make such a fuss about things."

Meanwhile the little hedgehog had wandered solemnly and a little sadly to the door and out down the steps. The water had stopped flowing and now filled the veranda like a lake. And the whole ceiling was covered with Outlandish Words.

ULLY THE PIPER

ANDRE NORTON

THE DALES OF HIGH HALLECK are many and some are even forgotten, save by those who live in them. During the great war with the invaders from overseas, when the lords of the dales and their armsmen fought, skulked, prospered or sank in defeat, there were small places left to a kind of slumber, overlooked by warriors. There, life went on as it always had, the dalesmen content in their islands of safety, letting the rest of the world roar on as it would.

In such a dale lay Coomb Brackett, a straggle of houses and farms with no right to the title of village, though so the indwellers called it. So tall were the ridges guarding it that few but the wild shepherds of the crags knew what lay beyond them, and many of their tales were discounted by the dalesmen. But there were also ill legends about those heights that had come down from the elder days when humankind first pushed this far north and west. For men were not the first to settle here, though story said that their predecessors had worn the outward seeming of men for convenience, their real aspect being such that no dalesman would care to look upon them by morn light.

dalesman would care to look upon them by morn light.

Those elder ones had withdrawn, seeking a refuge in the Beyond Wilderness, yet at times they returned on strange pilgrimages. Did not the dalesmen keep certain feast days – or nights – when they took offerings up to rocks which bore queer markings that had not been chiselled there by wind and weather? The reason for those offerings no man now living could tell, but that luck followed their giving was an established fact.

But the dale was good enough for the men of Coomb Brackett. Its fields were rich, a shallow river winding through them. Orchards of fruit flourished and small woodland copses held nut trees which also bore crops in season. Fat sheep fed placidly in the uplands, cattle ambled to the river to drink and went then to graze once more. Men sowed in spring, harvested in early autumn and lay snug in their homesteads in winter. As they often said to one another, who wanted more in this life?

They were as plump as their cattle and almost as slow moving at times. There was little to plague them, for even the Lord of Fartherdale, to whom they owed loyalty, had not sent his tithemen for a tale of years. There was a rumour that the lord was dead in the far-off war. Some of the prudent put aside a folding of woollen or a bolting of linen, well sprinkled with herbs to keep it fresh, against the day when the tithes might be asked again. But for the most part they spun their flax and wool, wove it into stout cloth for their own backs, ate their beef and mutton, drank ale brewed from their barley and wine from their fruit, and thought that trouble was something which struck at others far beyond their protecting heights.

There was only one among them who was not satisfied with things as they comfortably were, because for him there was no comfort. Ully of the hands was not the smallest, nor the youngest of the lads of Coomb Brackett – he was the different one. Longing to be as the rest filled him sometimes with a pain he could hardly bear.

He sat on his small cart and watched the rest off to the feasting on May Day and Harvest Home; and he watched them dance Rings Around following the smoking great roast at Yule – his clever hands folded in upon themselves until the nails bit sorely into the flesh of his palms.

There had been a tree to climb when he was so young he could not rightly recollect what life had been like before that hour. After he fell he had learned what it meant to go hunched of back and useless of leg, able to get from one place to another only by huddling on his cart and pushing it along the ground with two sticks.

He was mender-in-chief for the dale, though he could never mend himself. Aught that was broken was brought to him so that his widowed mother could sort out the pieces, and then Ully worked patiently hour by hour to make it whole again. Sometimes he thought that more than his body had been broken in that fall, and that slowly pieces of his spirit were flaking away within him. For Ully, being chained to his cart, was active in his mind and had many strange ideas he never shared with the world.

Only on a night such as this, when it was midsummer and the youth of the village were streaming up into the hills to set out first fruit, new bread, a flagon of milk and another of wine on the offering rock . . . He did not want to sit and think his life away! He was young in spirit, torn by such longings as sometimes made him want to howl and beat with his fists upon the ground, or pound the body which imprisoned him. But for the sake of his mother he never gave way so, for she would believe him mad, and he was not that – yet.

He listened to the singing as the company climbed, giving the rallying call to the all-night dancing:

"High dilly, High dally,
Come lilly, Come lally!
Dance for the ribbons –
Dance for new shoes!"

Who would dance so well this night that he would return by morn's light wearing the new shoes, she the snood of bright ribbons?

Not Stephen of the mill; he was as heavy-footed in such frolicking as if he carried one of the filled flour sacks across his ox-strong shoulders. Not Gretta of the inn, who so wanted to be graceful. (Ully had seen her in the goose meadow by the river practising steps in secret. She was a kind maid and he wished her as well as he did any of those he thought of as the straight people.)

No, this year, as always, it would be Matt of High

Ridge Garth, and Morgana, the smith's daughter. Ully frowned at the hedge which hid the upper road from him, crouched low as he was.

Morgana he knew little of, save that she saw only what she wished to see and did only what it pleased her to do. But Matt he disliked, for Matt was rough of hand and tongue, caring little what he left broken or torn behind his heavily tramped way – whether it was something which could be mended, or the feelings of others, which could not. Ully had had to deal with both kinds of Matt's destruction, and some he had never been able to put right.

They were still singing.

Ully set his teeth hard upon his lower lip. He might be small and crooked of body, but he was a man; and a man did not wail over his hurts. It was so fine a night he could not bear as yet to go back to the cottage. The scent of his mother's garden arose about him, seeming even stronger in the twilight. He reached within his shirt and brought out his greatest triumph of mending, twisted it in his clever fingers and then raised it to his lips.

The winter before, one of the rare strangers who ever came over the almost-obliterated ridge road had stopped at the inn. He had brought news of battles and lords they had never heard of. Most of Coomb Brackett, even men from the high garths, had come to listen, though to them it was more tale than reality.

At last the stranger had pulled out his pipe of polished wood and had blown sweet notes on it. Then he had laid it aside as Morgana came to share his bench; she took it as her just due that the first smiles of any man were for her. Matt, jealous of the outsider, had slammed down his tankard so hard that he had jarred the pipe on the floor and broken it.

There had been hot words then, and Matt had sullenly paid the stranger a silver piece. But Gretta had picked up the pieces and brought them to Ully, saying wistfully that the music the stranger had made on it was so sweet she longed to hear its like again.

Ully had worked hard to put it together and when it was complete once again he had taken to blowing an odd note or two. Then he tried even more, imitating a bird's song, the sleepy murmur of the river, the wind in the trees. Now he played the song he had so put together note by note, combining the many voices of the dale itself. Hesitatingly he began, then grew more confident. Suddenly he was startled by a clapping of hands and jerked his head painfully around to see Gretta by the hedge.

"Play – oh, please play more, Ully! A body could dance as light as a wind-driven cloud to music like that."

She took up her full skirt in her hands and pointed her toes. But then Ully saw her smile fade, and he knew well her sorrow, the clumsy body which would not obey the lightness of mind. In a moment she was smiling again and ran to him, holding out her work-calloused hand.

"Such music we have never had, Ully. You must come along and play for us tonight!"

He shrank back, shaking his head, but Gretta coaxed. Then she called over her shoulder.

"Stephen, Will! Come help me with Ully, he can

pipe sweeter than any bird in the bush. Let him play for our dancing tonight and we shall be as well-served as they say the old ones were with their golden pipes!"

Somehow Ully could not refuse them, and Stephen and Will pushed the cart up to the highest meadow where the token feast had been already spread on the offering rock and the fire flamed high. There Ully set pipe to lips and played.

But there were some not so well pleased at his coming. Morgana, having halted in the dance not far away, saw him and cried out so that Matt stepped protectingly before her.

"Ah, it's only crooked Ully," she cried spitefully. "I had thought it some one of the monsters out of the old tales crawled up from the woods to spy on us." And she gave an exaggerated shiver, clinging to Matt's arm.

"Ully?" Matt laughed. "Why does Ully crawl here, having no feet to dance upon? Why stare at his betters? And where did you get that pipe, little man?" He snatched at the pipe in Ully's hands. "It looks to me like the one I had to pay a round piece for when it was broken. Give it here now; for if it is the same, it belongs to me!"

Ully tried to hold on to the pipe, but Matt's strength was by far the greater. The resting dancers had gathered close to the offering rock where they were opening their own baskets and bags to share the midnight feast. There was none to see what chanced here in the shadow. Matt held up the pipe in triumph.

"Good as new, and worth surely a silver piece again. Samkin the peddler will give me that and I shall not be out of pocket at all."

"*My* pipe, crooked man! I had to pay for it, didn't I? Mine to do with as I will."

Helpless anger worked in Ully as he tried to raise himself higher, but his movements only set the wheels of the cart moving and he began to roll down the slope of the meadow backwards. Morgana cried out and moved as if to stop him. But Matt, laughing, caught her back.

"Let him go, he will come to no harm. And he has no place here now, has he? Did he not even frighten you?"

He put the pipe into his tunic and threw an arm about her waist, leading her back to the feast. Halfway there they met Gretta.

"Where is Ully?"

Matt shrugged. "He is gone."

"Gone? But it is a long way back to the village and he—" She began to run down the slope of the hill calling, "Ully, Ully!"

The runaway cart had not gone that way, but in another direction, bumping and bouncing towards the small wood which encircled half the high meadow, its green arms held out to embrace the open land.

Ully crouched low, afraid to move, afraid to try to catch at any of the shrubs or low-hanging branches as he swept by, lest he be pulled off to lie helpless on the ground.

In and out among the trees spun the cart, and Ully began to wonder why it had not upset, or run against a trunk or caught in some vine. It was almost as if it were being guided. When he tried to turn and look to the fore, he could see nothing but the dark wood.

were being guided. When he tried to turn and look to the fore, he could see nothing but the dark wood.

Then with a rush, the cart burst once more into the open. No fire blazed here, but the moon seemed to hang oddly bright and full just above, as if it were a fixed lamp. Heartened somehow, Ully dared to reach out and catch at a tuft of thick grass, a vine runner, and pulled the cart around so that he no longer faced the wood through which he had come, but rather an open glade where the grass grew short and thick as if it were mown. Around was a wall of flowers and bushes, while in the middle was a ring of stones, each taller than Ully, and so blazingly white in the moonlight that they might have been upright torches.

Ully's heart ceased to pound so hard. The peace and beauty of the place soothed him as if soft fingers stroked his damp face and ordered his tousled hair. His hands resting on his shrunken knees twitched, he so wanted his pipe.

But there was no pipe. Softly Ully began to hum his tune of the dale: bird song, water ripple, wind. Then his hum became a whistle. It seemed to him that all the beauty he had ever dreamed of was gathered here, just as he had fitted together broken bits with his hands.

Great silvery moths came out of nowhere and sailed in and out among the candle pillars, as if they were weaving some unseen fabric, netting a spell. Hesitatingly Ully held out one hand and one of the moths broke from the rest and lit fearlessly on his wrist, fanning wings which might have been tipped with stardust for the many points of glitter there. It was so light he was hardly aware that it rested so, save that he saw it. Then it took to the air again.

Ully wiped the hand across his forehead, sweeping back a loose lock of hair, and as he did so . . .

The moths were gone; beside each pillar stood a woman. Small and slight indeed they were, hardly taller than a young child of Ully's kin, but these were truly women, for they were dressed only in their long hair. The bodies, revealed as they moved, were so perfectly formed that Ully knew he had never seen real beauty before. They did not look at him, but glided on their small bare feet in and out among the pillars, weaving their spell even as the moths had done. At times they paused, gathering up their hair with their two hands, to hold it well away from their bodies and shake it. It seemed to Ully that when they did so there was a shifting of glittering motes carried along in a small cloud moving away from the glade, though he did not turn his eyes to follow it.

Though none of them spoke, he knew what they wanted of him and he whistled his song of the dale. He must truly be asleep and dreaming, or else in that wild dash downslope he had fallen from the cart and suffered a knock from which this vision was born. But dream or hurt, he would hold to it as long as he could. This – this was such happiness as he had never known.

At last their dance grew slower and slower, until they halted, each standing with one hand upon a pillar side. Then they were gone; only the moths fluttered once again in the dimming light.

Ully was aware that his body ached, that his lips and mouth were dry and that all the weight of fatigue had suddenly fallen on him. But still he cried out against its ending.

There was movement by the pillar directly facing him and someone came farther into the pale light of new dawn. She stood before him, and for the last time she gathered up her hair in both hands, holding it out shoulder high. Once, twice, thrice, she shook it. But this time there were no glittering motes. Rather he was struck in the face by a blast of icy air, knocked from his cart so his head rapped against the ground, dazing him.

He did not know how long it was before he tried to move. But he did struggle up, braced on his forearms. Struggle – he writhed and fought for balance.

Ully who could not move his shrivelled legs, nor straighten his back – why – he was straight! He was as straight as Stephen, as Matt! If this were a dream . . .

He arched up, looked for the woman to babble questions, thanks, he knew not what. But there was no one by the pillar. Hardly daring to trust the fact that he was no longer bowed into a broken thing, he crawled, feeling strength flow into him with every move, to the foot of the pillar. He used that to draw himself to his feet, to stand again!

His clothes were too confining for his new body. He tore them away. Then he was erect, the pillar at his back and the dawn wind fresh on his body. Still keeping his hold on the white stone, he took small cautious steps, circling his support. His feet moved and were firm under him; he did not fall.

Ully threw back his head and cried his joy aloud. Then he saw the glint of something lying in the centre of the pillar circle and he edged forward. A sod of green turf was half uprooted, and protruding from it was a pipe. But such a pipe! He had thought the one he mended was fine; this was such as a high lord might treasure!

He picked it loose of the earth, fearing it might well disappear out of his very fingers. Then he put it to his lips and played his thanks to what, or who, had been there in the night; he played with all the joy in him.

So playing he went home, walking with care at first because it was so new to him. He went by back ways until he reached the cottage and his mother. She, poor woman, was weeping. They had feared him lost when he had vanished from the meadow and Gretta had aroused the others to search for him without result. When she first looked at this new Ully his mother judged him a spirit from the dead, until he reassured her.

All Coomb Brackett marvelled at his story. Some of the oldest nodded knowingly, spoke of ancient legends of the old ones who had once dwelt in the dales, and how it was that they could grant blessings on those they favoured. They pointed out symbols on the pipe which were not unlike those of the tribute rock. Then the younger men spoke of going to the pillar glade to hunt for treasure. But Ully grew wroth and they respected him as one set apart by what had happened, and agreed it was best not to trouble those they knew so little of.

It would seem that Ully had brought back more than straight legs and a pipe. For that was a good year in the dale. The harvest was the richest in memory, and there were no ill happenings. Ully, now on his two feet, travelled to the farthest homestead to mend and play, for the pipe never left him. And it was true that when they listened to it the feet of all grew lighter as did their hearts, and any dancer more skilful.

But inside Matt there was no rest: Now he was no longer first among the youth; Ully was more listened to. He began to talk himself, hinting dire things about gifts from unknown sources, and a few listened, those who are always discontent to see another prosper. Among them was Morgana, for she was no longer so courted. Even Gretta nowadays was sometimes partnered before her. And one day she broke through Matt's grumbling shortly.

"What one man can do, surely another can also. Why do you keep muttering about Ully's fortune? Harvest Eve comes soon and those old ones are supposed then to come again to view the wealth of the fields and take their due. Go to Ully's pillars and play; they may be grateful again!"

Matt had been practising on the pipe he had taken from Ully, and he did well enough with the rounds and the lays the villagers had once liked; though the few times he had tried to play Ully's own song the notes had come sourly, off key.

The more Matt considered Morgana's suggestion, the better it seemed, and the old thought of treasure clung in his mind. There could be deals with the old ones if a man were shrewd. Ully was a simple fellow who had not known how to handle such. His thoughts grew ambitious.

So when the feast came Matt lagged behind the rest and turned aside to take a brambly way he judged would bring him to Ully's oft-described ring of pillars.

Leaving much of his shirt hanging in tatters on the briers and his skin redstriped by thorns, he came at last into the glade.

There were the pillars right enough, but they were not bright and white and torchlike. Instead, each seemed to squat direfully in a mass of shadow which flowed about their bases as if something unpleasant undulated there. But Matt dropped down beneath one of the trees to wait. He saw no moths, though there were vague flutterings about the crowns of the pillars. At last, thinking Ully fashioned out of his own imagination much of his story, Matt decided to try one experiment before going back to the feasting villages to proclaim just how much a lie his rival was.

But the notes he blew on his pipe were shrill squeaks; and when he would have left, he found to his horror and dismay that he could not move, his legs were locked to the ground as Ully's had once been. Nor could he lower the pipe from his lips, but was compelled by a will outside his own to keep up that doleful, sorry wailing. His body ached, his mouth was dry, and fear was laid as a lash upon him. He saw things around those pillars.

He would close his eyes! But again he could not, but must pipe and watch, until he was close to the brink of madness. Then his leaden arms fell, the pipe spun away from his lax fingers, and he was dimly aware the dawn had come.

From the pillar before him sped a great bloated thing with an angry buzzing – such a fly as he had seen gather to drink the blood spilled at a butchering – yet this was greater than six of those put into one.

It flew straight into his face, stinging him. He tried to beat it away, but could only manage to crawl on his hands and knees; the fly continued to buzz about him as a sheepdog might herd a straggler.

Somehow Matt finally struggled to his feet, but it was long before he could walk erect. For many days his face was so swollen that he would not show it in the village, nor would he ever tell what happened to him.

But for many a year thereafter Ully's pipe led the people of Coomb Bracket to their feasting and played for their dancing. Sometimes, it was known, he slipped away by himself to the place of pillars and there played for other ears, such as did not side mortal heads.

MILO CONDUCTS THE DAWN

NORTON JUSTER
from The Phantom Tollbooth

Milo is a boy who doesn't know what to do with himself. Everything bores him, until one day a huge parcel arrives containing a toy tollbooth (the kind of thing you put money in when you are driving on a road or a bridge which is not publicly owned). Milo, in a bored way, pretends to put money in and pretends to drive past it. Instantly he finds himself in the midst of strange adventures. He meets Tock, his Watchdog, who has a large clock in one side of him, and the two eventually meet a boy called Alec whose feet never touch the ground. Alec acts as their guide.

THE SUN WAS DROPPING slowly from sight, and stripes of purple and orange and crimson and gold piled themselves on top of the distant hills. The last shafts of light waited patiently for a flight of wrens to find their way home, and a group of anxious stars had already taken their places.

"Here we are!" cried Alec, and, with a sweep of his arm, he pointed towards an enormous symphony orchestra. "Isn't it a grand sight?"

There were at least a thousand musicians ranged in

a great arc before them. To the left and right were the violins and cellos, whose bows moved in great waves, and behind them, in numberless profusion, the piccolos, flutes, clarinets, oboes, bassoons, horns, trumpets, trombones and tubas were all playing at once. At the very rear, so far away that they could hardly be seen, were the percussion instruments, and lastly, in a long line up one side of a steep slope, were the solemn bass fiddles.

On a high podium in front stood the conductor, a tall, gaunt man with dark, deep-set eyes and a thin mouth placed carelessly between his long, pointed nose and his long, pointed chin. He used no baton, but conducted with large, sweeping movements which seemed to start at his toes and work slowly up through his body and along his slender arms and end finally at the tips of his graceful fingers.

"I don't hear any music," said Milo.

"That's right," said Alec; "you don't listen to this concert – you watch it. Now, pay attention."

As the conductor waved his arms, he moulded the air like handfuls of soft clay, and the musicians carefully followed his every direction.

"What are they playing?" asked Tock, looking up inquisitively at Alec.

"The sunset, of course. They play it every evening, about this time."

"They do?" said Milo quizzically.

"Naturally," answered Alec; "and they also play morning, noon, and night, when of course, it's morning, noon, or night. Why, there wouldn't be any colour in the world unless they played it. Each instrument plays a different one," he explained, "and depending, of course, on what season it is and how the weather's to be, the conductor chooses his score and directs the day. But watch: the sun has almost set, and in a moment you can ask Chroma himself."

The last colours slowly faded from the western sky, and, as they did, one by one the instruments stopped, until only the bass fiddles, in their sombre slow movement, were left to play the night and a single set of silver bells brightened the constellations. The conductor let his arms fall limply at his sides and stood quite still as darkness claimed the forest.

"That was a very beautiful sunset," said Milo, walking to the podium.

"It should be," was the reply, "we've been practising since the world began." And, reaching down, the speaker picked Milo off the ground and set him on the music stand. "I am Chroma the Great," he continued, gesturing broadly with his hands, "conductor of colour, maestro of pigment, and director of the entire spectrum."

"Do you play all day long?" asked Milo when he had introduced himself.

"Ah yes, all day, every day," he sang out, then pirouetted gracefully around the platform. "I rest only at night, and even then *they* play on."

"But what would happen if you stopped?" asked Milo, who didn't quite believe that colour happened like that.

"See for yourself," roared Chroma, and he raised both hands high over his head. Immediately the instruments that were playing stopped, and at once all colour vanished. The world looked like an enormous colouring book that had never been used. Everything appeared in simple black outlines, and it looked as if someone with a set of paints the size of a house and a brush as wide could stay happily occupied for years. Then Chroma lowered his arms. The instruments began again and the colour returned.

"You see what a dull place the world would be without colour?" he said, bowing until his chin almost touched the ground. "But what pleasure to lead my violins in a serenade of spring green or hear my trumpets blare out the blue sea and then watch the oboes tint it all in warm yellow sunshine. And rainbows are best of all – and blazing neon signs, and taxicabs with stripes, and the soft, muted tones of a foggy day. We play them all."

While Chroma was speaking, Milo sat with his eyes open wide, and Alec, Tock, and the Humbug looked on in wonder.

"Now I really must get some sleep," Chroma yawned. "We've had lightning, fireworks, and parades for the last few nights, and I've had to be up to conduct them. But tonight is sure to be quiet." Then, putting his large hand on Milo's shoulder, he said, "Be a good fellow and watch my orchestra till morning, will you? And be sure to wake me at 5.23 for sunrise. Good night, good night, good night."

With that he leaped lightly from the podium and, in three long steps, vanished into the forest.

One by one, the hours passed, and at exactly 5.22 (by Tock's very accurate clock) Milo carefully opened one eye and, in a moment, the other. Everything was still purple, dark blue, and black, yet scarcely a minute remained to the long, quiet night.

He stretched lazily, rubbed his eyelids, scratched his head, and shivered once as a greeting to the early-morning mist.

"I must wake Chroma for the sunrise," he said softly. Then he suddenly wondered what it would be like to lead the orchestra and to colour the whole world himself.

The idea whirled through his thoughts until he quickly decided that since it couldn't be very difficult, and since they probably all knew what to do by themselves anyway, and since it did seem a shame to wake anyone so early, and since it might be his only chance to try, and since the musicians were already poised and ready, he would – but just for a little while.

And so, as everyone slept peacefully on, Milo stood on tiptoes, raised his arms slowly in front of him, and made the slightest movement possible with the index finger of his right hand. It was now 5.23 a.m.

As if understanding his signal perfectly, a single piccolo played a single note and off in the east a solitary shaft of cool lemon light flicked across the sky. Milo smiled happily and then cautiously crooked his finger again. This time two more piccolos and a flute joined in and three more rays of light danced lightly into view. Then with both hands he made a great circular sweep in the air and watched with delight as all the musicians began to play at once.

The cellos made the hills glow red, and the leaves and grass were tipped with a soft pale green as the violins began their song. Only the bass fiddles rested as the entire orchestra washed the forest in colour.

Milo was overjoyed because they were all playing for him, and just the way they should.

"Won't Chroma be surprised?" he thought, signalling the musicians to stop. "I'll wake him now."

But, instead of stopping, they continued to play even louder than before, until each colour became more brilliant than he thought possible. Milo shielded his eyes with one hand and waved the other desperately, but the colours continued to grow brighter and brighter and brighter, until an even more curious thing began to happen.

As Milo frantically conducted, the sky changed slowly from blue to tan and then to a rich magenta red. Flurries of light-green snow began to fall, and the leaves on the trees and bushes turned a vivid orange.

All the flowers suddenly appeared black, the grey rocks became a lovely soft chartreuse, and even peacefully sleeping Tock changed from brown to a magnificent ultramarine. Nothing was the colour it should have been, and yet, the more he tried to straighten things out, the worse they became.

"I wish I hadn't started," he thought unhappily as a pale-blue blackbird flew by. "There doesn't seem to be any way to stop them."

He tried very hard to do everything just the way Chroma had done, but nothing worked. The musicians played on, faster and faster, and the purple sun raced quickly across the sky. In less than a minute it had set once more in the west and then, without any pause, risen again in the east. The sky was now quite yellow and the grass a charming shade of lavender. Seven times the sun rose and almost as quickly disappeared as the colours kept changing. In just a few minutes a whole week had gone by.

At last the exhausted Milo, afraid to call for help and on the verge of tears, dropped his hands to his sides. The orchestra stopped. The colours disappeared, and once again it was night. The time was 5.27 a.m.

"Wake up, everybody! Time for the sunrise!" he shouted with relief, and quickly jumped from the music stand.

"What a marvellous rest," said Chroma, striding to the podium. "I feel as though I'd slept for a week. My, my, I see we're a little late this morning. I'll have to cut my lunch hour short by four minutes."

He tapped for attention, and this time the dawn proceeded perfectly.

"You did a fine job," he said, patting Milo on the head. "Some day I'll let you conduct the orchestra yourself."

Tock wagged his tail proudly, but Milo didn't say a word, and to this day no one knows of the lost week but the few people who happened to be awake at 5.23 on that very strange morning.

"We'd better be getting along," said Tock, whose alarm had begun to ring again, "for there's still a long way to go."

Chroma nodded a fond goodbye as they all started back through the forest, and in honour of the visit he made all the wild flowers bloom in a breathtaking display.

"I'm sorry you can't stay longer," said Alec sadly.

"There's so much more to see in the Forest of Sight. But I suppose there's a lot to see everywhere, if only you keep your eyes open."

WHO GOES DOWN THIS DARK ROAD?

JOAN AIKEN

IT SEEMS SINGULAR, remembering that first interview with Mrs King, to think that I had no kind of premonition or foreknowledge – yet how could I have had? If I had known, or guessed, that my intervention would result in my being brought here – would end in this tedious incarceration – I might have let well alone. But I did not.

Amanda King had not made any particular impression on me, save as a very *good* girl. Among the children in the beginners' group she was not distinguished for brightness at her lessons, nor for liveliness in class; she did not have that spontaneous vivacity and wit that some small children possess, nor was she in any way remarkable when the children played games, or sang songs, or acted plays, or told stories. And yet, by the time Mrs King came to see me, I was aware of Amanda as a particularly stable and pleasant member of the group. *Stable* seems an odd term to apply to a six-year-old, yet stability seemed to be Amanda's paramount quality. She was always punctual, polite and friendly; indeed she had charming manners. I had at first assumed that it was Mrs King who prompted the daily – and very tastefully arranged – posies, sometimes from the Kings' garden, sometimes wild flowers; but by degrees I realized that this was Amanda's own idea. Her appearance was in no way striking, yet there was something neat and attractive about her: her dark-blue school pinafore and white blouse were always clean and crisp, her fair hair shining, beautifully brushed and neatly plaited, her big grey eyes serious and attentive to what was going on. She seemed a model pupil, and, though she never came top in any subject apart from spelling and deportment, seemed unlikely ever to cause either parents or teachers the slightest worry.

It was, therefore, a considerable surprise when Mrs King came to see me, visibly distressed, one afternoon after school when I was setting up the model Saxon village for next day's intermediate class.

"Oh, Mr Thorneycroft, I'm ever so sorry to trouble you when I know how hard you work for the children, but me and Mr King are that worried about Amanda, we don't know what to do for the best."

"About *Amanda*?" I was really amazed. "But she's the best little girl in the school."

"I know, sir, and so she's always been at home, but just lately something's got into her; something – well, peculiar. She's turned that obstinate, sir, I can't give you any idea!"

"Well, even the best children go through awkward phases," I began vaguely and consolingly. "What form does it take with Amanda, Mrs King?"

"Sir, it's to do with her hair."

"Her hair?"

Then it did occur to me that for the last week or two, Amanda's hair had not been so shiningly neat and symmetrically plaited as hitherto. And indeed that very morning, I now recalled, Amanda had turned up with the two corn-blonde plaits shorn off, and her hair hanging loose and rather short about her small serious face. I had made some remark on it and she had said, "Mum thought it would be easier to keep tidy if it was short."

The child next to her, Lily Thatcher, called out, "You oughter sleep with the plaits under your pillow, Mandy, then you'll dream about the fellow you're going to marry!" which raised a laugh, but Amanda, rather oddly, I now recalled, said that she had buried the plaits in the garden.

"What about her hair, then, Mrs King?"

"Well, sir – I don't know how to put it so you won't think either I or the child is crazy—" I noticed with astonishment that the placid-seeming Mrs King had tears in her eyes— "but she's got this notion that there's people living in her hair."

Various possibilities flashed through my mind. I said delicately, "You're quite sure, Mrs King, that it's not a simple case of nits, head parasites – something like that?"

"Sir! How could you think such a thing? There's some families in the village I wouldn't put it past them, but my Amanda's always been perfectly clean – I've washed her hair myself every Saturday night since she was born."

"I must say her hair always does look beautifully clean," I said quickly. "Well, if that is the case, you don't think it's possible that she *imagines* she has something of the sort? Children sometimes have such odd private worries—"

"No, sir, no, it's not like that. No, it's *people* she says are living on top of her head. In among the hair, like. She says—" Mrs King faltered, "she says the hair seems like a forest to them."

"She's playing a game with you, Mrs King," I suggested. "It's just a piece of pretence. I remember when I was a boy I had an imaginary bear – oh, I carried him around with me for years!"

"A game it may be, sir, but it's dead serious to her," Mrs King said worriedly. "Every day I have the very deuce of the job, you'll pardon me, sir, to get her hair brushed. 'Don't *do* that, Mum, you'll drive them out of the forest,' she says, and she screams and screams; it makes my Joe really wild, he's threatened to give her a good hiding if she won't be more reasonable. And lately, sir – oh, I've begun to wonder if she's going mental." Mrs King here fairly burst out crying. "She talks such rubbish, sir! All about chariots and temples and sacred stones and armies and navies – it's not right, sir, it really isn't. And sometimes what she says doesn't make sense at all, it's just doubledutch, you can't make head nor tail of it, and she'll go on like that for hours."

"Did you mention this to Dr Button?"

"Well, I did, sir – I didn't take Amanda to the surgery for fear of scaring her, I just told him, and he fairly snapped my head off and said she was a perfectly healthy child and not to fuss him with a bit of kid's moonshine."

This sounded true to form. I said cautiously, "Well, what did you want me to do, Mrs King?"

"Oh, sir, if you could just *talk* to Amanda about it a bit! She thinks the world of you, sir, if you could just reason this nonsense out of her head—"

"Very aptly put, Mrs King."

She looked at me rather blankly, so I promised that I would see what I could do. "Supposing I take Amanda for a walk, Mrs King, tomorrow, after school – I could ask her to show me where she picks her delightful bunches of flowers. Then it won't seem too like a formal interview."

"Oh, Mr Thorneycroft, I don't know how to thank you—"

I pointed out that I hadn't done anything yet, but she went away evidently relieved to have pushed the responsibility onto somebody else, even if only temporarily.

Next afternoon Amanda agreed, with grave politeness, to take me across the Common and show me where she picked her cowslips and ladies' smocks. I thought there was no sense in deferring the question, so as soon as we were away from the village, I said, "Your mother asked me to talk to you, Amanda, about this idea you have that – er, that people are living in your hair."

She looked up at me calmly, with a surprisingly adult expression in her grey eyes, and said, "Yes, I thought perhaps she had."

I said, gently, not wanting to seem unsympathetic or mocking, "What sort of people are they, Amanda?"

She answered at once, "They're a tribe of Gauls, the Veneti. They were defeated, you see, by the Romans, in a big sea-battle, and driven out of their homes. They built a new town, but then it was destroyed – it sank in the sea. And so they collected up what they could of their belongings – and now they live in my hair. It's like a forest to them, you see."

I was startled, to say the least.

"But, Amanda – how did you come to know about the Veneti?"

"I can hear them," she said matter-of-factly. "Talking. Through my skull."

"But they were a long time ago! More than two thousand years."

"I suppose they got through it fast, somehow. Some people go quicker than others."

I said, "How could they all get onto your head, though? They were full-sized people – a whole tribe of them. How could they all camp on one little corn-coloured nut?"

She gave me a look as closely approaching to impatience as natural politeness would permit.

"Things seem a different size, don't you see, when they're in different places. If I saw you a long way off – you'd look small, wouldn't you? Or if I saw you beside a *huge* monster." Her eyes widened, and I remembered that, after all, she was still only a six-year-old. The word *relative* was probably outside her vocabulary.

"What sort of language do they talk, these people, Amanda?" This fable she had spun for herself was wonderfully coherent so far; I wondered where she read or heard of the Veneti, who, I recalled, had been vanquished by Caesar in Brittany.

"Well, they talk two languages," she told me.

"Can you remember any of the words?"

She reeled off a string of jargon which was meaningless to me full of X sounds and CH sounds; I became more and more interested remembering medical cases of glossolalia, "speaking with tongues", which sometimes occur in religious fanatics or mental patients – but in an otherwise matter-of-fact little girl of six?

"And what is the other language?"

She then startled me out of my wits by replying, "*Una salus victis nullam sperare salutem*" (there is but one safe thing for the vanquished; not to hope for safety).

"Good heavens, Amanda! Where did you hear that?"

"One of them up there said it." She pointed to her flaxen locks.

"Can you remember any more?"

"*Quid nunc it per iter tenebricosum*—"

"*Illuc*," I said it with her, "*unde negant redire quemquam*."

"You know that too?" she said, turning the grey eyes on me.

"I have heard it, yes. What was the people's town called, Amanda – the town that sank in the sea?"

"It was called Is."

"Do you know the names of the gods they worship?"

"They must not be spoken or written down. There is a serpent's egg that must be thrown into the air."

"And caught in a white cloak?"

"Yes. But just now their holy men are very worried," she said, turning to me, frowning – she looked absurdly like her mother.

"Why are they worried, Amanda?"

"They have signs from – from the ones who can tell the future – that there is going to be another very bad happening – and that they are going to have to move again, their circle of sacred stones and all the people with their things. Oh!" she cried, clasping her hands to her fair head, "I do *hope* Mum isn't going to cut off all my hair! She said she might do that! Please tell her not to, Mr Thorneycroft!"

"All right, Amanda – don't worry. I'll tell her."

"Look," she said, cheering up, "this is where the cowslips grow."

We both picked a bunch and started for home. I was very silent and thoughtful but Amanda, having had my promise about the hair-cutting, skipped along beside me quite light-heartedly with her bunch of cowslips, humming in a tuneless but not unpleasing little voice.

I, needless to say, was wondering what to do, and hardly looked where I was going. Which is why I didn't hear the car till it was right behind us.

It was young, feckless Colin Gaddock, who works in the petrol station over at Maynards Cross; he always comes home at a crazy pace, hell-bent on getting to his evening's enjoyment. His wing mirror caught the child's jacket as he shot past us and she was dragged, shrieking, five hundred yards up the road before he could brake to a stop.

He's doing time for manslaughter now; I'd like to think it has taught him a lesson, but fear that he's the kind of hopeless lout who will presently come out of jail and do exactly the same thing again.

I could never go into a butcher's shop again. The sight of a piece of steak . . .

People said I'd had a breakdown, and everyone was very sorry for me. But actually it's simpler than that. What happened was, that the Veneti transferred from Amanda's head to mine.

And I'm a bit bothered now because their Druids are predicting another catastrophe.

THE HOUSE OF HARFANG

C. S. LEWIS
from The Silver Chair

Jill Pole and Eustace Scrubb have been sent to the magic land of Narnia by the great Lion, Aslan, to look for the lost prince of Narnia. Aslan gives them a companion, Puddleglum, a web-footed person called a marsh-wiggle; and he also gives them four clear instructions for finding the prince. They make a mess of following the first two instructions and as a result they arrive, cold and exhausted, at Harfang, the castle of the giants. The giants seem very glad to see them.

JILL'S ROOM WAS about the size of a church, and would have been rather grim if it had not had a roaring fire on the hearth and a very thick crimson carpet on the floor. And here delightful things began to happen to her. She was handed over to the queen's old nurse, who was, from the giants' point of view, a little old woman almost bent double with age, and, from the human point of view, a giantess small enough to go about an ordinary room without knocking her head on the ceiling. She was very capable, though Jill did wish she wouldn't keep on clicking her tongue and saying things like "Oh la, la! Ups-a-daisy" and "There's a duck" and "Now we'll be all right, my poppet". She filled a giant foot-bath with hot water and helped Jill into it. If you can swim (as Jill could) a giant bath is a lovely thing. And giant towels, though a bit rough and coarse, are lovely too, because there are acres of them. In fact you don't need to dry at all, you just roll about on them in front of the fire and enjoy yourself. And when that was over, clean, fresh, warmed clothes were put on Jill: very splendid clothes and a little too big for her, but clearly made for humans not giantesses. "I suppose if that woman in the green kirtle comes here, they must be used to guests of our size," thought Jill.

She soon saw that she was right about this, for a table and chair of the right height for an ordinary grown-up human were placed for her, and the knives and forks and spoons were the proper size too. It was delightful to sit down, feeling warm and clean at last. Her feet were still bare and it was lovely to tread on the giant carpet. She sank in it well over her ankles and it was just the thing for sore feet. The meal – which I suppose we must call dinner, though it was nearer tea time – was cock-a-leekie soup, and hot roast turkey, and a steamed pudding, and roast chestnuts, and as much fruit as you could eat.

The only annoying thing was that the nurse kept coming in and out, and every time she came in, she brought a gigantic toy with her – a huge doll, bigger than Jill herself, a wooden horse on wheels, about the size of an elephant, a drum that looked like a young gasometer, and a woolly lamb. They were crude, badly made things, painted in very bright colours, and Jill hated the sight of them. She kept on telling the nurse she didn't want them, but the nurse said, "Tut-tut-tut-tut. You'll want 'em all right when you've had a bit of a rest, I know! Te-he-he! Beddy bye, now. A precious poppet!"

The bed was not a giant bed but only a big four-poster, like what you might see in an old-fashioned hotel; and very small it looked in that enormous room. She was very glad to tumble into it.

"Is it still snowing, nurse?" she asked sleepily.

"No. Raining now, ducky!" said the giantess. "Rain'll wash away all the nasty snow. Precious poppet will be able to go out and play tomorrow!" And she tucked Jill up and said goodnight.

I know nothing so disagreeable as being kissed by a giantess. Jill thought the same, but was asleep in five minutes.

The rain fell steadily all the evening and all the night, dashing against the windows of the castle, and Jill never heard it but slept deeply, past supper time and past midnight. And then came the deadest hour of the night and nothing stirred but mice in the house of the giants. At that hour there came to Jill a dream. It seemed to her that she awoke in the same room and saw the fire, sunk low and red, and in the firelight the great wooden horse. And the horse came of its own will, rolling on its wheels across the carpet, and stood at her head. And now it was no longer a horse, but a lion as big as the horse. And then it was not a toy lion, but a real lion, The Real Lion, just as she had seen him on the mountain beyond the world's end. And a smell of all sweet-smelling things there are filled the room.

But there was some trouble in Jill's mind, though she could not think what it was, and the tears streamed down her face and wet the pillow. The Lion told her to repeat the signs, and she found that she had forgotten them all. At that, a great horror came over her. And Aslan took her up in his jaws (she could feel his lips and his breath but not his teeth) and carried her to the window and made her look out. The moon shone bright; and written in great letters across the world or the sky (she did not know which) were the words UNDER ME. After that, the dream faded away, and when she woke, very late next morning, she did not remember that she had dreamed at all.

She was up and dressed and had finished breakfast in front of the fire when the nurse opened the door and said, "Here's pretty poppet's little friends come to play with her." In came Scrubb and the Marsh-wiggle.

"Hullo! Good morning," said Jill. "Isn't this fun? I've slept about fifteen hours, I believe. I do feel better, don't you?"

"I do," said Scrubb, "but Puddleglum says he has a headache. Hullo! Your window has a window seat. If we got up on that, we could see out." And at once they all did so: and at the first glance Jill said, "Oh, how perfectly dreadful!"

The sun was shining and, except for a few drifts, the snow had been almost completely washed away by the rain. Down below them, spread out like a map, lay the flat hill-top which they had struggled over yesterday afternoon; seen from the castle, it could not be mistaken for anything but the ruins of a gigantic city. It had been flat, as Jill now saw, because it was still, on the whole, paved, though in places the pavement was broken. The criss-cross banks were what was left of the walls of huge buildings which might once have been giants' palaces and temples. One bit of wall, about five hundred feet high, was still standing; it was that which she had thought was a cliff. The things that looked like factory chimneys were enormous pillars, broken off at unequal heights; their fragments lay at their bases like felled trees of monstrous stone. The ledges which they had climbed down on the north side of the hill – and also, no doubt the other ledges which they had climbed up on the south side – were the remaining steps of giant stairs. To crown all, in large, dark lettering across the centre of the pavement, ran the words UNDER ME.

The three travellers looked at each other in dismay, and, after a short whistle, Scrubb said what they were all thinking, "The second and third signs muffed." And at that moment Jill's dream rushed back into her mind.

"It's my fault," she said in despairing tones. "I – I'd given up repeating the signs every night. If I'd been thinking about them I could have seen it was the city, even in all that snow."

"I'm worse," said Puddleglum. "I *did* see, or nearly. I thought it looked uncommonly like a ruined city."

"You're the only one who isn't to blame," said Scrubb. "You *did* try to make us stop."

"Didn't try hard enough, though," said the Marsh-wiggle. "And I'd no call to be trying. I ought to have done it. As if I couldn't have stopped you two with one hand each!"

"The truth is," said Scrubb, "we were so jolly keen on getting to this place that we weren't bothering about anything else. At least I know I was. Ever since we met that woman with the knight who didn't talk, we've been thinking of nothing else. We'd nearly forgotten about Prince Rilian."

"I shouldn't wonder," said Puddleglum, "if that wasn't exactly what she intended."

"What I don't quite understand," said Jill, "is how we didn't see the lettering? Or could it have come there since last night. Could he – Aslan – have put it there in the night? I had such a queer dream." And she told them all about it.

"Why, you chump!" said Scrubb. "We did see it. We got into the letter E in ME. That was your sunk lane. We walked along the bottom stroke of the E, due north – turned to our right along the upright – came to another turn to the right – that's the middle stroke – and then went onto the top left-hand corner, or (if you like) the north-eastern corner of the letter, and came back. Like the bally idiots we are." He kicked the window seat savagely, and went on, "So it's no good, Pole. I know what you were thinking because I was thinking the same. You were thinking how nice it would have been if Aslan hadn't put the instructions on the stones of the ruined city till after we'd passed it. And then it would have been his fault, not ours. So likely, isn't it? No. We must just own up. We've only four signs to go by, and we've muffed the first three."

"You mean I have," said Jill. "It's quite true. I've spoiled everything ever since you brought me here. All the same – I'm frightfully sorry and all that – all the same, what *are* the instructions? UNDER ME doesn't seem to make much sense."

"Yes it does, though," said Puddleglum. "It means we've got to look for the prince under that city."

"But how can we?" asked Jill.

"That's the question," said Puddleglum, rubbing his big, frog-like hands together. "How can we *now*? No doubt, if we'd had our minds on our job when we were at the Ruinous City, we'd have been shown how – found a little door, or a cave, or a tunnel, met someone to help us. Might have been (you never know) Aslan himself. We'd have got down under those paving-stones somehow or other. Aslan's instructions always work: there are no exceptions. But how to do it *now* – that's another matter."

"Well, we shall just have to go back, I suppose," said Jill.

"Easy, isn't it?" said Puddleglum. "We might try opening that door to begin with." And they all looked at the door and saw that none of them could reach the handle, and that almost certainly no one could turn it if they did.

"Do you think they won't let us out if we ask?" said Jill. And nobody said, but everybody thought, *Supposing they don't.*

It was not a pleasant idea. Puddleglum was dead against any idea of telling the giants their real business and simply asking to be let out; and of course the children couldn't tell without his permission, because they had promised. And all three felt pretty sure that there would be no chance of escaping from the castle by night. Once they were in their rooms with the doors shut, they would be prisoners till morning. They might, of course, ask to have their doors left open, but that would rouse suspicions.

"Our only chance," said Scrubb, "is to try to sneak away by daylight. Mightn't there be an hour in the afternoon when most of the giants are asleep? – and if we could steal down into the kitchen, mightn't there be a back door open?"

"It's hardly what I call a chance," said the Marsh-wiggle. "But it's all the chance we're likely to get." As a matter of fact, Scrubb's plan was not quite so hopeless as you might think. If you want to get out of a house without being seen, the middle of the afternoon is in some ways a better time to try it than in the middle of the night. Doors and windows are more likely to be open; and if you *are* caught, you can always pretend you weren't meaning to go far and had no particular plans. (It is very hard to make either giants or grown-ups believe this if you're found climbing out of a bedroom window at one o'clock in the morning.)

"We must put them off their guard, though," said Scrubb. "We must pretend we love being here and are longing for this Autumn Feast."

"That's tomorrow night," said Puddleglum. "I heard one of them say so."

"I see," said Jill. "We must pretend to be awfully excited about it, and keep on asking questions. They think we're absolute infants anyway, which will make it easier."

"Gay," said Puddleglum with a deep sigh. "That's what we've got to be. Gay. As if we hadn't a care in the world. Frolicsome. You two youngsters haven't always got very high spirits. I've noticed. You must watch me, and do as I do. I'll be gay. Like this" – and he assumed a ghastly grin. "And frolicsome" – here he cut a most mournful caper. "You'll soon get into it, if you keep your eyes on me. They think I'm a funny fellow already, you see. I dare say you two thought I was a trifle tipsy last night, but I do assure you it was – well, most of it was – put on. I had an idea it would come in useful, somehow."

The children, when they talked over their adventures afterwards, could never feel sure whether this last statement was quite strictly true; but they were sure that Puddleglum thought it was true when he made it.

"All right. Gay's the word," said Scrubb. "Now, if we could only get someone to open this door. While we're fooling about and being gay, we've got to find out all we can about this castle."

Luckily, at that very moment the door opened, and the giant nurse bustled in saying, "Now, my poppets. Like to come and see the king and all the court setting out on the hunting? Such a pretty sight!"

They lost no time in rushing out past her and climbing down the first staircase they came to. The noise of hounds and horns and giant voices guided them, so that in a few minutes they reached the courtyard. The giants were all on foot, for there are no giant horses in that part of the world, and the giants' hunting is done on foot; like beagling in England. The hounds also were of normal size. When Jill saw that there were no horses she was at first dreadfully disappointed, for she felt sure that the great fat queen would never go after the hounds on foot; and it would never do to have her about the house all day. But then she saw the queen in a kind of litter supported on the shoulders of six young giants. The silly old creature was all got up in green and had a horn at her side. Twenty or thirty giants, including the King, were assembled, ready for the sport, all talking and laughing fit to deafen you: and down below, nearer Jill's level, there were wagging tails, and barking, and loose slobbery mouths and noses of dogs thrust into your hand. Puddleglum was just beginning to strike what he thought a gay and gamesome attitude (which might have spoiled everything if it had been noticed) when Jill put on her most attractively childish smile, rushed across to the queen's litter and shouted up to the queen.

"Oh, please! You're not going *away*, are you? You will come back?"

"Yes, my dear," said the queen. "I'll be back tonight."

"Oh, *good*. How lovely!" said Jill. "And we *may* come to the feast tomorrow night, mayn't we? We're so longing for tomorrow night! And we do love being here. And while you're out, we may run over the whole castle and see everything, mayn't we? Do say yes."

The queen did say yes, but the laughter of all the courtiers nearly drowned her voice.

The others admitted afterwards that Jill had been wonderful that day. As soon as the king and the rest of the hunting party had set off, she began making a tour of the whole castle and asking questions, but all in such an innocent, babyish way that no one could suspect her of any secret design. Though her tongue was never still you could hardly say she talked: she *prattled* and giggled. She made love to everyone – the grooms, the porters, the housemaids, the ladies-in-waiting, and the elderly giant lords whose hunting days were past. She submitted to being kissed and pawed about by any number of giantesses, many of whom seemed sorry for her and called her "a poor little thing" though none of them explained why. She made especial friends with the cook and discovered the all-important fact that there was a scullery door which let you out through the outer wall, so that you did not have to cross the courtyard or pass the great gatehouse. In the kitchen she pretended to be greedy, and ate all sorts of scraps which the cook and scullions delighted to give her. But upstairs among the ladies she asked questions about how she would be dressed for the great feast, and how long she would be allowed to sit up, and whether she would dance with some very, very small giant. And then (it made her hot all over when she remembered it afterwards) she would put her head on one side in an idiotic fashion which grown-ups, giant and otherwise, thought very fetching, and shake her curls and fidget, and say, "Oh, I do wish it was tomorrow night, don't you? Do you think the time will go quickly till then?" And all the giantesses said she was a perfect little darling; and some of them dabbed their eyes with enormous handkerchiefs as if they were going to cry.

"They're dear little things at that age," said one giantess to another. "It seems almost a pity . . ."

Scrubb and Puddleglum both did their best, but girls do that kind of thing better than boys. Even boys do it better than Marsh-wiggles.

At lunchtime something happened which made all

three of them more anxious than ever to leave the castle of the Gentle Giants. They had lunch in the great hall at a little table of their own, near the fireplace. At a bigger table, about twenty yards away, half a dozen old giants were lunching. Their conversation was so noisy, and so high up in the air, that the children soon took no more notice of it than you would of hooters outside the window or traffic noises in the street. They were eating cold venison, a kind of food which Jill had never tasted before, and she was liking it.

Suddenly Puddleglum turned to them, and his face had gone so pale that you could see the paleness under the natural muddiness of his complexion. He said, "Don't eat another bite."

"What's wrong?" asked the other two in a whisper.

"Didn't you hear what those giants were saying? 'That's a nice tender haunch of venison,' said one of them. 'Then that stag was a liar,' said another. 'Why?' said the first one. 'Oh,' said the other. 'They say that when he was caught he said, *Don't kill me, I'm tough. You won't like me.*'"

For a moment Jill did not realize the full meaning of this. But she did when Scrubb's eyes opened wide with horror and he said:

"So we've been eating a *Talking* stag."

This discovery didn't have exactly the same effect on all of them. Jill, who was new to that world, was sorry for the poor stag and thought it rotten of the giants to have killed him. Scrubb, who had been in that world before and had at least one Talking beast as his dear friend, felt horrified; as you might feel about a murder. But Puddleglum, who was Narnian born, was sick and faint, and felt as you would feel if you found you had eaten a baby.

"We've brought the anger of Aslan on us," he said. "That's what comes of not attending to the signs. We're under a curse, I expect. If it was allowed, it would be the best thing we could do, to take these knives and drive them into our own hearts."

And gradually even Jill came to see it from his point of view. At any rate, none of them wanted any more lunch. And as soon as they thought it safe they crept quietly out of the hall.

It was now drawing near to that time of the day on which their hopes of escape depended, and all became nervous. They hung about in passages and waited for things to become quiet. The giants in the hall sat on a dreadfully long time after the meal was over. The bald one was telling a story. When that was over, the three travellers dawdled down to the kitchen. But there were still plenty of giants there, or at least in the scullery, washing up and putting things away. It was agonizing, waiting till these finished their jobs and, one by one, wiped their hands and went away. At last only one old giantess was left in the room. She pottered about, and pottered about, and at last the three travellers realized with horror that she did not intend to go away at all.

"Well, dearies," she said to them. "That job's about through. Let's put the kettle there. That'll make a nice cup of tea presently. Now I can have a little piece of a rest. Just look into the scullery, like good poppets, and tell me if the back door is open."

"Yes, it is," said Scrubb.

"That's right. I always leave it open so as Puss can

get in and out, the poor thing."

Then she sat down on one chair and put her feet up on another.

"I don't know as I mightn't have forty winks," said the giantess. "If only that blamey hunting party doesn't come back too soon."

All their spirits leaped up when she mentioned forty winks, and flopped down again when she mentioned the return of the hunting party.

"When do they usually come back?" asked Jill.

"You never can tell," said the giantess. "But there; go and be quiet for a bit, my dearies."

They retreated to the far end of the kitchen, and would have slipped out into the scullery there and then if the giantess had not sat up, opened her eyes, and brushed away a fly. "Don't try it till we're sure she's really asleep," whispered Scrubb. "Or it'll spoil everything." So they all huddled at the kitchen end, waiting and watching. The thought that the hunters might come back at any moment was terrible. And the giantess was fidgety. Whenever they thought she had really gone to sleep, she moved.

"I can't bear this," thought Jill. To distract her mind, she began looking about her. Just in front of her was a clean wide table with two clean pie-dishes on it, and an open book. They were giant pie-dishes of course. Jill thought that she could lie down just comfortably in one of them. Then she climbed up on the bench beside the table to look at the book. She read:

MALLARD. This delicious bird can be cooked in a variety of ways.

"It's a cookery book," thought Jill without much interest, and glanced over her shoulder. The giantess's eyes were shut but she didn't look as if she were properly asleep. Jill glanced back at the book. It was arranged alphabetically: and at the very next entry her heart seemed to stop beating. It ran—

MAN. This elegant little biped has long been valued as a delicacy. It forms a traditional part of the Autumn Feast, and is served between the fish and the joint. Each Man—

but she could not bear to read any more. She turned round. The giantess had waked up and was having a fit of coughing. Jill nudged the other two and pointed to the book. They also mounted the bench and bent over the huge pages. Scrubb was still reading about how to cook Men when Puddleglum pointed to the next entry below it. It was like this:

MARSH-WIGGLE. Some authorities reject this animal altogether as unfit for giants' consumption because of its stringy consistency and muddy flavour. The flavour can, however, be greatly reduced if—

Jill touched his feet, and Scrubb's, gently. All three looked back at the giantess. Her mouth was slightly open and from her nose there came a sound which at the moment was more welcome to them than any music; she snored. And now it was a question of tiptoe work, not daring to go too fast, hardly daring to breathe, out through the scullery (giant sculleries smelt horrid), out at last into the pale sunlight of a winter afternoon.

They were at the top of a rough little path which ran steeply down. And, thank heavens, on the right side of the castle; the City Ruinous was in sight. In a few minutes they were back on the broad, steep road which led down from the main gate of the castle. They were also in full view from every single window on that side. If it had been one, or two, or five windows there'd be a reasonable chance that no one might be looking out. But there were nearer fifty than five. They now realized, too, that the road on which they were, and indeed all the ground between them and the City Ruinous, didn't offer as much cover as would hide a fox; it was all coarse grass and pebbles and flat stones. To make matters worse, they were now in the clothes that the giants had provided for them last night: except Puddleglum, whom nothing would fit. Jill wore a vivid green robe, rather too long for her, and over that a scarlet mantle fringed with white fur. Scrubb had scarlet stockings, blue tunic and cloak, a gold-hilted sword, and a feathered bonnet.

"Nice bits of colour, you two are," muttered Puddleglum. "Show up very prettily on a winter day. The worst archer in the world couldn't miss either of you if you were in range. And talking of archers, we'll be sorry not to have our own bows before long, I shouldn't wonder. Bit thin, too, those clothes of yours, are they?"

"Yes, I'm freezing already," said Jill.

A few minutes ago when they had been in the kitchen, she had thought that if only they could once get out of the castle, their escape would be almost complete. She now realized that the most dangerous part of it was still to come.

"Steady, steady," said Puddleglum. "Don't look back. Don't walk too quickly. Whatever you do, don't run. Look as if we were just taking a stroll, and then, if anyone sees us, he might, just possibly, not bother. The moment we look like people running away, we're done."

The distance to the City Ruinous seemed longer than Jill would have believed possible. But bit by bit they were covering it. Then came a noise. The other two gasped. Jill, who didn't know what it was, said, "What's that?"

"Hunting horn," whispered Scrubb.

"But don't run even now," said Puddleglum. "Not till I give the word."

This time Jill couldn't help glancing over her shoulder. There, about half a mile away, was the hunt returning from behind them on the left.

They walked on. Suddenly a great clamour of giant voices arose; then shouts and hollas.

"They've seen us. Run," said Puddleglum.

Jill gathered up her long skirts – horrible things for running in – and ran. There was no mistaking the danger now. She could hear the music of the hounds. She could hear the king's voice roaring out, "After them, after them, or we'll have no man-pies tomorrow."

She was last of the three now, cumbered with her dress, slipping on loose stones, her hair getting in her mouth, running-pains across her chest. The hounds were much nearer. Now she had to run uphill, up the stony slope which led to the lowest step of the giant stairway. She had no idea what they would do when they got there, or how they would be any better off even if they reached the top. But she didn't think about that. She was like a hunted animal now; as long as the pack was after her, she must run till she dropped.

The Marsh-wiggle was ahead. As he came to the lowest step he stopped, looked a little to his right, and all of a sudden darted into a little hole or crevice at the bottom of it. His long legs, disappearing into it, looked very like those of a spider. Scrubb hesitated and then vanished after him. Jill, breathless and reeling, came to the place about a minute later. It was an unattractive hole – a crack between the earth and the stone about three feet long and hardly more than a foot high. You had to fling yourself flat on your face and crawl in. You couldn't do it so very quickly either. She felt sure that a dog's teeth would close on her heel before she had got inside.

"Quick, quick. Stones. Fill up the opening," came Puddleglum's voice in the darkness beside her. It was pitch black in there, except for the grey light in the opening by which they had crawled in. The other two were working hard. She could see Scrubb's small hands and the Marsh-wiggle's big, frog-like hands black against the light, working desperately to pile up stones. Then she realized how important this was and began groping for large stones herself, and handing them to the others. Before the dogs were baying and yelping at the cave mouth, they had it pretty well filled; and now, of course, there was no light at all.

"Farther in, quick," said Puddleglum's voice.

"Let's all hold hands," said Jill.

"Good idea," said Scrubb. But it took them quite a long time to find one another's hands in the darkness. The dogs were sniffing at the other side of the barrier now.

"Try if we can stand up," suggested Scrubb. They did and found that they could. Then, Puddleglum holding out a hand behind him to Scrubb, and Scrubb holding a hand out behind him to Jill (who wished very much that she was the middle one of the party and not the last), they began groping with their feet and stumbling forwards into the blackness. It was all loose stones underfoot. Then Puddleglum came up to a wall of rock. They turned a little to their right and went on. There were a good many more twists and turns. Jill had now no sense of direction at all, and no idea where the mouth of the cave lay.

"The question is," came Puddleglum's voice out of the darkness ahead, "whether, taking one thing with another, it wouldn't be better to go back (if we can) and give the giants a treat at that feast of theirs, instead of losing our way in the guts of a hill where, ten to one, there's dragons and deep holes and gases and water and— Ow! Let go! Save yourselves. I'm—"

After that all happened quickly. There was a wild cry, a swishing, dusty, gravelly noise, a rattle of stones, and Jill found herself sliding, sliding, hopelessly sliding, and sliding quicker every moment down a slope that grew steeper every moment. It was not a smooth, firm slope, but a slope of small stones and rubbish. Even if you could have stood up, it would have been no use.

Any bit of that slope you had put your foot on would have slid away from under you and carried you down with it. But Jill was more lying than standing. And the farther they all slid, the more they disturbed all the stones and earth, so that the general downward rush of everything (including themselves) got faster and louder and dustier and dirtier. From the sharp cries and swearing of the other two, Jill got the idea that many of the stones which she was dislodging were hitting Scrubb and Puddleglum pretty hard. And now she was going at a furious rate and felt sure she would be broken to bits at the bottom.

Yet somehow they weren't. They were a mass of bruises, and the wet sticky stuff on her face appeared to be blood. And such a mass of loose earth, shingle, and larger stones was piled up round her (and partly over her) that she couldn't get up. The darkness was so complete that it made no difference at all whether you had your eyes open or shut. There was no noise. And that was the very worst moment Jill had ever known in her life. Supposing she was alone: supposing the others. . . Then she heard movements around her. And presently all three, in shaken voices, were explaining that none of them seemed to have any broken bones.

"We can never get up that again," said Scrubb's voice.

"And have you noticed how warm it is?" said the voice of Puddleglum. "That means we're a long way down. Might be nearly a mile."

No one said anything. Some time later Puddleglum added, "My tinder-box has gone."

After another long pause Jill said, "I'm terribly

thirsty."

No one suggested doing anything. There was so obviously nothing to be done. For the moment, they did not feel it quite so badly as one might have expected; that was because they were so tired.

Long, long afterwards, without the slightest warning, an utterly strange voice spoke. They knew at once that it was not the one voice in the whole world for which each had secretly been hoping; the voice of Aslan. It was a dark, flat voice – almost, if you know what that means, a pitch-black voice. It said, "What make you here, creatures of the Overworld?"

MARTHA IN THE WITCH'S POWER

K. M. BRIGGS
from Hobberdy Dick

This story takes place in the time of Oliver Cromwell. Hobberdy Dick is a hobgoblin and it is the nature of hobgoblins always to live in a house. Hobberdy Dick lives in an old manor house in Oxfordshire where, to his sorrow, he sees the old Cavalier family forced to depart and a new Puritan family, the Widdisons, move in. Mrs Widdison has dreams of grandeur. She takes pleasure in hiring for her waiting-woman the last surviving member of the Cavalier family, Anne Seckar. Hobberdy Dick loves Anne. He also comes to love Mrs Widdison's stepson Joel and her second daughter, Martha, because both of them take to the old country ways. The trouble is, Martha takes to these ways too wholeheartedly. On Midsummer Eve she goes with a local girl, Marian Barnard, to look for magic fernseed and is carried away by a witch. Ann, Joel and the man-servant, George Batchford, search frantically for Martha. So does Hobberdy Dick – in his own way.

Taynton Lob, who was couched snug in his own church tower. The difficulty was to persuade him to stir abroad on Midsummer Eve, and on so perilous an errand. He reminded Dick how they had been put to flight a year ago last May Day, and that witchcraft was much stronger at this season; but the Lob was good-natured, and Dick, strengthened by a human blessing, overbore his objections. He gave Lob a leaf from his elder twig, and they set out together. There was no one of much consequence at Barrington, so they made straight up the hill towards Stow. At Iccomb they turned aside to pick up Patch of Iccomb, who had a fairy horn with which he could summon such other hobs as might be stirring abroad. He was a brisk fellow, and glad of the prospect of a bicker. The moon had set, however, before they reached Stow churchyard, and found old Grim, playing a subdued and melancholy air upon the bones.

It took a long time to explain the matter to him; Patch's horn had summoned some half-dozen spirits before Dick and Lob succeeded in convincing him that Martha had been carried off not by the fairies but by witches. When he fully understood them his partisanship was aroused. This was no mere matter between humans, for whom Grim cared little enough by this time, but an attempt against the realm of fairy, in which Hobberdy Dick himself had nearly been carried away.

"A murrion on them!" he cried. "And may the lightning blast their circle and the fire freeze aneath their cauldron! What right have they to meddle with the likes of we?"

He drew himself up to a greater height than they had ever seen him, and green fire flashed from his eye sockets. His companions shrank back from him with something like amazement. They began to recollect the days when Grim's Ditch had stretched from the forest to Alvescot, and he had been a god rather than a hob.

"What shall us do, Grim?" said Hobberdy Dick, with even greater respect than usual.

"Second cock-crow be at hand," said Grim. "All those that be bound by it leap home to bed; those that be free scour round the barrows that have lost their spirits. There's more that use the hollow hills than the like of we. And meet me at Rollright tomorrow night when the moon casts the shadow of the stones."

He shook himself, and a shaggy, black dog, as large as a calf and with fiery eyes, stood for a moment in his place, and then sprang over the churchyard wall and was gone. Four of the spirits vanished in obedience to his command, the remaining five drew into the shelter of Grim's tomb and consulted together.

"'Twas at Shipton Barrow that Mother Darke did set eye on her last," said Dick. "That be a favourite place for the witches, for 'tis by Habber Gallows Hill; but they do shift their ground here and there. Then there's the Long Barrow near Leafield; will 'ee look there, Lull, 'tis not far from Kingstanding; and there's the old work beyond Cornbury, where Drip did use to bide afore he was laid; would 'ee look there too."

"And I'll do Maugerbury Camp and Cornhill," said Patch, "and there's Knollbury Camp and Lyneham; Hairy Tib of Bruern can do them both; and have a look-see at the Hawkstone, Tib, while you'm about it."

"'Tis not likely they'll cross the Windrush," said Dick, "but I'll go to the Asthall Mound, and the Great Camp at Windrush."

"And I'll go to Eastington Barrow and Norbury," said another Lob, "and see if I can pick up any news at Woeful Lake. There's a nixie there do know more than most."

"I'll go to Shipton Barrow," said the Taynton Lob bravely. "It seems to me 'tis there they're most like to be; and they haven't got ahold of my name like they have of Dick's."

"No, Lob, thee's a cunning one," said Tib of Bruern, "and have holden on to thy name so long that even the rest of we can hardly call it to mind."

Lob grinned at this compliment, and they parted on their various ways, moving furtively, and taking cover under elder trees whenever they could find them. Luckily the hedges had been little trimmed since the wars, and the hobs had seen to it that the elders sprang up apace. It was full day by the time that Hobberdy Dick got to Widford, where he paused for a short time to look in before crossing the river to Asthall Mound. The household was all in confusion, and none of the men to be seen; but George Batchford had looked to the stock before setting out. Dick fed the hens, whom Charity had forgotten, and then went downstream to cross the river by Swinbrook bridge. It was difficult to be sure by daylight, the ghosts were all at rest and there was no one to give information, but he could find no trace of the witches' visitation there, nor at Windrush. He crossed the Windrush at Barrington, and looked in to Taynton churchyard to see if the Lob was at home.

He was still away, however, and Dick went up to the Shipton Barrow, and met him there.

"They've been here within two-three nights," he said, "and in the old quarry yonder; but there's no saying if they were here last night, and there's no entering the mound till moonlight. Us must try it tonight."

"Till tonight, then," said Dick, and they parted.

Dick went pondering home. Suppose that Martha was spellbound within the barrow there, it would be no easy matter to free her. It was no hard thing to free a mortal from fairy land, for mortals had so many weapons. There was cold iron, and holy water, and bread and spittle and salt. Some of these the witches feared a little, but their mortal blood stood them in good stead, and they had a dozen ways of evading these counter-charms. Many times they stood firm even against Holy Writ, for they had their own ways of twisting it to ill. Besides, which of the hobs could use these human spells? And for the fairy weapons, the traitorous bogles who served the witches, and the poor spirits whom they had enslaved, could wield these with the best of them. To enlist mortal help would be best, and that would not be easy to do. If only the old lady were alive, he thought, she would know what was best to be done.

So poor Joel thought, whom Dick found already arrived when he returned. He was trying at once to devise a plan of action and to comfort and encourage his stepmother, who was entreating and scolding by turns and crying all the while. She would hardly give him time to consult with Anne and George Batchford, and find out what was best to do, and what had been done. At length he persuaded her to lie down and rest a little in Anne's care, for she was really ill and fevered with crying, while he went to fetch Marion Barnard. He explained to her father that she and Martha had sometimes gone about together, and gave him a shilling to allow her to come and show him the places where they had gone. He brought her back, pale and tongue-tied, and he and George Batchford went with her over the way which they had taken the night before. She was not quite sure where they had run into mist, but it was not far from Shipton Barrow. She changed colour when she saw how near it was, and said urgently, "Come away, come within doors, and I'll tell 'ee summat."

She would say no more until she had taken them right back to Widford; and in the stable there, well guarded by its horseshoes, she at length broke silence.

"'Twas up by that very barrow as Mother Darke comed after us on May Eve, wheedling and coaxing of us to come back with her. And she did come on close beside us till Martha struck her face with an elder twig, and she did vanish clean away, and us did run home so fast as we could run. And I can tell you no more, but I know she had a mind to Martha." She burst out crying as she spoke, and sobbed bitterly, "But Martha was too true-hearted to go along with the likes of she."

"We know she was," said Joel. "Do you know anything of this old woman, George?"

"Mother Darke be the wickedest old hag in Wychwood," said George Batchford, "and that's saying a deal. No man don't know where she bides, or I'd a fetched a wisp of her thatch and burned it right now. 'Tis a sure way to bring a witch if she have ill-willed you."

"'Tis best not to meet spells with spells," said Joel. "There must be some right way of freeing her. Don't cry, Marion. What you have told us may be a good help to us. Run to Charity in the kitchen, and she will give you a piece of cake and a drink of milk before you go home."

When she had gone, still sobbing, across the yard George Batchford and Joel looked questioningly at each other. George Batchford's face was pale and grim, and he had a bandage over one eye, for the gipsies had actively resented the search of their camp.

"Do you think it can be so, George?" said Joel. "What could the witches want with a good child like Martha, and would they be so mad as to rouse Justice against them? Why a few years back the very name of a witch was fatal to anyone."

"Aye, in most places," said George Batchford. "But there's old, old things there, and more hiding places than the keepers know of. As for what use they'd make of her, they witches has darker purposes than the likes of we can guess. Maybe they're after the Widford treasure, there was a sight of it hidden here in the old days they do say. But never fear, master, we'll get her back, and before we're much older. There's those about are good friends to us, and while the young mistress is in the house naught can go far amiss."

"In the meantime," said Joel, "we will search the Barrow again, and the quarries behind it."

"Best wait till moonrise," said George Batchford,

"and go carefully. Us don't want to frighten them away. I'll attend to the stock."

Marion's news gave more satisfaction to Hobberdy Dick than to the others, for it confirmed Lob's findings. It was now nearly certain that Martha had been caught near the Barrow, and in all probability she was still beneath it. The Barrow was one of the hollow places that had long lost its proper occupant; and when a gentle spirit deserts a place an evil one is almost certain to possess it. Joel and George Batchford were to go there at night, and George could be trusted to take salt and a horseshoe and elder branches. He wondered if he would bring a Bible, and if he knew what verses to read. If he did Dick thought that between them they could free Martha. But he was not sure of the verses, nor did he know how he could convey them, unless one of these humans would settle down and go to sleep, and that they showed no signs of doing, except Mrs Widdison, whose mind was impermeable, awake or asleep. Dick was wiser than the mortals. He knew that he had done all that he could do until he had held counsel with old Grim, and that he would need all his strength and energy that night. He curled himself up on a beam of the well-guarded stable and went to sleep.

As soon as the moon was strong enough to cast a dark shadow of the Rollright Stones on the grass the lobs met in conclave. Dick and Lob of Taynton came first, with Patch of Iccomb, who joined them as they climbed the hill. All were assembled, with the exception of one small, nighthaunting hob who was not to be seen when a dark, gaunt form came loping over the grass, and Grim, assuming his proper shape, crouched in the shadow of the tallest stone. The hobs gave their reports in turn. What evidence there was corroborated Dick's and the Taynton Lob's. Witches had passed from every point in a direction centring on the Shipton Barrow, though there was no direct evidence that their meeting had been at Gallows Hill.

"But Gallows Hill or no," said Dick, "Shipton Barrow's the hollow place nearest to it. If they be gone underground 'tis likely 'tis there they'll be. But how to get at 'em is another story; and 'tis there we look to thee, Grim."

"Give I a drink of may dew," said old Grim, "and then grip hands in a circle; for I have a power of work behind me, and 'tis a clear head I need, and all the strength your hands can give to say my tale aright."

They dispersed, and returned in a minute with hands abrim with may dew, which each offered in turn to old Grim. Then they crouched in a circle, hand locked in hand, and swayed slightly. Old Grim, with his eyes closed, swayed with them, then stopped rigid and opened his eyes, from which a green light now blazed. "I've been about and about," he said, "this way and that; and I've learned all there is to know about Mother Darke. She'm a learned witch, the head of all the witches in these parts, but she've pretty well reached the end of her tether. She'm a two-ways witch, and such is always in more peril, for their devils loathe 'em. She've sold her soul right enough, and has her things what suck her, same as any old black witch as you might name. But her's not content with that, for her's as proud as one we'll not mention. So her's dug her circles and carved her sigils, and bound her spirits to her, good and bad. And her's so testy and tetchy, they must skip this way and that with never a civil word, till they hate her very shoestrings, one and all. But she've over-reached herself, so she have, when she tried to bind an honest hob to her service. She knows right well how they hate her, and except for one or two impets that she suckles, there's not a one she dare treat with without she stands in her circle with her rod in her hand. And that, I take it, is how she've looked round for a milder spirit to treat with, and how she tried to catch our Dick. Tonight, I take it, in the full of the moon, the hill will open, and she'll be trying her spells, with the mortal child as scryer. 'Twill be easy for us to get into the hill, Dick, and if so be as you can get quietly close to the circle, I'll terrify her so her'll start a little back, and do 'ee snatch her rod so soon as it comes clear of the circle, and then her'll have no more power on 'ee never more."

"But what about Martha?" said Dick. "'Tis her we're seeking to free."

"I don't know naught about her," said Grim. "If so be you have the rod, 'tis likely you can free her, but I knows naught."

"I've heard tell," said Patch, "that human must free human, and it must be by book. They say there is a piece that will do it; but I don't know which. Maybe mortals could tell."

"There's no time to be lost," said Dick. "I must go get mortal help from Widford. Could 'ee give us a back, Grim," he said pleadingly. "I'd not ask it, but mortals move so fearful slow, and they must be up there afore the moon sets."

"Maybe," said the Taynton Lob, "the old witch's imps will tell on thee, Dick, as thee comes up to the circle, and then 'twill go hard. Maybe 'tis the very trap she've set."

"I can't help for that," said Dick. "It must be tried, whether or no."

"Hold out thy hand, Dick," said a voice, close at his ear. Dick held out his hands, something fell tickling into the palms, and the Shining Boy of Widley Copse appeared to the company. At the same moment Dick disappeared, as the precious fernseed touched his hands. The hobs laughed and cheered, and crowded round the Shining Boy with congratulations. Grim shook himself and leapt to his feet, Dick scrambled on to his shaggy back with some difficulty, keeping his fists still clenched, and the great creature bounded towards Widford.

By the time they reached it Joel, George Batchford and Jonathon Fletcher had set out for the Barrow, George loaded with every countercharm which occurred to him. The women servants were in the kitchen, Rachel and Diligence crouched down with them by the fire. Martha's bed was ready for her, with hot bricks in it, and a skillet was standing by the fire. No one was asleep there, for old Ursula was fidgeting to and fro, sending the servants on this errand or that, though there was nothing left to do. Even little Diligence, who had as a rule a great talent for sleep, was kept awake by her bustle. Neither Anne nor Mrs Widdison was in the room, and Dick went upstairs to look for them. Here at length fortune was propitious. Anne had longed with all her heart to go up to the Barrow with the men to look for Martha, but Mrs Widdison could not be left. Grief and suspense had made her really ill, and her tears could only be stayed by constant attention. Anne had succeeded at length in getting her to take some spoonfuls of milk and wine, and had read her to sleep. Now she was sitting with the Bible before her; but the enforced stillness, her wakeful night and busy, anxious day, had overpowered her senses, and she was dozing.

She had sat there only a minute, with her head bowed over her book, when she heard a voice say loud and clear beside her, "Search the Scriptures! Go up and read it at the old Barrow! Make haste! Make haste!"

She started, wide awake in a moment, or so it seemed to her, and rose to her feet without haste or delay. She had no doubt of the passage; the Bible was open at Luke 10, and in verses 17 to 20 she saw what would help her if anything could. She carried it with her, still open, and set off running, up the field track to the copse, straight across the Swinbrook road, and through the fields to Fulbrook Gap, and thence up the road to the Barrow. Dick did not wait for her. As soon as he saw that his message was delivered he ran back to Grim, and scrambled again upon his back. The moonlit fields flashed past them, and they were soon at the thorny thicket which hid the Barrow. It was a busy scene, to their eyes at least. The mortals were there, searching the small scrub of twisted thorns, and the friendly hobs were already in their places, hidden here and there where a propitious plant afforded shelter, and

and there where a propitious plant afforded shelter, and ready to give what help they could. The mortals saw neither them nor the pillars upon which the Barrow was raised, for strong blinding spells hid these from honest human eyes. Dick slid off the black dog's back, and Grim resumed his usual form. He held out his hand, and Dick opened his right hand into it. Invisible to mortal and fairy eyes alike, they went into the hill.

Shipton Barrow was small, but it gave entrance to a much wider space; and they saw a great but dark cave, without the gaieties of fairy habitation, lit only by corpselights and touchwood. This night Mother Darke was without colleagues – it may be that she pursued secrets too potent, or wealth too great, to be shared. But though she worked alone the cave was busy. Dick at first glance had seen Martha crouched on the ground and staring entranced into a crystal of moonstone. A raven was perched on a projecting tree-root, and two small green creatures in a basket of wool cocked their ears and watched. These were her familiars, and were chiefly to be feared by the hobs. Mother Darke was in a terrene circle, with her rod in her hand and surrounded by a diverse crowd of imps, those whom she addressed crouching before her, and those behind her clawing vainly at the circle. At her feet was the bath of blood, and terrible words streamed from her lips. A smaller circle had been made on the ground before her, and into this it was evident that something was to be conjured. Dick stole up to the circle behind the witch, as near as he could to the noxious spirits, and fixed his eyes upon the wand. He could no longer see Grim, but guessed where he would two circles and near to the witch, a monstrous shape appeared, with flaming jaws and eyes, larger than a panther and rampant, so that his great paw came higher than her head. It was utterly unexpected, and the witch faltered backward. Dick snatched for her wand, but her demons had been quicker. A claw caught her skirt and another her heel; there were unearthly yells and gibberings and squeaks, a sudden swirling chaos was opened beneath them, Dick leapt back just in time; the lights went out, and all was darkness and silence, except for the flapping and dismal cries of the raven, and small squeals from the green creatures. The hobs ran in from outside with a faint light of glow-worms, and found old Grim stretched upon the floor, exhausted by this final effort. But Martha knelt on by her crystal stone, and the wand which might have freed her was gone.

Joel and George Batchford had set off for the Barrow shortly after sundown, followed, rather under protest, by Jonathon Fletcher, who saw no sense in this lurking about draughty hillsides. They reached the Barrow at about ten, when the first stars were showing, and the strengthening moon had begun to cast a shadow. They searched the place again, treading cautiously and speaking in whispers; then they set Jonathon to watch behind the nearest hedgerow, under the shelter of a wild plum tree, and went on to search the quarries, both the old, disused ones near at hand and the newer quarries that were still being worked. Then they climbed to Habber Gallows Hill, where the bones of Ned Lightfoot of Leafield were still dangling, clear in the moonshine, to see if there was any fold or thicket which could conceal a witch's hovel. As they returned from this fruitless quest Jonathon came running across the open space to meet them.

"I saw something," he said, much shaken. "Something went past me into the thicket, and I heard as it might be a kind of laugh."

"Quick, where did it go?" said Joel.

"Into the thicket there, round the old mound; but I wouldn't venture there, not for a hundred pounds, and no more shouldn't you, master."

"There's more at stake here nor a hundred pound," said George Batchford sternly; but Jonathon still hung back. George tossed him a crust of bread for a guard, and he and Joel plunged again into the thicket, as quietly as might be. They searched the place to and fro, inch by inch, for what seemed hours, but there was no sign of human footing, though sometimes there were strange rustlings beside them, hard to account for in the stillness of that night. George noticed some stinkpot toadstools, and, tracing them round, found that they encircled the barrow. He began to sprinkle salt on them, one by one; but it was a slow business, for they were hard to find in the uncertain moonshine and thick undergrowth. Before he was half round them they heard a sound like a landslide in the quarry, with a more sinister echo like the shriek of a storm. They came together, heedless for the moment of the noise they made.

"Was it in the quarry, do you think?" said Joel.

"Nay," said George. "It sounded to me more like under our feet. God guard the little maiden."

There was a rush past them, a little dancing of faint

light, and as they strained their ears they thought they heard a confusion of faint sounds, high pitched and almost inaudible like the cries of bats.

"She's here! She's here!" cried Joel in despair. "And we can't get through to her. What can we do, George?"

"Sprinkle salt and pray, master," said George. "'Tis the likeliest thing to avail now."

They stood together, each murmuring his prayers, though George Batchford's were mostly an adaptation of the White Paternoster. Their devotions were broken by the sound of a girl's voice speaking breathlessly in the direction where they had left Jonathon Fletcher. The hope came to them that it was Martha, and they both ran towards it; but it was Anne Seckar, breathless and muddied, with an open Bible in her hand. She thrust it into Joel's, gasping, "Read, read from there; I have no breath."

The moonlight was not bright enough for him to read by it, and they spent some time lighting their lantern, while Anne lay panting on the turf. At length the light was strong enough, and Joel read. "Again," said Anne when he reached the end of the passage. He read it again, and began a third time; but he had not reached the end before a faint light appeared from the barrow in front of them, and Martha came walking steadily towards them, with her eyes open and her hands outstretched. Joel snatched her up in his arms and threw his cloak about her, and she seemed to come to herself.

Two solicitous processions set out from the Barrow that night in opposite directions, one carrying Martha and one old Grim of Stow. Dick was torn between them, but in the end his gratitude conquered, and he went with the hobs. They bore old Grim to his favourite tomb, washed him from head to foot with may dew, rubbed him down with wild thyme, and, as he revived, gave him as much dew to drink as he could quaff. Gradually his shrivelled form expanded, and he looked around him with a livelier air. Indeed old Grim was the brisker, the stronger and the more alert for that night's work for a hundred years to come.

In the meantime George Batchford and Joel carried Martha home by turns. She was still dazed and silent. Jonathon Fletcher hurried on ahead to tell the good news. The household came out in a clamour of relief and curiosity, and Mrs Widdison, running downstairs in her stuff gown, caught Martha in her arms and kissed her repeatedly, exclaiming, "You naughty, naughty child! Where have you been? You deserve to be well whipped. I have been nearly dead with anxiety for you, and it is unknown what your father will say. Where have you been?"

"She is not fully herself, madam," said Anne Seckar. "We had better give her some warm milk and put her to bed, had we not? We will tell you about it when she is asleep."

Martha drank the warmed milk that was waiting for her, and as she gave back the cup looked at Anne and said, "Where is the deep pool that I was looking in? Didn't I ought to be back there? I was waiting for someone."

ABU ALI MEETS A DRAGON

NOEL LANGLEY
from The Land of Green Ginger

Abu Ali, the son of Aladdin, has borrowed his father's famous lamp and set out adventuring. Unfortunately, Abdul the Slave of the Lamp has forbidden Abu Ali to rub the lamp more than once so Abu Ali has to do things the hard way. He heads first for Samarkand to find Silver Bud, the beautiful daughter of Sulkpot Ben Nagnag, a rich and greedy jeweller. On the way he runs across two rival suitors, Rubdub Ben Thud and Tintac Ping Foo, who conspire to steal his horse. Undeterred, Abu Ali and a new-found friend, Omar Khayyam, travel by donkey to the heavily-guarded house of Sulkpot Ben Nagnag. Abu Ali scales the garden wall, lands right on top of Kublai Snoo (one of the guards), and proceeds to tie him up . . .

"WHAT *ARE* YOU DOING?" asked a surprised and charming voice behind him.

Abu Ali looked around, quickly, and fell absolutely and everlastingly in Love at First Sight with Silver Bud, who was gazing at him in wide-eyed bewilderment.

"*Oh*!" exclaimed Abu Ali, struck speechless by her beauty. And so he should have been, Gentle Reader.

No one, before or since, has *ever* been so beautiful. Think of all the most beautiful blossoms you have ever seen blooming, and Silver Bud was a thousand times more beautiful than the Blossom of your Heart's Delight.

"Why have you tied up Kublai Snoo?" she inquired politely, in a voice that was sweeter than all the Songbirds you have ever heard, and all the prettiest Music ever played.

Indeed, her voice so enraptured the already enraptured Abu Ali, that he had to pinch himself rapidly before he could find *his* voice.

"Because I don't want to be Boiled in Oil," he answered, gazing at her in rapturous wonder.

"If you don't want to be Boiled in Oil," she said very reasonably, "what are you doing *here*?"

"I came to seek *you*!" he cried, falling on one knee. "To Serve you with my Life, Beloved Silver Bud!"

"Oh, dear! That's what it nearly always costs," sighed Silver Bud regretfully. "Who are *you*?"

"My name is Abu Ali," said Abu Ali devoutly. "And Humble though I may Appear to you, I have sworn a vow to rescue you from this Durance Vile, and take you away to Happiness and Freedom!"

"Indeed, though I hardly know you, I see you are very brave," confessed Silver Bud, touched to her tender-hearted heart, "and, also very gallant! I couldn't bear to see you Boiled in Oil! Please go before they find you!"

"Never, Silver Bud, Fairest of the Fair!" cried Abu Ali, valiantly, rising to his feet. "Death before Dishonour! Trust me, that is all I ask! Trust me enough to Fly from Here with me!"

"*Now*?" asked Silver Bud. "This very *minute*?"

"Now!" nodded Abu Ali. "This very *minute*!"

"Certainly!" said Silver Bud, delighted. "How?"

"All we have to do," said Abu Ali swiftly, "is to climb this tree on *this* side of the Wall, then climb down Omar Khayyam on the other! Ready?"

"Ready!" cried Silver Bud obediently; but just as she placed her tiny foot on the first bough of the tree, an Ear-Splitting Roar of Rage shook the air, and Sulkpot Ben Nagnag came bouncing across the Garden with his slippers slapping on his bunioned feet.

"Ho, there! Guards!" he was shouting wildly. "Ho, there! Guards! Stop them! Stop them, I say! Arrest that Scoundrel!"

Guards appeared like Magic from every corner, and in Less Time than it Takes to Tell, Abu Ali was overpowered and dragged before Sulkpot, though he fought like a tiger and kicked the Captain four times on the same leg before he was subdued.

"Caught you in the Nick of Time!" snarled Sulkpot savagely to Silver Bud. "Well, what do you have to say? Explain yourself, young lady, *if* you can!"

"Well, really, father!" protested Silver Bud in a voice of perfect calm. "My Friend and I were simply going to climb this tree to look at a bird's nest—"

"Enough! No more! Not another word!" roared her red-nosed Father, and directed the bulk of his fury at Abu Ali. "Who are you, Creature?" he shouted. "Don't answer me, you Insect! I'll have you Boiled Alive for this!"

"You can't!" cried Silver Bud protectively. "He's an

Old and Trusted Friend of mine! I *asked* him to go birds' nesting with me! You shan't Boil him in Oil! I *love* him!"

"You WHAT???" cried Abu Ali and Sulkpot Ben Nagnag together, but for very different reasons.

"I love him!" repeated Silver Bud, *quite* fearlessly.

Nobody had noticed Kublai Snoo yet.

"My Ears Deceive Me!" rumbled Sulkpot, now quite beside himself. "I shall choke, or something! Water! Bring me water! Ungrateful daughter! Do you realize what you said? Off to the Oil Vats with him! My Ears and Turban, I shall have a fit, a stroke, a seizure! I can feel them coming on! Away with him, Guards! No! Wait a minute! Who are you, hey? What's your name, you Beast, you Brat, you Burglar, you Brute, you Brigand, you Blackguard?"

"Chu-Chin-Chow, Laundryman!" returned Abu Ali with spirit.

"TAKE HIM AWAY!" screamed Sulkpot hoarsely, dancing with anguish on his bunions. "Boil him in Oil! Boil him in Oil!"

Nothing loath, the Guards obeyed.

"Stop!" cried Silver Bud, with such nobility of purpose that the Guards were awed into obeying her.

Then she faced Sulkpot with her head held high.

"If you Boil him in Oil," she announced clearly, "I shall Never Marry Anyone Else, not as Long as I live! I shall just pine away instead! And I mean it! I mean it! I *mean* it!"

Nobody had noticed Kublai Snoo yet; but the Uproar had brought the Wicked Princes Rubdub Ben Thud and Tintac Ping Foo into the Garden, and they were just in time to hear what Silver Bud said.

"*What's* that?" asked Tintac Ping Foo, extremely taken aback. "Can I believe my ears?"

"The echoes must be playing tricks!" said Rubdub Ben Thud, taken even further aback.

"Call some more Guards!" shouted Sulkpot Ben Nagnag, having been taken even further aback than that, and now at a loss. "Lots more Guards! I never *heard* of such a Thing! Can you be Defying *me*, Daughter?"

"Indeed, I can!" Silver Bud assured him. "I *am*!"

"These are all the Guards we have," said the Captain apologetically. "There *are* no more!"

"Good Grief! It's that Abu Ali Person!" cried Tintac Ping Foo suddenly, pointing. "He's here before us!"

"Imposserous!" cried Rubdub. "He has no Horse!"

"What's that?" asked Sulkpot Ben Nagnag swiftly. "You *know* this Crafty Cut-Throat?"

"Who? Him?" shrilled Tintac Ping Foo hastily. "I should hope *not*! Indeed! *Pff*!"

"The idea!" added Rubdub Ben Thud grandly. "*Really*!"

"In that case, Gentlemen, I apologize to you for this Unseemly Confusion!" said Sulkpot, rapidly pulling himself together from every direction. "Allow me to present to you my cherished daughter, Silver Bud, the Bride you Came to Seek!"

"*Ooh*!" said Rubdub appreciatively.

"*My*!" said Ping Foo, smirking.

"Don't trust them!" Abu Ali called to Silver Bud.

"I won't!" she promised him.

"Guards, remove that Knave!" shouted Sulkpot Ben

Nagnag.

"Leave him alone!" countered Silver Bud at once. "I claim the Right to choose the Bravest of the Three to be my Husband!"

"Me!" cried Tintac Ping Foo instantly.

"Me!" cried Rubdub Ben Thud, only a second later.

"Nonsense!" said Abu Ali flatly.

"Silence!" roared Sulkpot Ben Nagnag.

"The only way to prove which one is the bravest," continued Silver Bud firmly, "is to set all three a Difficult Task, and then I shall wed the One who does his Task best!"

"I agree!" cried Abu Ali. "Do you, Gentlemen?"

This was met by an Unaccountable Silence, which the Wicked Prince Tintac Ping Foo finally broke by giving a small cough.

"You said, a Difficult Task?" he asked Silver Bud uneasily.

"*You* heard!" said Abu Ali pointedly.

The Wicked Prince Rubdub Ben Thud thrust out his lower lip.

"We weren't given Adequate Notice of this!" he said, resentfully. "Not so much as a Hint! I refuse to commit myself until I've seen my Lawyer!"

"*There* speaks a coward!" cried Silver Bud in fine scorn.

"No, I'm not!" shouted Ben Thud. "But I have a Cold! My Mummie says I'm not to get my feet wet!"

"And I'm not allowed to talk to Strangers!" chimed in Ping Foo. "Otherwise, I'd take on *any* old Task; and *Win*!"

"Come, Daughter, you are beside yourself!" fumed

Sulkpot Ben Nagnag. "Choose between these two very Fine Princes, for you cannot have them Both!"

"Never!" cried Silver Bud. "Not till all Three have done a Difficult Task!"

"Extraordinary!" muttered Rubdub Ben Thud, more to himself than to Those Present. "Can't think what's got into People! What next, I wonder?"

"Father!" said Silver Bud firmly. "Set the Tasks!"

"But you're not *Serious*?" demanded Tintac Ping Foo in shrill amazement. "Why, you *can't* be!"

"It just gets more and more Irregular as we Go Along!" grumbled Rubdub. "And I'll have you know that Umbrage Has Been Taken!"

"Ah, the Trials and the Tribulations of a Father!" said Sulkpot self-pityingly. "You can see that I have no Choice, Gentlemen," he added apologetically. "I'm afraid I must ask you, Prince Tintac Ping Foo, to find and bring back – bring back – a – let me see; bring back an – ah, yes – bring back a Magic Carpet!"

"A Magic *Carpet*!" echoed Ping Foo in scandalized tones. "Whatever *for*? What on *Earth* would you do with it?"

"Make it fly!" said Silver Bud, promptly.

"And me?" inquired Rubdub Ben Thud uneasily. "What do *I* have to bring back?"

Sulkpot Ben Nagnag, never a very imaginative man, thought hard.

"Another Magic Carpet," he said at last.

"Unfair! Unfair!" squealed Rubdub at once.

"And what about the Upstart?" snapped Ping Foo spitefully. "What's *he* got to bring back?"

"Yes! Make it even *more* impossible!" said Rubdub

balefully.

"Don't worry – I will!" promised Sulkpot, scowling horribly at Abu Ali. "You, Creature, will bring back Three Tail Feathers from a Magic Phoenix Bird, which is believed to be Quite Extinct by Those Who Know!"

"Certainly!" said Abu Ali cheerfully. "Now may I be released?"

"Yes!" said Silver Bud quickly. "Release him, Guards!"

The Guards were glad to.

Still nobody had noticed Kublai Snoo.

"Magic Carpet!" muttered Rubdub Ben Thud ferociously to the Garden Wall. "I'd like to know where I'm Expected to Find an Idiotic Thing like *That*!"

Silver Bud laid her hand gently on Abu Ali's arm.

"I hope you'll find the Tail Feathers easily, and come back safely," she said tenderly.

"I will! I promise you I will!" vowed Abu Ali with all his heart.

"Goodbye," said Silver Bud in a small voice.

"Goodbye," said Abu Ali, and to avoid any display of Unheroic Feeling, he turned away quickly and was over the Wall in a jump.

When Samarkand lay far behind him, and both Abu Ali and the Donkey were beginning to feel exceedingly tired and hot, they came upon a Forest of Tall Trees, stretching away as far as the Eye could See, and no doubt farther, if one but knew.

"If," reasoned Abu Ali, bringing the Donkey to a halt, and gazing at the Forest, "if I ride *round* this Forest, it might take me the Best Years of my Life! On the other hand – allowing for the fact that there are hidden dangers in Forests, and perhaps Dragons – if it is wide but not deep, I could ride *through* it, and be out on the other side in No Time at All. I shall do this."

Whereupon he rode straight into the Forest, and soon the Donkey was trotting through wooded glades where the branches knotted their knuckles together over their heads, and small streams rippled out from behind bushes and rippled back behind others, and all was quiet and peaceful.

Then they came to a Clearing in the Forest, and there in the Clearing, dancing about and not noticing them as yet, was a Huge, Horned, Scaly, Scowly, Nozzle-nosed, Claw-Hammered, Gaggle-toothed, People-hating, Smoke-snorting, Fire-eating, Flame-throwing, Penulticarnivorous, Bright Green Dragon.

And, as he danced, his bright green scales banged and clashed like cymbals, and he sang in a voice like a Bright Green Erupting Volcano:

"If you come into the Woods tonight
I'll give you a Horrible Fright!
I'll Howl and Scowl
And Gobble and Growl!
Your hair, it'll turn to White!
For I'm a Dragon,
Yes, I'm a Dragon!
(That's my Tail – that's what I'm draggin'!)
What'll I do?
If I meet you?
Hup-one-two!
I'll Eat Yer!"

Well, the Donkey was so Paralysed by the Spectacle

that it stood Rooted to the Spot, and Abu Ali was powerless to make it turn and run.

He simply had to sit there till the Dragon did a particularly complicated hop-skip-and-turn which brought him Face to Face with them. At once he switched off his Song in mid-sizzle, leaned his spiky elbow against a convenient tree, and surveyed them intently with his head on one side.

"You'll forgive me, I'm sure," said the Green Dragon in his best Party Manners, "but I don't recall having had the Previous Pleasure of your Acquaintance! Stranger in these Parts?"

"Yes," said Abu Ali, "and what is more, lost!"

"Lost, ha?" said the Dragon, with a Great Show of Sympathetic Concern. "Imagine that! Still, that's the Way it Goes! Here Today, and gone Tomorrow!" He smiled hard at the Donkey, and the Donkey dropped his ears uneasily. "A pleasing Donkey you're sitting on, Good Sir! Tasty, I should say off-hand! And plump!"

The Donkey's ears drooped even more uneasily, and the Green Dragon smiled even harder back.

"I'm searching," Abu Ali explained hastily, feeling anxious for the Donkey, "for the Magic Phoenix Birds, and any information you might be able to supply—"

"The Magic Phoenix Birds?" interrupted the Green Dragon expansively. "Why, of course! I know *exactly* where you'll find them! How fortunate we met, Good Sir!" And here he eyed the Donkey again, and was noticed by Abu Ali to Lick his Lips with his Long Green Tongue. "*Most* fortunate!"

"Then would you be kind enough to direct me to them?" asked Abu Ali. "If it's not asking too much?"

"No, no! *Indeed* it's not Asking too Much!" the Green Dragon assured him warmly. "I'll be Delighted, Good Sir! It's the Least I can Do in Return!"

"In return for what?" asked Abu Ali cautiously.

"In return for eating your Donkey with a Lettuce Salad and Tomato Sliced Thin!" said the Green Dragon as Blandly as a Beadle.

"Never!" cried Abu Ali resolutely.

"Come, Come!" said the Green Dragon. "Fair's fair! *You* want the Phoenix Birds! I want the Donkey! Exchange is no robbery! And he'd go *beautifully* with a Lettuce Salad and Tomato Sliced Thin!"

"He would not!" Abu Ali asserted. "He's as tough as leather!"

"To you, yes," the Green Dragon agreed. "To a Green Dragon, no! Tasty and Toothsome, Tender and Plump! And this must be borne in mind, Good Sir; if I don't eat your Donkey, I'll have to eat *you*!"

"Be that as it may," parried Abu Ali bravely, "and even supposing I *do* give you my Donkey, how do I know you'll still tell me where to find the Phoenix Birds, once you've eaten him? How do I know you *do* know where they are?"

"That's just a Chance you'll have to Take," said the Green Dragon airily. "Forsooth, one can never be sure of *anything* in this World, can one? That's what Makes it all so Exciting, I always say!"

Abu Ali pondered on his predicament for a moment, and then very reluctantly dismounted.

"Very well," he said. "There's the Donkey. But before I leave him to his Dreadful Fate, tell me where to find the Magic Phoenix Birds!"

"Nobody knows," said the Green Dragon, blithely, "so how should I?"

"That's Cheating!" cried Abu Ali hotly. "You don't get the Donkey!"

"Nonsense!" returned the Green Dragon stretching out a Long Green Claw for the Donkey. But Abu Ali was quicker. He slapped the Donkey so hard that it gave one Terrified Bray and galloped off into the Forest like a Streak of Lightning.

"*Well*!" said the Green Dragon, aghast. "*Imagine that*!"

"Butter-fingers!" said Abu Ali calmly. "That's the last *either* of us'll ever see of him!"

"Yes, I know it is!" exclaimed the Green Dragon angrily. "And I'm *furious*, simply *furious*! In fact," said the Green Dragon, with a Nasty Light coming into his Eye, "I'm *nearly* too furious to Eat You Instead! *Nearly*!" said the Green Dragon, beginning to creep towards Abu Ali. "But not *quite*! So bid Farewell to this Empty World of Shallow Pomp, because HERE I COME!"

He gave a Great Pounce, but Abu Ali skipped neatly behind a tree, and the Dragon tripped and fell on his smouldering nose.

"Now, wait!" Abu Ali urged him. "Pause! Consider! You're over-excited!"

"No, I'm not! I'm under-nourished!" snarled the Green Dragon, creeping towards him again.

He made another Pounce, and Abu Ali jumped aside, and the Green Dragon bumped his head so hard against a knot in the tree trunk that it bent one of his horns.

"*Oooh! Ahh! Ouch*!" cried the Green Dragon, sitting

back on his heels and rubbing his bent horn tenderly. "*Now* look what you made me do!"

Abu Ali peeped round the trunk warily.

"It serves you right!" he said. "Do you want to bend the *other* horn? If not, stand aside and let me be on my way!"

For answer, the Green Dragon turned his Head away indifferently and began to whistle, as if he were no longer Interested in the Proceedings.

Abu Ali was smart enough to remain where he was, and after a long pause, the Green Dragon looked back at him.

"Well, I never, did you ever!" exclaimed the Green Dragon in elaborate surprise. "You're not still there? I thought you'd gone *ages* ago!"

"No, you didn't!" returned Abu Ali. "You thought I'd be silly enough to venture out from behind this tree so you could eat me!"

"*Tcha*!" said the Dragon sulkily.

"And *Tcha* to you!" returned Abu Ali.

There was another pause.

"Come out from behind that tree, and I'll show you my Butterfly Collection," the Green Dragon invited in New, Honeyed Tones.

"No, thank you," said Abu Ali. "I have all the Butterflies I need, right here in my own Tum."

"Very well then, I'll Boil a Kettle on my Nose and we'll all have Tea!" offered the Dragon brightly.

"I'm not thirsty," said Abu Ali.

"Scorpions and Centipedes!" fumed the Dragon in a Fulminous Fury, and made another Sudden Pounce, missing Abu Ali again, but tripping himself against a root. "Wait till I getcha, that's all! This is a *fine* way to treat a Dragon! I'll teach you to make me Look Undignified! Come *here*!" He made another Pounce at Abu Ali, and caught his Claw in a Root, which tripped him up so beautifully that he sat back on his Tail with an undignified Thud.

"You realize that we can keep this up indefinitely, without either of us getting anywhere?" asked Abu Ali from the other side of the tree. "I'll stop, if you will!"

"*Tcha*!" the Green Dragon snorted.

"And a Boom-tcha-tcha! And a Boom-tcha-tcha!" said Abu Ali promptly.

"Don't *do* that!" screamed the Green Dragon. "I *loathe* being imitated!"

"If you mind *your* manners, I'll mind *mine*," offered Abu Ali.

The Green Dragon sat down again, tenderly nursing his Tail with one Claw and rubbing his bent horn with the other.

"You needn't think you'll get away!" he informed Abu Ali nastily. "Because you *won't*! The *Second* you come out from behind that tree, I'll have you down in Three Gulps! *Two* Gulps! I'm *Furious*!"

Abu Ali leaned against the other side of the tree-trunk and Reviewed the Situation Thoughtfully.

There was no doubt that the Green Dragon meant Exactly what he said; in which case, it was just a question of time before he was eaten with a Lettuce Salad and a Tomato Sliced Thin.

It was also quite out of the question to try and make a run for it, because once in the open, the Green Dragon would catch him easily.

Only one Source of Help remained to him. The One Rub of the Magic Lamp allowed him by Abdul.

Abu Ali drew the Lamp from his pocket and peeped round the tree.

The Green Dragon was still rubbing his foot and his bent horn, but he was watching Abu Ali intently.

"Hey there, Green Dragon!" called Abu Ali. "Did you ever hear of Aladdin's Magic Lamp?"

"What if I did?" sneered the Green Dragon. "I am an Educated Dragon, and not alarmed by Old Wives' Tales and other such Bucolic Balderdash!"

"Do you know what this is?" asked Abu Ali, holding up the Lamp.

The Green Dragon surveyed it uninterestedly.

"Well, goodie-goodie!" he said sarcastically. "So you remembered to bring your own Gravy!"

"This," said Abu Ali impressively, "is not a Gravy boat. It is the Magic Lamp! I have only to give it One Rub, and there will be an Awful Rumble of Thunder, the Ground will Split Open, and a Large and Terrible Djinn will appear in a Cloud of Smoke! What will you do then?"

The Green Dragon breathed on his Claw, and rubbed it nonchalantly against his Scales.

"Pardon me if I don't smile, I have a Chipped Lip!" he said contemptuously.

"Very well, I'll prove it!" said Abu Ali firmly. "One! Two!—"

"*One* Moment," the Green Dragon interrupted rudely. "It's only fair to tell you that I'm not being fooled by that Old Lamp! Instead of wasting my Valuable Time, why don't you act like a Man and come out from behind that tree—"

"Three!" said Abu Ali, and rubbed the Lamp.

For a moment the Dragon looked slightly uneasy, but when Nothing Happened to disturb the Peaceful Silence of the Forest, he relaxed again.

"Well? One, two, three *what*?" he jeered.

"Just you wait and see!" Abu Ali told him optimistically.

The Silence remained Undisturbed.

Abu Ali concealed his discomfiture behind a brave front and gave the Lamp another brisk rub.

"Try blowing down it!" suggested the Green Dragon disrespectfully.

The Silence continued.

"Har, har!" said the Dragon rudely. "What a Lamp! What do you keep in it? Glow-worms?"

Alas, Gentle Reader, Abu Ali had been so taken aback at the Failure of the Lamp that he forgot to keep his Weather Eye open. This enabled the Green Dragon to creep up on him unawares. Then with a Roar, he suddenly Pounced, and Abu Ali was just a moment too late to dodge. Before he knew it, he found himself pinned to the ground by Ten Large Green Claws.

"*Whoops*!" roared the Dragon triumphantly. "*Gotcha*! How shall I start? Shall I Bite you in Half, or start at the toes and Nibble you Hither and Yon?"

But the mocking words were no sooner out of his Jaws when a Loud Burst of Thunder suddenly shook the air.

The Green Dragon quickly turned his head and saw the ground slowly splitting open behind him.

"An Earthquake!" he gasped in a horrified voice.

"Imagine *that*!"

A Ball of Green Smoke suddenly shot up through the crack in the ground and hovered over the Green Dragon's head.

"Good Old Abdul!" cheered Abu Ali. "Just in time!"

"Ow, wow, *wow*!" screamed the Dragon. "A Volcano too! *Mother*!"

Whereupon he turned a complete somersault from Sheer Cowardice and tore away into the Forest as fast as his legs could carry him, and was never heard from again, not even by postcard.

Abu Ali sat up.

"Thank you, Abdul!" he said gratefully to the Green Cloud in the air above him.

The Green Cloud was behaving in a most peculiar way, however; as if a Great Struggle was going on inside it.

Abu Ali waited expectantly for a moment, but nothing new happened.

"Is that you, Abdul?" he inquired at last, just to make sure.

"I won't be a moment," the Cloud answered in a worried voice. "Something – seems – to have gone – wrong here – but – I'll – be done in a jiffy. *Bother*!"

The Cloud bounced about in the air, and began to bulge here and there.

"Is there anything I can do to help?" asked Abu Ali.

"Not a thing," replied the Cloud, beginning to sound a little desperate. "Really, this is absurd – wait a minute – I've got it – no, I haven't. Nuisance, nuisance – and it always looked so easy, too!"

The Cloud gave a sudden Lurch sideways, turned

upside down, and descended to Earth with a Bump, and a Voice that wasn't Abdul's said: "OOOCH!" very painfully.

Then the Green Smoke slowly dissolved away, leaving a Very Small, Round, Fat, Knee-high, Fourteen-carat, Rueful, Green-hued Djinn seated on the grass, looking more than slightly dazed.

Abu Ali stared at him in Blank Surprise.

"*Who* are *you*?" he asked at last.

"Boomalakka Wee," said the Very Small Djinn dejectedly.

"Then what happened to Abdul?" asked Abu Ali.

"Father was busy, so I came instead," said the Very Small Djinn apologetically. "I've always wanted to answer the Lamp, but he always said No, he didn't want me Hobnobbing with Mortals; but when you rubbed the Lamp just now, he was Sleeping off his Lunch, so I *had* to come instead."

He looked around him for a moment or two.

"Well, well, so this is Earth," he said, slightly disappointed. "I was told there was More of It. You may have noticed I had a little Trouble with that Cloud? Answering the Lamp's a lot more tricky than it looks. I forgot which was Up and which was Down. So the whole time I was trying to make it go Down I was really making it go Up. Which is why it Stood Still, of course. Naturally, it wouldn't go Up when it knew it ought to be going Down. But I think I may safely say I have Mastered It, so All is Well, and you can ask What Thou Wilt and I shall Obey!"

"That's more than kind of you," answered Abu Ali appreciatively, "but my request has already been answered!"

"Oh?" said Boomalakka swiftly. "By whom?"

"You!" said Abu Ali. "I was about to be eaten by a Green Dragon, and you scared him away. While you were still up in the Cloud, this was."

"Oh, good!" said Boomalakka Wee, cheering up at once. "I'm better at it than I thought! Well, now that I *am* here, can I be of any Other Assistance?"

"Well, if it's not too much to ask, I *do* need another Donkey," Abu Ali admitted. "Mine ran away."

"A Donkey?" repeated Boomalakka Wee confidently. "Nothing easier! Just watch carefully for a moment! A Donkey!"

He rubbed his fingertips together and waved them in the air.

"Presto!" said Boomalakka Wee impressively. "One Donkey!"

A moment or two passed by uneventfully.

"That's funny!" said Boomalakka Wee, wrinkling his forehead. "By rights there ought to be a Donkey here by now!"

"Try again," suggested Abu Ali. "You know how stubborn Donkeys are!"

"This one, especially!" agreed Boomalakka Wee, and rubbed his fingertips together again and waved them in the air.

"Presto! A Donkey!" he repeated, rather less confidently.

This time there was a noise that sounded like *Chug*, and a little puff of dust bounced up off the ground.

Boomalakka's chest swelled triumphantly.

"There you are, you see?" he said, his confidence

restored. "I *knew* I could do it!"

They bent over and looked.

"But isn't that a Mouse?" asked Abu Ali.

"It can't be!" said Boomalakka Wee.

"I rather think it is," said Abu Ali.

Boomalakka Wee examined it intently.

"Yes," he admitted at last, in a crestfallen voice. "It *is* a Mouse! But it's not what I *ordered*! I ordered a Donkey! You *heard* me!"

"I did indeed," said Abu Ali.

"'Presto! A Donkey!' I said."

"Your exact words."

"Exactly! My exact words! And now this Mouse!"

"Never mind. Try again," said Abu Ali encouragingly.

"Well, I would," confessed Boomalakka Wee, "but the thing is, if we *were* going to get a Donkey, we'd have got one the first Time, or Not at All!"

"Am I to gather from all this Beating About the Bush that you Won't Be Needing Me?" inquired the Mouse with icy politeness.

"You are. We won't," affirmed Boomalakka Wee.

"Then, if it's not Asking Too Much, would you be kind enough to Repatriate me?" requested the Mouse, still icily polite.

"Certainly," said Boomalakka Wee, "and I'm sorry we bothered you."

He rubbed his fingertips together and waved them in the air.

"Presto! No more Mouse!" he said.

They waited for a moment.

"I'm still here," said the Mouse with a touch of

asperity.

Boomalakka Wee turned to Abu Ali.

"Tell me, Master," he said earnestly. "Does it *have* to be a Donkey? I mean, if it came to a Pinch, could you make do with a Mouse Instead?"

"I'm afraid not," said Abu Ali regretfully.

"So I should hope!" the Mouse said tartly. "Make-do, indeed! Glory Ducketts, it's not as if I *wanted* to come, in the first place! Some People, and I mention no Names, might save a lot of Mice a great deal of Needless Inconvenience if they took the trouble to get their Spells right!"

"The Spell *was* right!" answered Boomalakka Wee hotly. "Except that I ordered a Donkey."

"I am no doubt Rather Dense," said the Mouse with mounting truculence. "May we take it a Step at a Time? The Spell was right, except that you ordered a Donkey. And what did you get? You got a Mouse. So *somebody* blundered. It can't possibly be You. So, I suppose it's *me*, for not being a Donkey?"

"I didn't say that!" returned Boomalakka Wee swiftly. "But what I *do* say now, is that I've known Mice who Kept their Place, and I've known Mice who didn't; and the Mice I admire least are the Mice who think they're ever so Bright and Witty!"

"To which type of Mouse do you infer that I belong?" demanded the Mouse icily.

"If the cap fits, wear it!" said Boomalakka Wee.

"Gentlemen, Gentlemen," Abu Ali restrained them peaceably.

"Gentlemen?" snapped the Mouse, rounding on Abu Ali. "I'd have thought *you'd* have known better!

Can't you tell a Lady when you see one?"

"I beg your pardon, Ma'am," said Abu Ali hastily.

"Granted as soon as asked," the Mouse replied in a slightly mollified voice. "And now may I go home? I have Friends who will Become Anxious!"

"Certainly!" Abu Ali assured her gallantly. "Send the Lady home, Boomalakka Wee!"

"I will when I can get a word in Edgeways," said Boomalakka Wee sulkily, and made the Magic Pass again.

Nothing happened that hadn't happened before – which was Nothing – and Boomalakka Wee blushed bright green with annoyance. He made the Magic Pass three times more, and then he sat down and cupped his chin in his hands.

"I can't think *why* it doesn't work!" he said disconsolately. "I've watched Father often enough!"

The Mouse gave a rather hollow laugh.

"It's come to a *Pretty* Pass, I *must* say," she declared, "when a Lady has to Start Life Afresh in a Strange Land, without so much as a Word of Warning or a Crumb of Cheese!"

"I suggest," said Abu Ali helpfully to Boomalakka Wee, "that you go back home to Abdul, explain the situation, and ask *him* what to do."

Boomalakka Wee brightened.

"Of course, yes!" he said, jumping up. "I should have thought of it myself!"

"How," inquired the Mouse, unexcited, "do *you* propose to get back, when you can't even send *me* back?"

Boomalakka Wee looked daggers at her.

"You *do* pour cold water on *everything*, don't you?" he said resentfully. "Well, just you watch, that's all!"

He stamped on the ground with one foot.

"Going *Down*!" he cried ringingly.

Nothing happened. Nothing whatever.

"So now," said the Mouse with morbid satisfaction, "*no one* can get back. We're here for ever. What fun. Tra-la-la. But, if ever I *do* get back," she added pugnaciously, "someone will Answer for This! I mention No Names, but just watch where my eyes rest!"

"Wait," said Abu Ali soothingly. "I have the solution. It's very simple. I'll rub the Lamp again, and Abdul will answer it, and then he'll put everything right!"

"No," said Boomalakka Wee in a small, sad voice. "No, he won't. He can't. Not till I get back. The Lamp works for only one person at a time; and as I can't get *back*, Father can't get *here*!"

"It just gets more and more gay," said the Mouse lugubriously. "I can't remember when I've laughed so hard. Hey-nonny-no."

"To sum up," said Abu Ali without reproach, "we are lost in the Middle of the Forest. We have no way of getting out except by walking. And we may run across a Green Dragon any moment now. Otherwise, everything's splendid."

"Yes, indeed, and it has even A Bright Side," agreed the Mouse, eyeing Boomalakka Wee expressively. "You could well say that you lost a Donkey, only to gain An Even Bigger One."

THE BOX OF DELIGHTS

JOHN MASEFIELD

It is Christmas and Kay Harker goes home by train. On the same train are some villains disguised as clergymen, who are hunting an old Punch and Judy man called Cole Haulings for the sake of the magic box he carries. "The wolves are running!" Kay is told. And they are. The clergymen take the old man prisoner in the snow and carry him off in an aeroplane, but, just in time, the old man gives Kay the magic box for safety. Kay tries to trace the villains even though he has houseguests to entertain. This keeps him so busy that it is a long time before he has leisure to look at the box. (The "shagreen" it is covered in is a kind of rough leather.)

NOW, AT LAST KAY FELT that he was free to look at the Box of Delights. He went up to his bedroom. He was very anxious not to be spied upon, and, remembering how those three spies had been peering in at the window the night before, and how the repulsive Rat had crept about in the secret passages finding out all sorts of things, he was not sure that he could guard himself from being seen. His bedroom had two doors in it opening onto different landings. He locked both doors and hung caps over the keyholes: he looked under the beds. Then, as in the past, when he had wished to hide from his governess, he crept under the valance of his dressing-table: no one could possibly see him there.

The box was of some very hard wood of a dense grain. It had been covered with shagreen, but the shagreen was black with age and sometimes worn away so as to show the wood beneath. Both wood and shagreen had been polished until they were as smooth as a polished metal. On the side of it there was a little counter-sunk groove, in the midst of which was a knob. "I press this to open," he repeated. "If I push it to the right I can go small, whatever that may mean. If I push it to the left I can go swift, and that I've tried. I do want to see what's inside it. I wonder, is this wood that it's made of lignum-vitae wood?"

"It's the wood the phoenix builds in," the box said.

"Is it really?" Kay said. "No wonder it smells like spice."

Then he saw that the groove was inlaid with gold and that the golden knob within the groove had been carven into the image of a rose bud, which was extraordinarily fragrant. "I say," Kay said to himself, "this is a wonderful box. Now I'll open it."

He pressed the tiny, golden rose bud and, at once, from within the box, there came a tiny crying of birds. As he listened he heard the stockdove brooding, the cuckoo tolling, blackbirds, thrushes, and nightingale singing. Then a far-away cock crowed thrice and the box slowly opened. Inside he saw what he took to be a book, the leaves of which were all chased and worked with multitudinous figures, and the effect that it gave him was that of staring into an opening in a wood. It was lit from within; multitudinous, tiny things were shifting there. Then he saw that the things which were falling were the petals of may blossom from giant hawthorn trees covered with flowers. The hawthorns stood on each side of the entrance to the forest, which was dark from the great trees yet dappled with light. Now, as he looked into it, he saw deer glide with alert ears, then a fox, motionless at his earth, a rabbit moving to new pasture and nibbling at a dandelion, and the snouts of the moles breaking the wet earth. All the forest was full of life: all the birds were singing, insects were humming, dragonflies darting, butterflies wavering and settling. It was so clear that he could see the flies on the leaves brushing their heads and wings with their legs. "It's all alive and it's full of summer. There are all the birds singing: there's a linnet; bullfinch; a robin; that's a little wren." Others were singing too: different kinds of tits; the woodpecker was drilling; the chiffchaff repeating his name; the yellow-hammer and garden-warbler were singing, and overhead, as the bird went swiftly past, came the sad, laughing cry of the curlew. While he gazed into the heart of summer and listened to the murmur and the singing, he heard another noise like the tinkling of little bells. As he wondered what these bells could be he decided that they were not bells, but a tinkling like the cry of many little long-tailed tits together. "Where did I hear that noise before quite recently?" Kay said to himself. It was not the noise of long-tailed tits: it was the noise of little chains chinking. He remembered that strange rider who had passed him in the street the day before. That rider, who seemed to have little silver chains dangling from his wrists, had jingled so. "Oh," Kay said, as he looked, "there's someone wonderful coming."

At first he thought that the figure was one of those giant red deer, long since extinct: it bore enormous antlers. Then he saw that it was a great man, antlered at the brow, dressed in deerskin and moving with the silent, slow grace of a stag; and, although he was so like a stag, he was hung about with little silver chains and bells.

Kay knew at once that this was Herne the Hunter, of whom he had often heard. "Hallo, Kay," Herne the Hunter said, "are you coming into my wild wood?"

"Yes, if you please, sir," Kay said. Herne stretched out his hand. Kay took it and at once he was glad that he had taken it, for there he was in the forest between the two hawthorn trees, with the petals of the may blossom falling on him. All the may blossoms that fell were talking to him, and he was aware of what all the creatures of the forest were saying to each other: what the birds were singing, and what it was that the flowers and trees were thinking. And he realized that the forest went on and on for ever, and all of it was full of life beyond anything that he had ever imagined; for in the trees, in each leaf, and on every twig, and in every inch of soil there were ants, grubs, worms; little, tiny, moving things, incredibly small yet all thrilling with life.

"Oh dear," Kay said, "I shall never know a hundredth part of all the things there are to know."

"You will, if you stay with me," Herne the Hunter said. "Would you like to be a stag with me in the wild wood?"

Now, next to being a jockey, Kay had longed to be a young stag. Now he realized that he had become one. He was there in the green wood beside a giant stag, so screened with the boughs that they were a part of a dappled pattern of light and shade, and the news of the wood came to him in scents upon the wind.

Presently the giant stag gave a signal. They moved off out of the green wood into a rolling grassland, where some fox cubs were playing with a vixen. They passed these and presently came down to a pool, where some moor-hens were cocking about in the water; a crested grebe kept a fierce eye upon them. They went out into the water. It was lovely, Kay thought, to feel the water cool upon the feet after running, and to be able to go paddling, although it had been winter only a minute before. "And it's lovely, too," he thought, "to have hard feet and not get sharp bits of twigs into one's soles." They moved through the water towards some reeds. Looking through the stalks of the reeds Kay saw that there were a multitude of wild ducks. "Would you like to be a wild duck, Kay?" Herne asked.

Now, next to being a jockey and a stag, Kay had longed to be a wild duck, and, at once, with a great clatter of feathers, the wild duck rose more and more and more, going high up, and, oh joy! Herne and Kay were with them, flying on wings of their own and Kay could just see that his neck was glinting green. There was the pool, blue as a piece of sky below them, and the sky above brighter than he had ever seen it.

They flew higher and higher in great sweeps, and, presently, they saw the sea like the dark blue on a map. Then they made a sweeping circle and there was the pool once more, blue like the sky. "Now for the plunge," Herne cried, and instantly they were surging down swiftly and still more swiftly, and the pool was rushing up to them, and they all went skimming into it with a long, scuttering, rippling splash. And there they all were paddling together, happy to be in the water again.

"How beautiful the water is," Kay said. Indeed it was beautiful, clear hill water, with little fish darting this way and that and the weeds waving, and sometimes he saw that the waving weeds were really fish. "Would you like to be a fish, Kay?" Herne asked.

And, next to being a jockey, a stag and a wild duck, Kay had always longed to be a fish. And then, instantly, Kay was a fish. He and Herne were there in the coolness and dimness, wavering as the water wavered, and feeling a cold spring gurgling up just underneath them and tickling their tummies.

While Kay was enjoying the water Herne asked, "Did you see the wolves in the wood?"

"No," Kay said.

"Well, they were there," Herne said. "That was why I moved. Did you see the hawks in the air?"

"No," Kay said.

"Well, they were there," Herne said. "And that was why I plunged. And d'you see the pike in the weeds?"

"No," Kay said.

"He is there," Herne said. "Look."

Looking ahead up the stream Kay saw a darkness of

weeds wavering in the water, and presently a part of the darkness wavered into a shape with eyes that gleamed and hooky teeth that showed. Kay saw that the eyes were fixed upon himself and suddenly the dark shadow leaped swiftly forward with a swirl of water. But Kay and Herne were out of the water. They were trotting happily together over the grass towards the forest; Herne a giant figure with the antlers of the red stag and himself a little figure with little budding antlers. And so they went trotting together into the forest to a great ruined oak-tree, so old that all within was hollow, though the great shell still put forth twigs and leaves.

Somehow, the figure of Herne, which had been so stag-like became like the oak tree and merged into the oak tree till Kay could see nothing but the tree. What had been Herne's antlers were now a few old branches and what had seemed silver chains dangling from Herne's wrists were now the leaves rustling. Then the oak tree faded and grew smaller till it was a dark point in a sunny glade. The glade shrank and there was Kay standing between the two hawthorn trees, which were shedding their blossoms upon him. Then these shrank till they were as tiny as the works of a watch and then Kay was himself again under the valance in his room at Seekings looking at the first page in the Book of Delights contained within the box. "My goodness," Kay said, "no wonder the old man treasured this box and called it a box of delights. Now, I wonder," he said, "how long I have been in that fairyland with Herne the Hunter?" He looked at his watch and found that he had been away only two minutes. It was now ten minutes to eleven. “My goodness,” Kay said, “all that took only two minutes.”

THE AMAZING FLIGHT OF THE GUMP

L. FRANK BAUM

from The Land of Oz

There has been a revolution in the emerald city of Oz. An army of girls has taken over and their leader, Jinjur, has declared herself queen. The Scarecrow, who is the rightful king of Oz, is trapped inside the palace along with the Tin Woodman (called Nick Chopper), the (Highly Magnified) Woggle-Bug, and a small boy called Tip. With Tip are two beings that Tip has brought alive with a magic powder: Jack Pumpkinhead, who has a wooden body and a pumpkin for a head, and the Saw-Horse, who is entirely made of wood. They all try to think of ways to escape.

"IT SEEMS TO ME," began the Scarecrow, when all were again assembled in the throne room, "that the girl Jinjur is quite right in claiming to be queen. And if she is right, then I am wrong, and we have no business to be occupying her palace."

"But you were the king until she came," said the Woggle-Bug, strutting up and down with his hands in his pockets, "so it appears to me that she is the interloper instead of you."

"Especially as we have just conquered her and put her to flight," added the Pumpkinhead, as he raised his hands to turn his face towards the Scarecrow.

"Have we really conquered her?" asked the Scarecrow, quietly. "Look out of the window, and tell me what you see."

Tip ran to the window and looked out.

"The palace is surrounded by a double row of girl soldiers," he announced.

"I thought so," returned the Scarecrow. "We are as truly their prisoners as we were before the mice frightened them from the palace."

"My friend is right," said Nick Chopper, who had been polishing his breast with a bit of chamois-leather. "Jinjur is still the queen, and we are her prisoners."

"But I hope she cannot get at us," exclaimed the Pumpkinhead, with a shiver of fear. "She threatened to make tarts of me, you know."

"Don't worry," said the Tin Woodman. "It cannot matter greatly. If you stay shut up here you will spoil in time, anyway. A good tart is far more admirable than a decayed intellect."

"Very true," agreed the Scarecrow.

"Oh, dear!" moaned Jack, "what an unhappy lot is mine! Why, dear father, did you not make me out of tin – or even out of straw – so that I would keep indefinitely."

"Shucks!" returned Tip, indignantly. "You ought to be glad that I made you at all." Then he added, reflectively, "Everything has to come to an end, some time."

"But I beg to remind you," broke in the Woggle-Bug who had a distressed look in his bulging, round eyes, "that this terrible Queen Jinjur suggested making a goulash of me Me! The only Highly Magnified and Thoroughly Educated Woggle-Bug in the wide, wide world!"

"I think it was a brilliant idea," remarked the Scarecrow, approvingly.

"Don't you imagine he would make a better soup?" asked the Tin Woodman, turning towards his friend.

"Well, perhaps," acknowledged the Scarecrow.

The Woggle-Bug groaned.

"I can see, in my mind's eye," said he, mournfully, "the goats eating small pieces of my dear comrade, the Tin Woodman, while my soup is being cooked on a bonfire built of the Saw-Horse and Jack Pumpkinhead's body, and Queen Jinjur watches me boil while she feeds the flames with my friend the Scarecrow!"

This morbid picture cast a gloom over the entire party, making them restless and anxious.

"It can't happen for some time," said the Tin Woodman, trying to speak cheerfully, "for we shall be able to keep Jinjur out of the palace until she manages to break down the doors."

"And in the meantime I am liable to starve to death, and so is the Woggle-Bug," announced Tip.

"As for me," said the Woggle-Bug, "I think that I could live for some time on Jack Pumpkinhead. Not that I prefer pumpkins for food; but I believe they are somewhat nutritious, and Jack's head is large and plump."

"How heartless!" exclaimed the Tin Woodman,

greatly shocked. "Are we cannibals, let me ask? Or are we faithful friends?"

"I see very clearly that we cannot stay shut up in this palace," said the Scarecrow, with decision. "So let us end this mournful talk and try to discover a means to escape."

At this suggestion they all gathered eagerly around the throne, wherein was seated the Scarecrow, and as Tip sat down upon a stool there fell from his pocket a pepper-box, which rolled upon the floor.

"What is this?" asked Nick Chopper, picking up the box.

"Be careful!" cried the boy. "That's my Powder of Life. Don't spill it, for it is nearly gone."

"And what is the Powder of Life?" inquired the Scarecrow, as Tip replaced the box carefully in his pocket. "It's some magical stuff old Mombi got from a crooked sorcerer," explained the boy. "She brought Jack to life with it, and afterward I used it to bring the Saw-Horse to life. I guess it will make anything live that is sprinkled with it; but there's only about one dose left."

"Then it is very precious," said the Tin Woodman.

"Indeed it is," agreed the Scarecrow. "It may prove our best means of escape from our difficulties. I believe I will think for a few minutes; so I will thank you, friend Tip, to get out your knife and rip this heavy crown from my forehead."

Tip soon cut the stitches that had fastened the crown to the Scarecrow's head, and the former monarch of the Emerald City removed it with a sigh of relief and hung it on a peg beside the throne.

"That is my last memento of royalty," said he, "and

I'm glad to get rid of it. The former king of this city, who was named Pastoria, lost the crown to the Wonderful Wizard, who passed it on to me. Now the girl Jinjur claims it, and I sincerely hope it will not give her a headache."

"A kindly thought, which I greatly admire," said the Tin Woodman, nodding approvingly.

"And now I will indulge in a quiet think," continued the Scarecrow, lying back in the throne.

The others remained as silent and still as possible, so as not to disturb him; for all had great confidence in the extraordinary brains of the Scarecrow.

And, after what seemed a very long time indeed to the anxious watchers, the thinker sat up, looked upon his friends with his most whimsical expression, and said, "My brains work beautifully today. I'm quite proud of them. Now, listen! If we attempt to escape through the doors of the palace we shall surely be captured. And, as we can't escape through the ground, there is only one other thing to be done. We must escape through the air!"

He paused to note the effect of these words; but all his hearers seemed puzzled and unconvinced.

"The Wonderful Wizard escaped in a balloon," he continued. "We don't know how to make a balloon, of course; but any sort of thing that can fly through the air can carry us easily. So I suggest that my friend the Tin Woodman, who is a skilful mechanic, shall build some sort of a machine, with good strong wings, to carry us; and our friend Tip can then bring the Thing to life with his magical powder."

"Bravo!" cried Nick Chopper.

"What splendid brains!" murmured Jack.

"Really quite clever!" said the Educated Woggle-Bug.

"I believe it can be done," declared Tip, "that is, if the Tin Woodman is equal to making the Thing."

"I'll do my best," said Nick, cheerily, "and, as a matter of fact, I do not often fail in what I attempt. But the Thing will have to be built on the roof of the palace, so it can rise comfortably into the air."

"To be sure," said the Scarecrow.

"Then let us search through the palace," continued the Tin Woodman, "and carry all the material we can find to the roof, where I will begin my work."

"First, however," said the Pumpkinhead, "I beg you will release me from this horse, and make me another leg to walk with. For in my present condition I am of no use to myself or to anyone else."

So the Tin Woodman knocked a mahogany centre-table to pieces with his axe and fitted one of the legs, which was beautifully carved, on to the body of Jack Pumpkinhead, who was very proud of the acquisition.

"It seems strange," said he, as he watched the Tin Woodman work, "that my left leg should be the most elegant and substantial part of me."

"That proves you are unusual," returned the Scarecrow, "and I am convinced that the only people worthy of consideration in this world are the unusual ones. For the common folks are like the leaves of a tree, and live and die unnoticed."

"Spoken like a philosopher!" cried the Woggle-Bug, as he assisted the Tin Woodman to set Jack upon his feet.

"How do you feel now?" asked Tip, watching the Pumpkinhead stump around to try his new leg.

"As good as new," answered Jack, joyfully, "and quite ready to assist you all to escape."

"Then let us get to work," said the Scarecrow, in a businesslike tone.

So, glad to be doing anything that might lead to the end of their captivity, the friends separated to wander over the palace in search of fitting material to use in the construction of their aerial machine.

When the adventurers reassembled upon the roof it was found that a remarkably queer assortment of articles had been selected by the various members of the party. No one seemed to have a very clear idea of what was required, but all had brought something.

The Woggle-Bug had taken from its position over the mantelpiece in a great hallway the head of a Gump, which was adorned with wide-spreading antlers; and this, with great care and greater difficulty, the insect had carried up the stairs to the roof. This Gump resembled an Elk's head, only the nose turned upward in a saucy manner and there were whiskers upon its chin, like those of a billy-goat. Why the Woggle-Bug selected this article he could not have explained, except that it had aroused his curiosity. Tip, with the aid of the Saw-Horse, had brought a large, upholstered sofa to the roof. It was an old-fashioned piece of furniture, with high back and ends, and it was so heavy that, even by resting the greatest weight upon the back of the Saw-Horse, the boy found himself out of breath when at last the clumsy sofa was dumped upon the roof.

The Pumpkinhead had brought a broom, which was the first thing he saw. The Scarecrow arrived with a coil of clothes-lines and ropes which he had taken from the courtyard, and in his trip up the stairs he had become so entangled in the loose ends of the ropes that both he and his burden tumbled in a heap upon the roof and might have rolled off if Tip had not rescued him.

The Tin Woodman appeared last. He also had been to the courtyard, where he had cut four great, spreading leaves from a huge palm-tree that was the pride of all the inhabitants of the Emerald City.

"My dear Nick!" exclaimed the Scarecrow, seeing what his friend had done; "you have been guilty of the greatest crime any person can commit in the Emerald City. If I remember rightly, the penalty for chopping leaves from the royal palm-tree is to be killed seven times and afterward imprisoned for life."

"It cannot be helped now," answered the Tin Woodman, throwing down the big leaves upon the roof. "But it may be one more reason why it is necessary for us to escape. And now let us see what you have found for me to work with."

Many were the doubtful looks cast upon the heap of miscellaneous material that now cluttered the roof, and finally the Scarecrow shook his head and remarked:

"Well, if friend Nick can manufacture, from this mess of rubbish, a Thing that will fly through the air and carry us to safety, then I will acknowledge him to be a better mechanic than I suspected."

But the Tin Woodman seemed at first by no means

sure of his powers, and only after polishing his forehead vigorously with the chamois-leather did he resolve to undertake the task.

"The first thing required for the machine," said he, "is a body big enough to carry the entire party. This sofa is the biggest thing we have, and might be used for a body. But, should the machine ever tip sideways, we would all slide off and fall to the ground."

"Why not use two sofas?" asked Tip. "There's another one just like this downstairs."

"That is a very sensible suggestion," exclaimed the Tin Woodman. "You must fetch the other sofa at once."

So Tip and the Saw-Horse managed, with much labour, to get the sofa to the roof; and when the two were placed together, edge to edge, the backs and ends formed a protecting rampart all around the seats.

"Excellent!" cried the Scarecrow. "We can ride within this snug nest quite at our ease."

The two sofas were now bound firmly together with ropes and clothes-lines, and then Nick Chopper fastened the Gump's head to one end.

"That will show which is the front end of the Thing," said he, greatly pleased with the idea. "And, really, if you examine it critically, the Gump looks very well as a figurehead. These great palm leaves, for which I have endangered my life seven times, must serve us as wings."

"Are they strong enough?" asked the boy.

"They are as strong as anything we can get," answered the Woodman, "and although they are not in proportion to the Thing's body, we are not in a position to be very particular."

So he fastened the palm leaves to the sofas, two on each side.

Said the Woggle-Bug, with considerable admiration:

"The Thing is now complete, and only needs to be brought to life."

"Stop a moment!" exclaimed Jack. "Are you not going to use my broom?"

"What for?" asked the Scarecrow

"Why, it can be fastened to the back end for a tail," answered the Pumpkinhead. "Surely you would not call the Thing complete without a tail."

"Hm!" said the Tin Woodman, "I do not see the use of a tail. We are not trying to copy a beast, or a fish, or a bird. All we ask of the Thing is to carry us through the air."

"Perhaps, after the Thing is brought to life, it can use a tail to steer with," suggested the Scarecrow. "For if it flies through the air it will not be unlike a bird, and I've noticed that all birds have tails which they use for a rudder while flying."

"Very well," answered Nick, "the broom shall be used for a tail," and he fastened it firmly to the back end of the sofa body.

Tip took the pepper-box from his pocket.

"The Thing looks very big," said he, anxiously; "and I am not sure there is enough powder left to bring all of it to life. But I'll make it go as far as possible."

"Put most on the wings," said Nick Chopper; "for they must be made as strong as possible."

"And don't forget the head!" exclaimed the Woggle-Bug.

"Or the tail!" added Jack Pumpkinhead.

"Do be quiet," said Tip, nervously; "you must give me a chance to work the magic charm in the proper manner."

Very carefully he began to sprinkle the Thing with the precious powder. Each of the four wings was first lightly covered with a layer; then the sofas were sprinkled, and the broom given a slight coating.

"The head! The head! Don't, I beg of you, forget the head!" cried the Woggle-Bug, excitedly.

"There's only a little of the powder left," announced Tip, looking within the box. "And it seems to me it is more important to bring the legs of the sofas to life than the head."

"Not so," decided the Scarecrow. "Every thing must have a head to direct it; and since this creature is to fly, and not walk, it is really unimportant whether its legs are alive or not."

So Tip abided by this decision and sprinkled the Gump's head with the remainder of the powder.

"Now," said he, "keep silence while I work the charm!"

Having heard old Mombi pronounce the magic words, and having also succeeded in bringing the Saw-Horse to life, Tip did not hesitate an instant in speaking the three cabalistic words, each accompanied by the peculiar gesture of the hands.

It was a grave and impressive ceremony.

As he finished the incantation the Thing shuddered throughout its huge bulk, the Gump gave the screeching cry that is familiar with those animals, and then the four wings began flapping furiously.

Tip managed to grasp a chimney, else he would have been blown off the roof by the terrible breeze raised by the wings. The Scarecrow, being light in weight, was caught up bodily and borne through the air until Tip luckily seized him by one leg and held him fast. The Woggle-Bug lay flat upon the roof and so escaped harm, and the Tin Woodman, whose weight of tin anchored him firmly, threw both arms around Jack Pumpkinhead and managed to save him. The Saw-Horse toppled over upon his back and lay with his legs waving helplessly above him.

And now, while all were struggling to recover themselves, the Thing rose slowly from the roof and mounted into the air.

"Here! Come back!" cried Tip, in a frightened voice, as he clung to the chimney with one hand and the Scarecrow with the other. "Come back at once, I command you!"

It was now that the wisdom of the Scarecrow, in bringing the head of the Thing to life instead of the legs, was proved beyond a doubt. For the Gump, already high in the air, turned its head at Tip's command and gradually circled around until it could view the roof of the palace.

"Come back!" shouted the boy, again.

And the Gump obeyed, slowly and gracefully waving its four wings in the air until the Thing had settled once more upon the roof and become still.

"This," said the Gump, in a squeaky voice not at all proportioned to the size of its great body, "is the most novel experience I ever heard of. The last thing I remember distinctly is walking through the forest and hearing a loud noise. Something probably killed me then, and it certainly ought to have been the end of me. Yet here I am, alive again, with four monstrous wings and a body which I venture to say would make any respectable animal or fowl weep with shame to own. What does it all mean? Am I a Gump, or am I a juggernaut?" The creature, as it spoke, wiggled its chin whiskers in a very comical manner.

"You're just a Thing," answered Tip, "with a Gump's head on it. And we have made you and brought you to life so that you may carry us through the air wherever we wish to go."

"Very good!" said the Thing. "As I am not a Gump, I cannot have a Gump's pride or independent spirit. So I may as well become your servant as anything else. My only satisfaction is that I do not seem to have a very strong constitution, and am not likely to live long in a state of slavery."

"Don't say that, I beg of you!" cried the Tin Woodman, whose excellent heart was strongly affected by this sad speech. "Are you not feeling well today?"

"Oh, as for that," returned the Gump, "it is my first day of existence; so I cannot judge whether I am feeling well or ill." And it waved its broom tail to and fro in a pensive manner.

"Come, come!" said the Scarecrow, kindly, "do try to be more cheerful and take life as you find it. We shall be kind masters, and will strive to render your existence as pleasant as possible. Are you willing to carry us through the air wherever we wish to go?"

"Certainly," answered the Gump. "I greatly prefer to navigate the air. For should I travel on the earth and meet with one of my own species, my embarrassment would be something awful!"

"I can appreciate that," said the Tin Woodman, sympathetically.

"And yet," continued the Thing, "when I carefully look you over, my masters, none of you seems to be constructed much more artistically than I am."

"Appearances are deceitful," said the Woggle-Bug, earnestly. "I am both Highly Magnified and Thoroughly Educated."

"Indeed!" murmured the Gump, indifferently.

"And my brains are considered remarkably rare specimens," added the Scarecrow, proudly.

"How strange!" remarked the Gump.

"Although I am of tin," said the Woodman, "I own a heart altogether the warmest and most admirable in the whole world."

"I'm delighted to hear it," replied the Gump, with a slight cough.

"My smile," said Jack Pumpkinhead, "is worthy of your best attention. It is always the same."

"*Semper idem*," explained the Woggle-Bug, pompously; and the Gump turned to stare at him.

"And I," declared the Saw-Horse, filling in an awkward pause, "am remarkable because I can't help it."

"I am proud, indeed, to meet with such exceptional masters," said the Gump, in a careless tone. "If I could but secure so complete an introduction to myself, I would be more than satisfied."

"That will come in time," remarked the Scarecrow. "To 'Know Thyself' is considered quite an accomplishment, which it has taken us, who are your elders, months to perfect. But now," he added, turning to the others, "let us get aboard and start upon our journey."

"Where shall we go?" asked Tip, as he clambered to a seat on the sofas and assisted the Pumpkinhead to follow him.

"In the South Country rules a very delightful queen called Glinda the Good, who I am sure will gladly receive us," said the Scarecrow, getting into the Thing clumsily. "Let us go to her and ask her advice."

"That is cleverly thought of," declared Nick Chopper, giving the Woggle-Bug a boost and then toppling the Saw-Horse into the rear end of the cushioned seats. "I know Glinda the Good, and believe she will prove a friend indeed."

"Are we all ready?" asked the boy.

"Yes," announced the Tin Woodman, seating himself beside the Scarecrow.

"Then," said Tip, addressing the Gump, "be kind enough to fly with us to the Southward; and do not go higher than to escape the houses and trees, for it makes me dizzy to be up so far."

"All right," answered the Gump, briefly.

It flapped its four huge wings and rose slowly into the air; and then, while our little band of adventurers clung to the backs and sides of the sofas for support, the Gump turned toward the south and soared swiftly and majestically away.

ON THE GREAT WALL

RUDYARD KIPLING

from Puck of Pook's Hill

Dan and Una live in Sussex. One day, quite by accident, they "break the hills" and summon Puck, the last one left of the People of the Hills. He is "a small, brown, broad-shouldered, pointy-eared person with a snub nose, slanting blue eyes, and a grin that ran right across his freckled face." He tells them, "By right of Oak, Ash and Thorn are you free to come and go and look and know where I shall show or best you please. You shall see What you shall see and you shall hear What you shall hear, though it shall have happened three thousand year." Thereafter they are constantly meeting with people who had lived in Sussex before them. Among these is a young Roman officer, Parnesius, whose family once had a villa in the nearby Isle of Wight.

Parnesius tells them how he was sent to Hadrian's Wall for daring to contradict the future Roman Emperor, Maximus.

"When I left Rome for Lalage's sake
    By the Legions' Road to Rimini,
She vowed her heart was mine to take

With me and my shield to Rimini –
(Till the Eagles flew from Rimini!)
And I've tramped Britain and I've tramped Gaul
And the Pontic shore where the snowflakes fall
As white as the neck of Lalage –
As cold as the heart of Lalage!
And I've lost Britain and I've lost Gaul,"

(the voice seemed very cheerful about it),

"And I've lost Rome, and worst of all,
I've lost Lalage!"

THEY WERE STANDING by the gate to Far Wood when they heard this song. Without a word they hurried to their private gap and wriggled through the hedge almost atop of a jay that was feeding from Puck's hand.

"Gently!" said Puck. "What are you looking for?"

"Parnesius, of course," Dan answered. "We've only just remembered yesterday. It isn't fair."

Puck chuckled as he rose. "I'm sorry, but children who spend the afternoon with me and a Roman Centurion need a little settling dose of magic before they go to tea with their governess. Ohé, Parnesius!" he called.

"Here, Faun!" came the answer from Volaterrae. They could see the shimmer of bronze armour in the beech crotch, and the friendly flash of the great shield uplifted.

"I have driven out the Britons." Parnesius laughed like a boy. "I occupy their high forts. But Rome is merciful! You may come up." And up they three all scrambled.

"What was the song you were singing just now?" said Una, as soon as she had settled herself.

"That? Oh, 'Rimini'. It's one of the tunes that are always being born somewhere in the empire. They run like a pestilence for six months or a year, till another one pleases the legions, and then they march to *that*."

"Tell them about the marching, Parnesius. Few people nowadays walk from end to end of this country," said Puck.

"The greater their loss. I know nothing better than the Long March when your feet are hardened. You begin after the mists have risen, and you end, perhaps, an hour after sundown."

"And what do you have to eat?" Dan asked, promptly.

"Fat bacon, beans, and bread, and whatever wine happens to be in the rest houses. But soldiers are born grumblers. Their very first day out, my men complained of our water-ground British corn. They said it wasn't so filling as the rough stuff that is ground in the Roman ox-mills. However, they had to fetch and eat it."

"Fetch it? Where from?" said Una.

"From that newly-invented water-mill below the forge."

"That's Forge Mill – *our* Mill!" Una looked at Puck.

"Yes, yours," Puck put in. "How old did you think it was?"

"I don't know. Didn't Sir Richard Dalyngridge talk about it?"

"He did, and it was old in his day," Puck answered. "Hundreds of years old."

"It was new in mine," said Parnesius. "My men looked at the flour in their helmets as though it had been a nest of adders. They did it to try my patience. But I – addressed them, and we became friends. To tell the truth, they taught me the Roman Step. You see, I'd only served with quick-marching auxiliaries. A legion's pace is altogether different. It is a long, slow stride, that never varies from sunrise to sunset. 'Rome's race – Rome's pace,' as the proverb says. Twenty-four miles in eight hours, neither more nor less. Head and spear up, shield on your back, cuirass-collar open one hand's breadth – and that's how you take the Eagles through Britain."

"And did you meet any adventures?" said Dan.

"There are no adventures South the Wall," said Parnesius. "The worst thing that happened to me was having to appear before a magistrate up North, where a wandering philosopher had jeered at the Eagles. I was able to show that the old man had deliberately blocked our road; and the magistrate told him, out of his own Book, I believe, that, whatever his Gods might be, he should pay proper respect to Caesar."

"What did you do?" said Dan.

"Went on. Why should *I* care for such things, my business being to reach my station? It took me twenty days.

"Of course, the farther north you go the emptier are the roads. At last you fetch clear of the forests and climb bare hills, where wolves howl in the ruins of our cities that have been. No more pretty girls; no more jolly magistrates who knew your father when he was young, and invite you to stay with them; no news at the temples and way-stations except bad news of wild beasts. There's where you meet hunters, and trappers for the circuses, prodding along chained bears and muzzled wolves. Your pony shies at them, and your men laugh.

"The houses change from gardened villas to shut forts with watch-towers of grey stone, and great stone-walled sheep-folds, guarded by armed Britons of the North Shore. In the naked hills beyond the naked houses, where the shadows of the clouds play like cavalry charging, you see puffs of black smoke from the mines. The hard road goes on and on – and the wind sings through your helmet-plume – past altars to legions and generals forgotten, and broken statues of gods and heroes, and thousands of graves where the mountain foxes and hares peep at you. Red-hot in summer, freezing in winter, is that big, purple heather country of broken stone.

"Just when you think you are at the world's end, you see a smoke from east to west as far as the eye can turn, and then, under it, also as far as the eye can stretch, houses and temples, shops and theatres, barracks and granaries, trickling along like dice behind – always behind – one long, low, rising and falling, and hiding and showing line of towers. And that is the Wall!"

"Ah!" said the children, taking breath.

"You may well," said Parnesius. "Old men who have followed the Eagles since boyhood say nothing in the empire is more wonderful than first sight of the Wall!"

"Is it just *a* Wall? Like the one round the kitchen garden?" said Dan.

"No, no! It is *the* Wall. Along the top are towers with guard-houses, small towers, between. Even on the narrowest part of it three men with shields can walk abreast, from guard-house to guard-house. A little curtain wall, no higher than a man's neck, runs along the top of the thick wall, so that from a distance you see the helmets of the sentries sliding back and forth like beads. Thirty feet high is the Wall, and on the Picts' side, the north, is a ditch, strewn with blades of old swords and spear-heads set in wood, and tyres of wheels joined by chains. The Little People come there to steal iron for their arrow-heads.

"But the Wall itself is not more wonderful than the town behind it. Long ago there were great ramparts and ditches on the south side, and no one was allowed to build there. Now the ramparts are partly pulled down and built over, from end to end of the Wall; making a thin town eighty miles long. Think of it! One roaring, rioting, cock-fighting, wolf-baiting, horse-racing town, from Ituna on the west to Segedunum on the cold eastern beach! On one side heather, woods and ruins where Picts hide, and on the other, a vast town – long like a snake, and wicked like a snake. Yes, a snake basking beside a warm wall!

"My cohort, I was told, lay at Hunno, where the Great North Road runs through the Wall into the Province of Valentia." Parnesius laughed scornfully. "The Province of Valentia! We followed the road, therefore, into Hunno town, and stood astonished. The place was a fair – a fair of peoples from every corner of the empire. Some were racing horses, some sat in wine shops, some watched dogs baiting bears, and many gathered in a ditch to see cocks fight. A boy not much older than myself, but I could see he was an officer, reined up before me and asked what I wanted.

"'My station,' I said, and showed him my shield." Parnesius held up his broad shield with its three Xs like letters on a beer-cask.

"'Lucky omen!' said he. 'Your cohort's the next tower to us, but they're all at the cockfight. This is a happy place. Come and wet the Eagles.' He meant to offer me a drink.

"'When I've handed over my men,' I said. I felt angry and ashamed.

"'Oh, you'll soon outgrow that sort of nonsense,' he answered. 'But don't let me interfere with your hopes. Go on to the statue of Roma Dea. You can't miss it. The main road into Valentia!' and he laughed and rode off. I could see the statue not a quarter of a mile away, and there I went. At some time or other the Great North Road ran under it into Valentia; but the far end had been blocked up because of the Picts, and on the plaster a man had scratched, 'Finish!' It was like marching into a cave. We grounded spears together, my little thirty, and it echoed in the barrel of the arch, but none came. There was a door at one side painted with our number. We prowled in, and I found a cook asleep, and ordered him to give us food. Then I climbed to the top of the Wall, and looked out over the Pict country, and I . . . thought," said Parnesius. "The bricked-up arch with 'Finish!' on the plaster was what shook me, for I was not much more than a boy."

"What a shame!" said Una. "But did you feel happy after you'd had a good—" Dan stopped her with a nudge.

"Happy?" said Parnesius. "When the men of the cohort I was to command came back unhelmeted from the cockfight, their birds under their arms, and asked me who I was? No, I was not happy; but I made my new cohort unhappy too . . . I wrote my mother I was happy, but, oh, my friends" – he stretched arms over bare knees – "I would not wish my worst enemy to suffer as I suffered through my first months on the Wall. Remember this: among the officers was scarcely one, except myself (and I thought I had lost the favour of Maximus, my general), scarcely one who had not done something of wrong or folly. Either he had killed a man, or taken money, or insulted the magistrates, or blasphemed the gods, and so had been sent to the Wall as a hiding place from shame and fear. And the men were as the officers. Remember, also, that the Wall was manned by every breed and race in the empire. No two towers spoke the same tongue, or worshipped the same gods. In one thing only we were all equal. No matter what arms we had used before we came to the Wall, *on* the Wall we were all archers, like the Scythians. The Pict cannot run away from the arrow, or crawl under it. He is a bowman himself. *He* knows!"

"I suppose you were fighting Picts all the time," said Dan.

"Picts seldom fight. I never saw a fighting Pict for half a year. The tame Picts told us they had all gone North."

"What is a tame Pict?" said Dan.

"A Pict – there were many such – who speaks a few words of our tongue, and slips across the Wall to sell ponies and wolf-hounds. Without a horse and a dog, *and* a friend, man would perish. The gods gave me all three, and there is no gift like friendship. Remember this" – Parnesius turned to Dan – "when you become a young man. For your fate will turn on the first true friend you make."

"He means," said Puck, grinning, "that if you try to make yourself a decent chap when you're young, you'll make rather decent friends when you grow up. If you're a beast, you'll have beastly friends. Listen to the Pious Parnesius on Friendship!"

"I am not pious," Parnesius answered, "but I know what goodness means; and my friend, though he was without hope, was ten thousand times better than I. Stop laughing, Faun!"

"O Youth Eternal and All-believing," cried Puck, as he rocked on the branch above. "Tell them about your Pertinax."

"He was that friend the gods sent me – the boy who spoke to me when I first came. Little older than myself, commanding the Augusta Victoria cohort on the tower next to us and the Numidians. In virtue he was far my superior."

"Then why was he on the Wall?" Una asked, quickly. "They'd all done something bad. You said so yourself."

"He was the nephew, his father had died, of a great rich man in Gaul who was not always kind to his mother. When Pertinax grew up, he discovered this, and so his uncle shipped him off, by trickery and force, to the Wall. We came to know each other at a ceremony in our temple – in the dark. It was the Bull Killing," Parnesius explained to Puck.

"*I* see," said Puck, and turned to the children. "That's something you wouldn't quite understand. Parnesius means he met Pertinax in church."

"Yes – in the cave we first met, and we were both raised to the Degree of Gryphons together." Parnesius lifted his hand towards his neck for an instant. "He had been on the Wall two years and knew the Picts well. He taught me first how to take heather."

"What's that?" said Dan.

"Going out hunting in the Pict country with a tame Pict. You are quite safe so long as you are his guest, and wear a sprig of heather where it can be seen. If you went alone you would surely be killed, if you were not smothered first in the bogs. Only the Picts know their way about those black and hidden bogs. Old Allo, the one-eyed, withered little Pict from whom we bought our ponies, was our special friend. At first we went only to escape from the terrible town, and talk together about our homes. Then he showed us how to hunt wolves and those great red deer with horns like Jewish candlesticks. The Roman-born officers rather looked down on us for doing this, but we preferred the heather to their amusements. Believe me," Parnesius turned again to Dan, "a boy is safe from all things that really harm when he is astride a pony or after a deer. Do you remember, O Faun," he turned to Puck, "the little altar I built to the Sylvan Pan by the pine forest beyond the brook?"

"Which? The stone one with the line from

Xenophon?" said Puck, in quite a new voice.

"No. What do *I* know of Xenophon? That was Pertinax – after he had shot his first mountain hare with an arrow – by chance! Mine I made of round pebbles in memory of my first bear. It took me one happy day to build." Parnesius faced the children quickly.

"And that was how we lived on the Wall for two years – a little scuffling with the Picts, and a great deal of hunting with old Allo in the Pict country. He called us his children sometimes, and we were fond of him and his barbarians, though we never let them paint us Pict fashion. The marks endure till you die."

"How's it done?" said Dan. "Anything like tattooing?"

"They prick the skin till the blood runs, and rub in coloured juices. Allo was painted blue, green, and red from his forehead to his ankles. He said it was part of his religion. He told us about his religion (Pertinax was always interested in such things), and as we came to know him well, he told us what was happening in Britain behind the Wall. Many things took place behind us in those days. And by the Light of the Sun," said Parnesius, earnestly, "there was not much that those little people did not know! He told me when Maximus crossed over to Gaul, after he had made himself emperor of Britain, and what troops and emigrants he had taken with him. We did not get the news on the Wall till fifteen days later. He told me what troops Maximus was taking out of Britain every month to help him to conquer Gaul; and I always found the numbers as he said. Wonderful! And I tell another strange thing!"

He jointed his hands across his knees, and leaned his head on the curve of the shield behind him.

"Late in the summer, when the first frosts begin and the Picts kill their bees, we three rode out after wolf with some new hounds. Rutilianus, our general, had given us ten days' leave, and we had pushed beyond the Second Wall – beyond the Province of Valentia – into the higher hills, where there are not even any of Rome's old ruins. We killed a she-wolf before noon, and while Allo was skinning her he looked up and said to me, 'When you are captain of the Wall, my child, you won't be able to do this any more!'

"I might as well have been made prefect of Lower Gaul, so I laughed and said, 'Wait till I am captain.' 'No, don't wait,' said Allo, 'Take my advice and go home – both of you.' 'We have no homes,' said Pertinax. 'You know that as well as we do. We're finished men – thumbs down against both of us. Only men without hope would risk their necks on your ponies. The old man laughed one of those short Pict laughs – like a fox barking on a frosty night. 'I'm fond of you two,' he said. 'Besides, I've taught you what little you know about hunting. Take my advice and go home.'

"'We can't,' I said. 'I'm out of favour with my general for one thing; and for another, Pertinax has an uncle.'

"'I don't know about his uncle,' said Allo, 'but the trouble with you, Parnesius, is that your general thinks well of you.'

"'Roma Dea!' said Pertinax, sitting up. 'Can you guess what Maximus thinks, you old horse-coper?'

"Just then (you know how near the brutes creep when one is eating?) a great dog-wolf jumped out behind us, and away our rested hounds tore after him, with us at their tails. He ran us far out of any country we'd ever heard of, straight as an arrow till sunset, towards the sunset. We came at long last to long capes stretching into winding waters, and on a grey beach below us we saw ships drawn up. Forty-seven we counted – not Roman galleys but the raven-winged ships from the north where Rome does not rule. Men moved in the ships, and the sun flashed on their helmets – winged helmets of the red-haired men from the north where Rome does not rule. We watched, and we counted, and we wondered, for though we had heard rumours concerning these Winged Hats, as the Picts called them, never before had we looked upon them.

"'Come away! Come away!' said Allo. 'My heather won't protect you here. We shall all be killed!' His legs trembled like his voice. Back we went – across the heather under the moon, till it was nearly morning, and our poor beasts stumbled on some ruins.

"When we woke, very stiff and cold, Allo was mixing the meal and water. One does not light fires in the Pict country except near a village. The little men are always signalling to each other with smokes, and a strange smoke brings them out buzzing like bees. They can sting, too!

"'What we saw last night was a trading-station,' said Allo. 'Nothing but a trading-station.'

"'I do not like lies on an empty stomach,' said Pertinax. 'I suppose' (he had eyes like an eagle's) – 'I suppose that is a trading-station also?' He pointed to a smoke far off on a hill-top, ascending in what we call the Picts' Call: puff – double-puff – double-puff – puff! They make it by raising and dropping a wet hide on a fire.

"'No,' said Allo, pushing the platter back into the bag. 'That is for you and me. Your fate is fixed. Come.'

"We came. When one takes heather, one must obey one's Pict – but that wretched smoke was twenty miles distant, well over on the east coast, and the day was as hot as a bath.

"'Whatever happens,' said Allo, while our ponies grunted along, 'I want you to remember me.'

"'I shall not forget,' said Pertinax. 'You have cheated me out of my breakfast.'

"'What is a handful of crushed oats to a Roman?' he said. Then he laughed his laugh that was not a laugh. 'What would *you* do if *you* were a handful of oats being crushed between the upper and lower stones of a mill?'

"'I'm Pertinax, not a riddle-guesser,' said Pertinax.

"'You're a fool,' said Allo. 'Your gods and my gods are threatened by strange gods, and all you can do is to laugh.'

"'Threatened men live long,' I said.

"'I pray the Gods that may be true,' he said. 'But I ask you again not to forget me.'

"We climbed the last hot hill and looked out on the eastern sea, three or four miles off. There was a small sailing galley of the North Gaul pattern at anchor, her landing-plank down and her sail half up; and below us, alone in a hollow, holding his pony, sat Maximus, emperor of Britain! He was dressed like a hunter, and he leaned on his little stick; but I knew that back as far as I could see it, and I told Pertinax.

"'You're madder than Allo!' he said. 'It must be the sun!'

"Maximus never stirred till we stood before him. Then he looked me up and down, and said, 'Hungry again? It seems to be my destiny to feed you whenever we meet. I have food here. Allo shall cook it.'

"'No,' said Allo. 'A Prince in his own land does not wait on wandering emperors. I feed my two children without asking your leave.' He began to blow up the ashes.

"'I was wrong,' said Pertinax. 'We are all mad. Speak up, O madman called emperor!'

"Maximus smiled his terrible tight-lipped smile, but two years on the Wall do not make a man afraid of mere looks. So I was not afraid.

"'I meant you, Parnesius, to live and die a centurion of the Wall,' said Maximus. 'But it seems from these,' he fumbled in his breast, 'you can think as well as draw.' He pulled out a roll of letters I had written to my people, full of drawings of Picts, and bears, and men I had met on the Wall. Mother and my sister always liked my pictures.

"He handed me one that I had called 'Maximus's Soldiers'. It showed a row of fat wine-skins, and our old doctor of the Hunno hospital snuffing at them. Each time that Maximus had taken troops out of Britain to help him conquer Gaul, he used to send the garrisons more wine – to keep them quiet, I suppose. On the Wall, we always called a wine-skin a 'Maximus'. Oh, yes; and I had drawn them in Imperial helmets.

"'Not long since,' he went on, 'men's names were sent up to Caesar for smaller jokes than this.'

"'True, Caesar,' said Pertinax, 'but you forget that was before I, your friend's friend, became such a good spearthrower.'

"He did not actually point his hunting spear at Maximus, but balanced it on his palm – so!

"'I was speaking of time past,' said Maximus, never fluttering an eyelid. 'Nowadays one is only too pleased to find boys who can think for themselves, *and* their friends.' He nodded at Pertinax. 'Your father lent me the letters, Parnesius, so you run no risk from me.'

"'None whatever,' said Pertinax, and rubbed the spearpoint on his sleeve.

"'I have been forced to reduce the garrisons in Britain, because I need troops in Gaul. Now I come to take troops from the Wall itself,' said he.

"'I wish you joy of us,' said Pertinax. 'We're the last sweepings of the empire – the men without hope. Myself, I'd sooner trust condemned criminals.'

"'You think so?' he said, quite seriously. 'But it will only be till I win Gaul. One must always risk one's life, or one's soul, or one's peace – or some little thing.'

"Allo passed round the fire with the sizzling deer's meat. He served us two first.

"'Ah!' said Maximus, waiting his turn. 'I perceive you are in your own country. Well, you deserve it. They tell me you have quite a following among the Picts, Parnesius.'

"'I have hunted with them,' I said. 'Maybe I have a few friends among the heather.'

"'He is the only armoured man of you all who

understands us,' said Allo, and he began a long speech about our virtues, and how we had saved one of his grandchildren from a wolf the year before."

"Had you?" said Una.

"Yes; but that was neither here nor there. The little green man orated like a – like Cicero. He made us out to be magnificent fellows. Maximus never took his eyes off our faces.

"'Enough,' he said. 'I have heard Allo on you. I wish to hear you on the Picts.'

"I told him as much as I knew, and Pertinax helped me out. There is never harm in a Pict if you but take the trouble to find out what he wants. Their real grievance against us came from our burning their heather. The whole garrison of the Wall moved out twice a year, and solemnly burned the heather for ten miles north. Rutilianus, our general, called it clearing the country. The Picts, of course, scampered away, and all we did was to destroy their bee-bloom in the summer, and ruin their sheep-food in the spring.

"'True, quite true,' said Allo. 'How can we make our holy heather-wine, if you burn our bee-pasture?'

"We talked long, Maximus asking keen questions that showed he knew much and had thought more about the Picts. He said presently to me, 'If I gave you the old Province of Valentia to govern, could you keep the Picts contented till I won Gaul? Stand away, so that you do not see Allo's face, and speak your own thoughts.'

"'No,' I said. 'You cannot remake that Province. The Picts have been free too long.'

"'Leave them their village councils, and let them furnish their own soldiers,' he said. 'You, I am sure, would hold the reins very lightly.'

"'Even then, no,' I said. 'At least not now. They have been too oppressed by us to trust anything with a Roman name for years and years.'

"I heard old Allo behind me mutter, 'Good child!'

"'Then what do you recommend,' said Maximus, 'to keep the north quiet till I win Gaul?'

"'Leave the Picts alone,' I said. 'Stop the heather-burning at once, and – they are improvident little animals – send them a shipload or two of corn now and then.'

"'Their own men must distribute it – not some cheating Greek accountant,' said Pertinax.

"'Yes, and allow them to come to our hospitals when they are sick,' I said.

"'Surely they would die first,' said Maximus.

"'Not if Parnesius brought them in,' said Allo. 'I could show you twenty wolf-bitten, bear-clawed Picts within twenty miles of here. But Parnesius must stay with them in hospital, else they would go mad with fear.'

"'*I* see,' said Maximus. 'Like everything else in the world, it is one man's work. You, I think, are that one man.'

"'Pertinax and I are one,' I said.

"'As you please, so long as you work. Now, Allo, you know that I mean your people no harm. Leave us to talk together,' said Maximus.

"'No need!' said Allo. 'I am the corn between the upper and lower millstones. I must know what the lower millstone means to do. These boys have spoken the truth as far as they know it. I, a prince, will tell you the rest. I am troubled about the men of the north.' He squatted like a hare in the heather, and looked over his shoulder.

"'I also,' said Maximus, 'or I should not be here.'

"'Listen,' said Allo. 'Long and long ago the Winged Hats' – he meant the Northmen – 'came to our beaches and said, "Rome falls! Push her down!" We fought you. You sent men. We were beaten. After that we said to the Winged Hats, "You are liars! Make our men alive that Rome killed, and we will believe you." They went away ashamed. Now they come back bold, and they tell the old tale, which we begin to believe – that Rome falls!'

"'Give me three years' peace on the Wall,' cried Maximus, 'and I will show you and all the ravens how they lie!'

"'Ah, I wish it too! I wish to save what is left of the corn from the millstones. But you shoot us Picts when we come to borrow a little iron from the Iron Ditch; you burn our heather, which is all our crop; you trouble us with your great catapults. Then you hide behind the Wall, and scorch us with Greek fire. How can I keep my young men from listening to the Winged Hats – in winter especially, when we are hungry? My young men will say, "Rome can neither fight nor rule. She is taking her men out of Britain. The Winged Hats will help us to push down the Wall. Let us show them the secret roads across the bogs." Do *I* want that? No!' He spat like an adder. '*I* would keep the secrets of my people though I were burned alive. My two children here have spoken truth. Leave us Picts alone. Comfort us, and cherish us, and feed us from far off – with the hand behind your back. Parnesius understands us. Let *him* have rule on the Wall, and I will hold my young men quiet for' – he ticked it off on his fingers – 'one year easily, the next year not so easily, the third year, perhaps! See, I give you three years. If then you do not show us that Rome is strong in men and terrible in arms, the Winged Hats, I tell you, will sweep down the Wall from either sea till they meet in the middle, and you will go. I shall not grieve over that, but well I know tribe never helps tribe except for one price. We Picts will go too. The Winged Hats will grind us to this!' He tossed a handful of dust in the air.

"'Oh, Roma Dea!' said Maximus, half aloud. 'It is always one man's work – always and everywhere!'

"'And one man's life,' said Allo. 'You are emperor, but not a god. You may die.'

"'I have thought of that too,' said he. 'Very good. If this wind holds, I shall be at the east end of the Wall by morning. Tomorrow, then, I shall see you two when I inspect, and I will make you captains of the Wall for this work.'

"'One instant, caesar,' said Pertinax. 'All men have their price. I am not bought yet.'

"'Do *you* also begin to bargain so early?' said Maximus. 'Well!'

"'Give me justice against my uncle Icenus, the duumvir of Divio in Gaul,' he said.

"'Only a life? I thought it would be money or an office. Certainly you shall have him. Write his name on these tablets – on the red side; the other is for the living!' And Maximus held out his tablets.

"'He is of no use to me dead,' said Pertinax. 'My mother is a widow. I am far off. I am not sure he pays her all her dowry.'

"'No matter. My arm is reasonably long. We will look through your uncle's accounts in due time. Now, farewell till tomorrow, O captains of the Wall!'

"We saw him grow small across the heather as he walked to the galley. There were Picts, scores, each side of him, hidden behind stones. He never looked left or right. He sailed away southerly, full spread before the evening breeze, and when we had watched him out to sea, we were silent. We understood! Earth bred few men like to this man.

"Presently Allo brought the ponies and held them for us to mount – a thing he had never done before.

"'Wait awhile,' said Pertinax, and he made a little altar of cut turf, and strewed heather-bloom atop, and laid upon it a letter from a girl in Gaul.

"'What do you do, O my friend?' I said.

"'I sacrifice to my dead youth,' he answered, and, when the flames had consumed the letter, he ground them out with his heel. Then we rode back to that Wall of which we were to be captains."

Parnesius stopped. The children sat still, not even asking if that were all the tale. Puck beckoned and pointed the way out of the wood. "Sorry," he whispered, "but you must go now."

"We haven't made him angry, have we?" said Una. "He looks so far off, and – and – thinky."

"Bless your heart, no. Wait till tomorrow. It won't be long. Remember, you've been playing *Lays of Ancient Rome*." And as soon as they had scrambled through their gap where oak, ash, and thorn grew, that was all they remembered.

THE WAKING OF THE KRAKEN

EVA IBBOTSON

from Which Witch?

The Wicked Wizard Arriman the Awful lives in a haunted mansion with his secretary, Mr Leadbetter (who has the misfortune to have been born with a tail), and his butler, Lester (a one-eyed ogre). It becomes clear to Arriman that he must marry and hand over the responsibility for doing evil to a son. So he holds a competition among the local witches. The one who can work the blackest magic will be his wife. Unfortunately, all the local witches are hideous, except for Belladonna, and Belladonna is only able to do white magic. Mabel Wrack, for instance, has scaly legs and an octopus for her familiar. And Mabel Wrack, watched by the two judges (an elderly ghoul called Mr Sniveller and a genie called Mr Chatterjee who lives in a bottle), has the first turn in the competition.

AND SO, AT LAST, after all the preparations and the fuss, the first day of the contest dawned.

Mabel Wrack – Witch Number One – had got up early and stood for two hours under the shower so that her legs did not dry out on her big day. She had dressed with care, fastening the sea slug brooch beneath her gown, but she was not nervous. Owing to Mrs Wrack having been a mermaid, Mabel was one-quarter fish, and, as is well known, fishes are cold-blooded and never get excited.

As everyone had expected, Mabel had decided to do her trick beside the sea. The place she had chosen was called the Devil's Cauldron: a sandy bay flanked by brooding granite cliffs and strewn with jagged rocks to which dark seaweed slimily clung.

Backing the sand was a strip of turf and it was here, at a trestle table which Lester had dragged out for them, that the judges sat. Arriman the Awful, wearing his robe with the constellations on it, was in the middle; Mr Chatterjee (inside his bottle on account of the nippy breeze) was on the magician's left, and on the right – pale and exhausted after a night of hideous wandering – drooped Mr Sniveller. The other witches, gowned and masked so that Arriman couldn't catch even an accidental glimpse of them, were huddled behind a clump of gorse bushes – all except Madame Olympia who had stayed snootily inside her caravan.

Arriman now got up to make a speech. He declared the Miss Witch of Todcaster contest open and welcomed all the competitors. He reminded them of the rules – any witch practising black magic on another witch or her familiars would be disqualified, the competitors must not show their faces and the judges' decision was final. Then he sat down and Mr Leadbetter, shouting through a megaphone like a film director, said, "Witch Number One – step forward!"

There was clapping from the other witches, and from some villagers who had come up the cliff path, and Mabel emerged from behind the gorse bushes. Only the lower part of her face showed beneath the mask, but it was enough to make Arriman hope frantically that she was going to go to sea in a sieve and drown.

"Present your list!" ordered Mr Leadbetter, and Mabel went up to the judges' table with her piece of paper. In the neat hand of a practised shopkeeper, Mabel had written:

1. *One gong (loud)*
2. *Some golden rings*
3. *A drowned sailor*

"The manager of the hotel was kind enough to lend us his gong," said Mr Leadbetter. "And we got the gold rings from Woolworths. But there is this matter of the drowned sailor."

"Hmm," said Arriman, looking rather sick. There is a place called Davy Jones's locker under the sea, where the bodies of drowned sailors are supposed to be kept, but he had never fancied it. Messy, it sounded, as though things would have been nibbled at, and, of all things, Arriman hated a *mess*.

Then he had an idea and smiled. "Hand me my wand, Leadbetter," he said, and shut his eyes. The next second a large grey skeleton stuck together with bits of wire swirled through the air and landed at the sea witch's feet.

"I wanted a *fresh* one," complained Miss Wrack. "One with some meat on him. It's for bait."

"If Witch Number One is not satisfied," snapped

Arriman, fire shooting from his nostrils, "she may withdraw from the contest."

"Oh, all right," said Mabel sulkily. "But he's a very funny shape."

This was certainly true. The skeleton had, in fact, belonged to the Biology Lab of a large comprehensive school in the Midlands, and the poor gentleman hadn't exactly been a sailor but an undertaker who liked messing about in boats and had fallen, in the year 1892, into the Shropshire Union Canal. Owing to the carelessness of the children, and the fact that the Biology master was the kind that couldn't keep order, the skeleton had got badly jumbled. The skull was back to front, three finger bones were missing and for some reason he seemed to have had three thighs.

"Announce the trick you will perform," Mr Leadbetter shouted through his megaphone.

Mabel Wrack turned to face the judges. She had taken Doris out of her bucket and thrown the familiar's tentacles carelessly round her shoulders like a mink stole, while she held the animal's round body under her arm, squeezing it for power and darkness like someone playing the bagpipes.

Then she spoke.

"I SHALL CALL FORTH THE KRAKEN FROM THE DEEP," she said.

There was a stunned silence. The Kraken! That dread and dangerous monster that has lain since the dawn of time beneath the surface of the sea, dragging ships to their doom, creating by its lightest movement, tidal waves that could drown cities!

"Oh, Terence," whispered Belladonna, "I'm scared,

aren't you? Fancy Mabel Wrack being able to do *that*!"

And indeed all the onlookers were a little bit ashamed. They had never taken the fishy witch too seriously and now . . .

Even Arriman the Awful was impressed. "Instruct Witch Number One to proceed," he said.

Mabel Wrack stepped forward to the edge of the ocean. The sea witch was no slouch and she had prepared her act with care. She would begin by peppering the sea with golden rings to fetch up the underwater spirits who were known to be extremely fond of jewellery and would then come and help her when she called them to her aid. As for the drowned sailor, he was meant to lure the Kraken from his lair and so make it easier for the spirits to find him.

She put Doris back in her bucket and threw the rings one by one into the foam. Then she raised her arms, and the skeleton of the undertaker who had liked messing about in boats rose slowly up in the air, turned a somersault and tumbled into the waves.

"Levitation," said Arriman. "Quite neat. Give her a mark for that, don't you think?" The thought of seeing a Kraken had quite cheered him up.

Next, Mabel picked up the gong and thumped it with a resounding wallop, which sent the sea birds flying up in terror. Then:

"Mighty Spirits of the Deep
Pray you waken from your sleep
Come as fast as you are able
Come and help your sister, Mabel,"

chanted Miss Wrack. She had decided to go into poetry for the contest. This may have been a mistake. Some witches have a feeling for poetry, some haven't. Miss Wrack hadn't.

"From thunderous reef and mighty grot
The dreaded Kraken must be got . . ."

"What's a grot?" whispered Mother Bloodwort pettishly from behind the gorse bushes.

"It's short for grotto, I think," Belladonna whispered back. "Sort of a cave." Though she knew that she had no chance of winning now – who could do anything more terrible than call up a Kraken – she was looking at Miss Wrack with shining eyes. There just wasn't a mean streak anywhere in Belladonna.

The pause which followed was an anxious one. Even Arriman wondered if he had been hasty. Would there be flooding? Whirlpools? Cannibalism? There are too many stories of witches summoning up evil forces which they cannot then control.

The pause lengthened. The ghoul, unable to take the strain, dropped off to sleep, and still the wind soughed, and the grey sea foamed and boiled against the rocks.

But now there was a change. The sky seemed to darken. The white crests of the waves died away to leave a creeping, wrinkled skin of water. The wind dropped. The sea birds fell silent.

What came next was a strange heaping up of the water into a mound which grew and grew and became a huge grey tower topped with foam. And now the tower reared upwards, bent, and turned to race – a great tunnel of boiling, churning water – towards the shore.

The witches huddled together. Terence's hand crept into Belladonna's, and at the judge's table, Arriman reached for the genie's bottle and screwed on the top.

Just in time. The towering wave had landed with a thunderous crash upon the strand. And when the foam and turmoil had died down, the onlookers blinked.

Miss Wrack had called on the Spirits of the Deep to help her find the Kraken and it was perhaps natural that these should be mermaids. But the four ladies who now sat on the beach were fleshy and no longer young, and they seemed to be rather pointlessly clutching a large black handbag, each of them holding on to it with a pudgy arm. The rings which Miss Wrack had sent them glistened on their fingers, and their lower halves were sensibly covered in tail cosies of knitted bladderwrack, but all of them were topless and Arriman had already flinched and closed his eyes.

Miss Wrack stepped closer – and her mouth opened in horror.

"Septic suckerfish!" she swore under her breath.

And indeed it was the most appalling luck! Of all the mermaids in the ocean, she had managed to call up her mother's four unmarried sisters: Aunt Edna, Aunt Gwendolyn, Aunt Phoebe and Aunt Jane!

For a moment, Mabel panicked. There is probably nothing less black or magical in the whole world than a person's aunt. Then she remembered that the top half of her face was covered by a mask. With luck, she would not be recognized. There had been a bit of a split in the family when her mother had opted for legs. So, disguising her voice as well as she could, she began:

"Summoned here, I bid thee hearken,
You have been sent to fetch the Kraken
Search the corners of the ocean—"

She broke off, trying to find a rhyme for "ocean", and also wondering a bit whether an ocean really *had* corners. But she needn't have bothered because all four of her aunts were talking at once, taking no notice of each other or of her.

"My dear, we're so glad you called! We've been worried sick!"

"Not knowing what to do for the best, you see."

"When that oil rig went through his mother's head—"

"Skull shattered; not a hope, poor soul—"

"It's *meant*, I said to Edna, didn't I, dear?"

"You did, Phoebe. It's *meant*, you said."

"*Someone* knows what's right."

The aunt who had just spoken broke off, edged closer, peered at Mabel Wrack. "Funny, I'd swear I'd seen you before. Those nostrils . . . that mouth . . ."

Still clutching their handbag, the mermaids waddled towards her on their tails.

"It can't be, of course. But isn't she the *spit* of poor Agatha!"

"The spit!" echoed Aunt Jane.

Mabel Wrack retreated backwards, but it was too late.

"It *must* be Agatha's little girl. The one she had with the fishmonger after the operation. It *is* her, I'm sure.

Mabel, wasn't she called?"

"Mabel! Dear little Mabel!"

Terribly excited, the aunts dropped their handbag at last and surrounded their niece with a great flopping of tails and waving of pink, plump arms.

"Stop it!" hissed Mabel furiously. "This is a competition. Keep *away*! And speak in verse, you're disgracing me."

There was a moment of outraged silence while Mabel continued to glare angrily at her relations. It was a silly thing for her to do. Mermaids are famous for being touchy, and so, of course, are maiden aunts.

"Oh, very well," said Aunt Edna haughtily. "We know when we aren't wanted, don't we?"

"It was you that called *us*, you know."

"Such airs – just because her father had legs and a shop."

As they spoke, the mermaids began to waddle huffily away, speaking over their shoulders as they went.

"We were going to stay and give you a few hints, but we won't bother now."

"Don't blame *us* if you don't know how much sieved sea squirt to give."

"Speak in verse, indeed!"

And with a last, offended sniff, the four mermaids dived back into the water and were gone.

"Stop!" shouted the desperate Miss Wrack. "Come back! You've left your handbag!"

It was a dreadful moment. The mermaids had gone, the mighty Kraken still slumbered beneath the deep, on the face of Arriman the Awful there was a look that froze the marrow in one's bones.

And now this handbag . . .

Only, *was* it a handbag? For even as they watched, the object on the sand seemed to give a kind of judder. Next it puffed itself out into a round, smooth dome like the top of a tadpole or of a small and very squidgy flying saucer. In the middle of this dome two slits now appeared and a pair of shining, tear-filled, sky-blue eyes stared upwards at Miss Wrack.

"Oh, my Gawd," said Lester, with whom the penny had already dropped.

The thing now went into a kind of private struggle and from its round, dark blancmange of a body there appeared, one by one, eight wavery, wobbly legs each ending in a blobshaped foot. Peering closer, the onlooker could see, at the rim of the saucer, a round hole from whose reddened edges the little finger bone of the undertaker sadly hung. Aunt Jane had given it to him to help him with his teething.

Even with the evidence there before their eyes, no one could quite believe it. They watched in silence as the "handbag" raised itself once more, tottered a few pathetic steps and fell in a despairing, quivering heap before Miss Wrack.

"Mummy?" it said in a piteous voice. "Mummy?"

The sea witch stepped back in disgust. Terence clung tightly to Belladonna to stop her running forward, the ghoul woke suddenly and said, "Spittle!" and Arriman the Awful rose from his seat.

"What in the name of devilry and darkness is that THING?" he thundered.

He knew, of course. You could say a lot about Arriman, but not that he was thick.

"That, sir," said the ogre, "is a Kraken. A baby Kraken. A very young baby Kraken indeed."

Hearing voices, feeling himself unwanted by the very witch who had called him from the sea, the Kraken, his eyes, his whole body streaming with tears, now began to totter wetly to the table where the judges sat. Three times he fell, his legs hopelessly knotted, and three times he rose again, leaving each time a glistening pool of water. Until he reached the chair of Arriman the Awful, Wizard of the North.

"Daddy?" said the Kraken, rolling his anguished eyes upwards. And again, "Daddy?"

Everybody waited.

Arriman looked downwards and shuddered. "Take it away, Lester. Remove it. Throw it back into the sea."

The ogre did not move.

"You heard me, Lester. It is dribbling on my feet."

"Sir," said the ogre. "That Kraken is an orphan. Its mother's had an oil rig through her head. It'll be two thousand years before that Kraken is old enough to swallow as much as a canoe. If you throw it back now, it'll die."

"So?" said Arriman nastily.

Over by the gorse bushes, Belladonna closed her eyes and prayed. Mr Chatterjee tried to swoosh out of his bottle, hit his head on the screwed-on top and fell back, his turban over his dark, kind face.

"Daddy?" said the Kraken, his voice only a whisper now – and raised from the top of his body, a tiny, trembling and hopeless-looking tail.

"Oh, a plague on the lot of you," cursed Arriman, and scooping up the Kraken, which immediately began to squeak and giggle because it was extremely ticklish, the furious magician left the judges' table and strode away towards the Hall.

THE CAVES IN THE HILLS

ELIZABETH GOUDGE
from Henrietta's House

Henrietta and her adopted brother, Hugh Anthony, live in the Cathedral Close at Torminster. It is Hugh Anthony's birthday and he is allowed to choose how they will celebrate it. He decides on a picnic party at Foxglove Combe up in the hills, but he does not want any children except Henrietta because he has had enough of children at school. The birthday guests gather, most of them over sixty, in a variety of carriages (plus one motor car) and Hugh Anthony decides to ride with the Dean of Torminster in the dean's elegant dog-cart. He feels he has a lot in common with the dean. All the carriages (and the motor car) set off for the hills. All (except one) get lost on the way.

This is what happens to Hugh Anthony and the dean.

"WHY, THERE IS A little house there!" exclaimed Hugh Anthony.

And so there was, a very ancient tumbledown house beside the figure of the mocking imp. The tiles on the roof were slipping and the small diamond-paned windows were broken in many places, and it was so they had not seen it at first. There was a tiny patch of garden, choked with weeds, before the front door, and to one side of it there was an old well with a huge toad sitting on the broken stone parapet.

"Astonishing! Astonishing!" repeated the dean. "It looks like the lodge of some big house. But all completely derelict. And how is it that I have never been here before?"

"There can't be anyone living there now," said Hugh Anthony.

And no sooner were the words out of his mouth than the door opened and there issued forth the very oldest old man that Hugh Anthony had ever set eyes on; and that is saying a good deal, because at this time the combined ages of the dean, the four canons and the archdeacon came to four hundred and ninety, for in Torminster life was so placid and peaceful that no one ever got tired and so never died. But this old man was at least a hundred, and in his youth must have been almost a giant, because even though bent with age he was still tall, almost as tall as the giant in the fairy tale who carried his heart in a paper bag. His matted grey hair was so long that it touched his shoulders and his forest of a beard spread all over his chest, and the straggling parts of it nearly touched his knees. He wore corduroy trousers such as labourers wear, tied beneath the knee with string, and a very old patched green coat. One could not see if he wore a waistcoat, because of the beard, and one could not see much of his face, because of the beard. But what one could see was alarming; a high brown hooked nose like a hawk's beak and flashing eyes beneath jutting white eyebrows. He might be old and bent but he was certainly not without vitality. He moved with an almost regal air and his eyes were as young as Hugh Anthony's.

"Good day, my good man," piped the dean in the genial yet patronizing tone that he always used with the lower orders. "Can you oblige me by telling me the way to Foxglove Combe?"

The old man now stood beside the gatepost with the carving of the mocking imp. "Eh?" he growled, and his growl was strange, deep, and very strong for one so aged.

The dean repeated himself.

"Eh?" said the old man. "I'm a little hard of hearing."

The dean gave an exclamation of annoyance, for deaf people always irritated him, cleared his throat and spoke as loudly as was compatible with dignity.

"Eh?" said the old man.

"Whoever owns this disgracefully neglected estate should have him sacked," said the dean angrily to Hugh Anthony. "What is the use of a lodge-keeper who cannot hear a word that is said to him?"

"*I'll* make him hear, Mr Dean," said Hugh Anthony with some arrogance, and cupping his hands round his mouth he bellowed, "Which way to Foxglove Combe?"

"What you need do be straight on through the wood," growled the old man. "Keep straight on. And may you enjoy it when you get there!"

"Open the gate, will you?" commanded the dean.

"Eh?" said the old man.

"The gate!" bellowed Hugh Anthony.

Growling, the old man fumbled with it. He took a long time, for his rheumaticky old hands found the fastening difficult to undo; so difficult that it seemed the gate could not be opened very often. The dean and Hugh Anthony sat high up above him and watched impatiently, Hugh Anthony keeping a tight hold upon Keeper, who in his eagerness to get inside the wood was whining and struggling and trying to get down. As the old man fumbled he muttered to himself. "Useless, am I?" he growled. "Ought to be sacked, ought I? Let them as don't keep civil tongues in their 'eads be careful! Let 'em be careful, I say!" And just as he spoke the last sentence with a quite extraordinary vindictiveness the gate swung open. The dean put his hand in his pocket, brought up a loose handful of change, pennies, shining shillings and halfcrowns and even one glittering half sovereign, chose out a penny and tossed it to the old man. Then he shook the reins and Black Beauty moved forward.

They had driven only a little way into the wood when the dog-cart gave a sudden lurch on the rough ground and the dean's light overcoat, hanging over the rail beside him, slid off on to the moss beside the track. They stopped again and Hugh Anthony jumped down to get it. Looking back at the little house, before he climbed up again he saw a window facing towards the wood that he had not noticed before. It was bigger than the other windows, and it was wide open, and upon its sill there stood a whole row of little wax figures. The old man must have shut the gate and hobbled back into the house very quickly, for he was there already in the room behind the wax figures, and he held something white in his hands and was moulding it quickly and eagerly into something or other. Another wax figure? Or perhaps two wax figures? For the first time in his life Hugh Anthony felt a little scared as he climbed back beside the dean and they drove on into the mysterious darkness of the enchantingly lovely wood.

The dean and Hugh Anthony and Keeper, who had quieted down now that he was where he wanted to be, drove on through the wood, awed to silence by its beauty. The dog-cart wheels, and the hoofs of Black Beauty, made no sound upon the grassy track. The branches of the trees were so thickly interlaced over their heads that the light was dim and green, as though they were in one of the vaulted aisles of a cathedral lost at the bottom of the sea.

"Strange to find such tall trees so high in the hills," said the dean.

"Yes," said Hugh Anthony.

And they drove on until at last they came to a sort of crossroads.

"Now which way?" wondered the dean, and he reined Black Beauty to a standstill.

Straight on and to the left the roads climbed steeply among boulders and rowan trees to unseen heights of grandeur, to the right the way lay level through the woods.

"To the right is easier going," said the dean.

"The old man said to keep straight on," Hugh Anthony reminded him. "I expect, when we get to the top, we shall be on the hill above Foxglove Combe."

"I hope so," said the dean soberly.

So they went straight on and Black Beauty had to go very slowly, so steep and rough was the track. And as they climbed, the trees thinned out and towering cliffs rose on each side of them, and down the centre of the gorge ran a stream of very clear water, just like the water that ran down the gutters beside the cobbled streets of Torminster.

"There are no rocks like this at Foxglove Combe," said Hugh Anthony.

"No," said the dean.

But still, as in a dream, they went on, until the track became so narrow that there was no room for Black Beauty and the dog-cart. But still they felt that they must go on, so they got out and left Black Beauty upon a patch of green turf beside the stream, where she would have plenty to eat and drink, and went on foot; Hugh Anthony and Keeper, who was now nearly crazy with joy, leaping from stone to stone beside the stream, the dean following more slowly, looking about him at the heather and the rowans, drawing great breaths of the cool, sweet scent of ferns and moss and running water, and beginning to feel ridiculously young and vigorous. He had forgotten now that they were supposed to be going for a picnic at Foxglove Combe, he had forgotten that he was an old man, he had even forgotten that he was the dean of Torminster, with an important position in the world, a large balance at the bank and lots of cares and worries. Being high up in the hills does make people forget things like these, for the world of men drops away below like a stone thrown down into a pond, and the years of busy-ness that have made one old fall away with them.

"Look, Mr Dean, look!" cried Hugh Anthony, pointing upwards, and the dean saw, half hidden by a rowan tree, the entrance to a cave. He made no demur when Hugh Anthony raced back to him and vigorously pushed him up the slope towards it, for he was feeling a boy again and no boy can hold out against the invitation of a cave. One must go inside. What else is it there for?

At first sight the cave seemed a small one, at the first cursory glance you might have thought that what you saw was all there was, but it did not take Hugh Anthony two minutes to discover the boulder at the back of the cave, with hidden behind it the low archway of a narrow passage leading off at right angles.

"But it's all dark," he said. "Have you any matches?"

"Matches would last us no time," said the dean. "Fetch one of the lamps from the dog-cart."

Hugh Anthony raced back to the place where they had left Black Beauty, and detached one of the two oil lamps from the dog-cart. When he got back he found that the dean, with the aid of matches, had already penetrated some way down the narrow passage, though it was so low that he had to bend nearly double to get along at all. Neither of them was surprised at the dean behaving in this undignified manner for since entering the wood nothing had surprised them, and they were in that frame of mind in which one is prepared for anything except the abandonment of an adventure.

"Give me the lamp," commanded the dean, and lit it with the last match.

"Should I go first?" Hugh Anthony not so much

requested as demanded.

"What? What? No," said the dean.

"Beast!" said Hugh Anthony under his breath, but good-humouredly, as though speaking to a boy of his own age. And they went on, the dean leading.

The passage brought them to a second cave, larger than the first one. They straightened themselves and looked about them, and had they been in a less adventurous frame of mind they might have been a little scared, for the lamplight gleamed upon a pool of water, inky black and evidently very deep, in the middle of the floor, and from the high vaulted roof there hung a quantity of large and horrible bats. From somewhere in the far distance there came a very eerie sound; rushing water in the depths of the earth.

"Look!" cried Hugh Anthony excitedly, kneeling beside the still, inky pool. "There are white fishes here. Quite white. Like ghosts."

The dean put the oil lamp on the ground and knelt beside him and together they watched fascinated as the strange white shapes swam round and round in the black water, their ghostly bodies rippling back and forth as though they were weaving some never-ending pattern upon the black loom of the water.

"Why are they white?" whispered the awed Hugh Anthony.

"Because they live in darkness," said the dean. "Colour lives only where the light can penetrate. It cannot live in eternal night. They have lived here for perhaps hundreds of years, swimming round and round like this in perpetual darkness."

And as they watched that strange motion of the

fishes it seemed to the dean that the loom upon which they were weaving was the loom of time, and that his century was being twisted in and out of another, the two mixed up as though they were one.

And just at that moment, when they were so dreamily and peacefully contemplating the swaying fishes, something horrible happened. All the bats suddenly let go of the vaulted roofs and fell upon them. Great leathery wings beat about their heads and brushed against their faces. Beating them off with their hands they had the feel of the rat-like bodies against their fingertips. The air was full of the sound of the beating wings and a queer inhuman crying, and there was a a horrible smell. Desperately beating off a loathsome creature who seemed as big as the dreadful Apollyon in one of the pictures in Grandfather's *Pilgrim's Progress*, Hugh Anthony lurched sideways and knocked the lamp into the pool.

"Keep still," whispered the dean. "It was the light that attracted them. Now it is out they'll go back to the roof."

But crouching down in the pitch darkness, with the wings still beating over his head, Hugh Anthony wondered if it *was* the light that had made those bats fall off the roof, for in the very moment of their falling his mind's eye had seen a queer little picture of pins being stuck into two wax images.

Gradually, almost imperceptibly, the sound of the beating wings grew fainter, and they could hear again that distant sound of water rushing along in the depths of the earth. That horrible smell lessened too, and those queer inhuman cries, and at last it was still and quiet again. Hugh Anthony plunged his arm into the pool, searching for the lamp; but it seemed the pool was so deep as to be bottomless. His gay adventurous mood had deserted him now. Ever since the bats fell he had been most horribly afraid . . . But he wasn't going to own it.

"I can't find that lamp," he said; and could have kicked himself because his voice was shaking.

"No matter, no matter," said the dean. "It would be of no use now for the water would have washed out the oil. We'll get to the wall and feel our way around it till we find the opening to the passage." His voice was not shaking like Hugh Anthony's, and it had an amused tone in it. He had remembered again that he was dean of Torminster and his mind's eye had suddenly shown him a picture of himself in his top hat and his eyeglass groping about in this ridiculous cave. He chuckled suddenly, the chuckle starting low down inside him where the mocking imp was, and rising up to issue in a hoot of mirth that astonished Hugh Anthony . . . He had not known that the dean could laugh like that.

One would have thought it would have been quite easy to find that passage by groping, but it wasn't, for so many boulders stood out from the irregular walls of the cave that one could not quite know whether one was feeling the walls or not.

"Be very careful," said the dean once, "not to step backwards into that pool."

And they went on groping for what, seemed like hours, and the darkness pressed upon them like a weight.

"I've got it," said the dean suddenly, and Hugh

"I've got it," said the dean suddenly, and Hugh Anthony groped his way to the calm confident voice and grasped the dean's coat tails in a passion of relief.

The passage had seemed a long one when they had made their way along it with the lamp but it seemed infinitely longer now they had to grope their way in the pitch dark. It seemed endless; though there did come a time when the roof was not so low, so that the dean could stand upright.

"Yet I don't remember standing upright when we came this way before," he said.

"You just didn't notice," said Hugh Anthony.

"And I don't remember hearing that rushing water so clearly either," said the dean.

"No," said Hugh Anthony.

And suddenly the dean nearly fell over on his nose, because they were going down a flight of steps.

"Hugh Anthony," he said, "there were two passages leading out of the cave, and we've come down the wrong one."

"Yes," said Hugh Anthony.

"I think," said the dean, "that it would be a good idea to sit down and discuss our situation."

So they sat down on the steps, one behind the other.

"We are in a difficult position," said the dean. "If we go back and try again we may never find the right passage, while if we go on we may find another way back into the world again. On the other hand we may not. Difficult. Difficult."

"Grandfather once told me about a dog," said Hugh Anthony, "who went into a cave at Badger's Hole and away. But it took him a week to get from one cave to the other, and he was very thin when he came out." And his voice ended suddenly on a squeak.

"No squeaking," said the dean sternly. "Our position is humiliating as well as difficult, but it has occurred to me during the last five minutes that we are an arrogant couple and that a little humiliation will do us no harm. But we must keep our heads. It is perfectly possible, with effort, to lose one's pride and yet retain one's sense. You use yours and tell me whether to go forward or back."

"Yes, Mr Dean," said Hugh Anthony humbly, and without squeaking. "It's funny to have steps right inside a hill, isn't it? They're real steps. Somebody made them. You feel."

The dean felt. "What? What? Good boy," he ejaculated. "Sensible boy. You're right. Who made them? Whoever he is he may be down there now. We'll go on and see."

"But he may have made them hundreds of years ago," said Hugh Anthony.

"It struck me some while back," said the dean, "that the age in which we live is getting interwoven with another age. At the bottom of these steps we may be in it."

Hugh Anthony suffered another moment of panic. Was this queer adventure turning the dean light-headed? Then he thrust away his fear and they went on groping their way down through the darkness.

"Where's that dog of yours?" said the dean suddenly. "Eh? Eh?"

Hugh Anthony stopped abruptly. Where was

Keeper? He had forgotten all about him! Yes, actually, what with the cave and the bats and one thing and another he had forgotten all about his precious dog. For the first time in his life, bitter self-reproach seized him. If he could forget that he had a dog then he did not deserve to have one. People who forget about their dogs are the most despicable people alive upon this earth.

"Where did you see him last?" asked the dean.

"Beside the stream in the Combe," said Hugh Anthony in a small voice. "He was jumping up and down and barking and he was so happy."

"He didn't follow us into the cave, did he?"

"No, I don't think so. He may have. I didn't notice."

"He's all right," consoled the dean. "Don't worry. Dogs are always all right. He'll wait with Black Beauty and the dog-cart . . . Ouch! Bless my soul!"

There was a queer slithering sound, and then Hugh Anthony had a feeling that the dean was not there, but he had no time to wonder where he was for with his next step downwards he suddenly found that he wasn't there either. He was falling through space, for the steps had come to an end as though they had been sliced off with a knife. It might have been alarming if one had had the time to be alarmed, but one hadn't. Hugh Anthony had scarcely taken in that he wasn't there when he found that he was there, sitting quite comfortably, though perhaps a little shakily, on a pile of something soft that felt and smelt like dried bracken.

"Are you there too, Mr Dean?" he asked, and he had to shout because the sound of rushing water had increased enormously since he had so abruptly left the steps.

"I am here," the dean called back. "And, by some miracle, unhurt. Yes, quite unhurt. Are you unhurt? Eh? Eh?"

"I'm all right," shouted Hugh Anthony. "This is bracken we've fallen on."

"Bracken? Bracken?" said the dean in an astonished voice. "And I believe – yes – yes – that I can dimly see the outline of a small boy sitting on it."

"And I can see *you*, Mr Dean," Hugh Anthony called back. "And your top hat has fallen off. I can see you because there's light coming from somewhere."

Slowly, as they recovered from the shock of their fall, they became aware of the dim green light that filled the cave where they were. It came from high up over their heads and was daylight filtering through a curtain of green ferns that covered a small opening in the cave's roof. Gradually, sitting there in an awed silence, they became aware of their surroundings, and what they saw would have astonished them beyond measure had they not long ago reached that condition of mind when nothing astonishes. All adventurers reach this condition sooner or later. It is only people who live humdrum lives who get surprised if things seem a bit odd. If once you push your mind and body a little further than they are accustomed to be pushed you get used to things getting odder and odder the further you go.

What the dean and Hugh Anthony saw was a large cave with an underground stream running swiftly through it, deep and strong, flowing out through a small dark cavern to the right and disappearing again into the darkness to the left. It had made a deep bed for itself across the floor of the cave, and as the spray flashed upwards from a boulder in its path they could see that the water was bright and clear and beautiful. Ferns were growing in the nooks and crannies of the walls of the cave, and beside the stream was a huge boulder shaped like a throne, with a smaller rock beside it, and in front of it a large stone with a flat top on which stood several mugs made of horn and a big metal jug. There was a loaf on a wooden platter on the rock too, and a basket of plaited rushes full of fruit. Near the throne, beside the river, was a small boat made out of the hollowed-out trunk of a tree, with two wooden oars inside it.

The dean and Hugh Anthony sat for a long while, blinking like owls after their long time in darkness, and then with one consent they turned and looked up at the steps from which they had fallen. They were even higher up than they had imagined, abruptly broken off by some landslide of rock perhaps a hundred years ago. A stout rope-ladder hung from them, but of course that had been no good when they had not known it was there. Then they looked at the pile of bracken upon which they sat. It had been built up to make a sort of wide bed, and on the extreme edges of this bed sat the dean and Hugh Anthony. Had either of them fallen a few inches one side or the other he would have fallen upon the hard floor of the cave.

"Incredible! Incredible!" muttered the dean. "How is it that we are not dead? Eh? Ought to be dead. Ought to be dead."

And suddenly Hugh Anthony's mind's eye saw

another little picture. When those bats had fallen off the roof it had seen the old man pushing pins into two wax figures, now it saw the same wax figures and the old man taking the pins out. And then his mind's eye was not seeing that picture any more but was seeing exactly what he and the dean looked like with their ruffled hair and their popping astonished eyes, sitting on the extreme edges of the pile of bracken with their legs sticking straight out in front of them, and they looked so comical that he laughed and laughed, rolling about on the bracken in a paroxysm of mirth. It was the first good laugh at himself that he had ever had, and he enjoyed it very much and it made him feel very hungry, so hungry that presently his mind saw no more pictures but became wholly concentrated upon the fact that his stomach had a hole in it just the size of a large piece of crusty bread.

"Incredible!" the dean was still muttering. "A miracle of salvation. A miracle. A miracle."

But Hugh Anthony was no longer interested in miracles. "Do you think that meal down there has been put ready for us?" he asked. "After all, it's my birthday."

The dean stuck in his eyeglass again, that had been jerked out of his eye by his fall, and had a look. "It has certainly been put ready for somebody," he said. "Do you see that rock like a throne, and the smaller seat beside it? They seem meant for a birthday king and his admiring vassal; or for a small boy saint and his humble adorer; or for St Hugh and the lowliest of his monks . . . You realize, Hugh Anthony, that we've fallen into the robbers' citadel?"

Hugh Anthony's eyes grew wider and wider. "But

you said it didn't exist," he gasped. "You said it was a legend."

"I was mistaken," said the dean. "I have been mistaken, Hugh Anthony, about many things in life. Happy the man who lives long enough to acknowledge his ignorance. Had I died a moment ago I should have died the most self-satisfied and narrow-minded man who ever lived. What a condition in which to enter eternity!"

"But the food!" said Hugh Anthony. "The bread and the fruit. *That's* not hundreds of years old. Who put it there?"

"I don't know," said the dean. "I don't know anything. I am an ignorant old man."

"Well, anyway, let's eat it," said Hugh Anthony. "Let's sit in the seats and eat it."

So they got up and made their way down to the flat rock beside the stream, and the dean made Hugh Anthony sit in the throne because he was birthday king, while he sat humbly on the small rock beside him, and they investigated the food. The big metal jug was full of a brown liquid which the dean said was beer, the modern equivalent of an ancient drink called mead, the bread was fresh and crusty, the basket was full of juicy whortleberries. They fell to without further pause. The bread was delicious. The dean took a very long pull at the beer, and then another, and said it was grand. Hugh Anthony, after a few gulps, choked and did not like it very much, so the dean finished it, but the juicy fruit slaked his thirst.

"I suppose you realize, my boy," said the dean, "that it will be very difficult for us to get out of this cave? If we climb up the rope ladder and go back to the cave of the bats we may never find the way out. There is no way of reaching the hole in the roof. We could get in the boat and drift down the stream, but we do not know where that would take us. The situation is once more difficult. Yes, difficult. Difficult."

But Hugh Anthony was not much worried; the food was so good, the nicest birthday tea he had ever eaten. One can't be worried while devouring good food. "How does the man who put this food here get in?" he asked with his mouth full. "That remains to be seen," said the dean, looking in the jug and finding he had finished the beer. "It would not surprise me, Hugh Anthony, if when he turns up we find that he does not belong to this century at all. Perhaps this beer that I have drunk *is* mead. Perhaps when we fell down those steps, it was as I thought it might be and we fell down several centuries . . . Hugh Anthony, have I drunk too much of this mead?"

"Oh, no, Mr Dean," said Hugh Anthony, humouring the old boy. But privately he thought that the dean had. And he knew they were still in their own century because the bread knife was exactly like the one they had at home. It had "Made in Sheffield" on it.

BIGGER THAN THE BAKER'S BOY

E. NESBIT
from Five Children and It

This story was written in the days when people had numerous servants (nursemaids, cooks and so forth) and when a baby carriage was known as a mail-cart. The five children – Anthea, Jane, Cyril, Robert and their baby brother, the Lamb, are on holiday in the country without their parents. The older four find a sand fairy – the Psammead – in an old quarry and the Psammead, very grumpily, agrees to give them one wish every day. But somehow, none of them ever manages to wish for the right thing.

"LOOK HERE," said Cyril. "I've got an idea."

"Does it hurt much?" said Robert sympathetically.

"Don't be a jackape! I'm not humbugging."

"Shut up, Bobs!" said Anthea.

"Silence for the Squirrel's oration," said Robert.

Cyril balanced himself on the edge of the water-butt in the backyard, where they all happened to be, and spoke.

"Friends, Romans, countrymen – and women – we found a Sammyadd. We have had wishes. We've had wings, and being beautiful as the day – ugh! – that was pretty jolly beastly if you like – and wealth and castles, and that rotten gypsy business with the Lamb. But we're no forrader. We haven't really got anything worth having for our wishes."

"We've had things happening," said Robert, "that's always something."

"It's not enough, unless they're the right things," said Cyril firmly. "Now I've been thinking—"

"Not really?" whispered Robert.

"In the silent what's-its-names of the night. It's like suddenly being asked something out of history – the date of the Conquest or something; you know it all right all the time, but when you're asked it all goes out of your head. Ladies and gentlemen, you know jolly well that when we're all rotting about in the usual way heaps of things keep cropping up, and then real earnest wishes come into the heads of the beholder—"

"Hear, hear!" said Robert.

"—of the beholder, however stupid he is," Cyril went on. "Why, even Robert might happen to think of a really useful wish if he didn't injure his poor little brains trying so hard to think. Shut up, Bobs, I tell you! You'll have the whole show over."

A struggle on the edge of a water-butt is exciting, but damp. When it was over, and the boys were partially dried, Anthea said, "It really was you began it, Bobs. Now honour is satisfied, do let Squirrel go on. We're wasting the whole morning."

"Well, then," said Cyril, still wringing the water out

of the tails of his jacket, "I'll call it pax if Bobs will."

"Pax then," said Robert sulkily. "But I've got a lump as big as a cricket ball over my eye."

Anthea patiently offered a dust-coloured handkerchief, and Robert bathed his wounds in silence. "Now, Squirrel," she said.

"Well then – let's just play bandits, or forts, or soldiers, or any of the old games. We're dead sure to think of something if we try not to. You always do."

The others consented. Bandits was hastily chosen for the game. "It's as good as anything else," said Jane gloomily. It must be owned that Robert was at first but a half-hearted bandit, but when Anthea had borrowed from Martha the red-spotted handkerchief in which the keeper had brought her mushrooms that morning, and had tied up Robert's head with it so that he could be the wounded hero who had saved the bandit captain's life the day before, he cheered up wonderfully. All were soon armed. Bows and arrows slung on the back look well; and umbrellas and cricket stumps stuck through the belt give a fine impression of the wearer's being armed to the teeth. The white cotton hats that men wear in the country nowadays have a very brigandish effect when a few turkey's feathers are stuck in them. The Lamb's mail-cart was covered with a red-and-blue checked tablecloth, and made an admirable baggage wagon. The Lamb asleep inside it was not at all in the way. So the banditti set out along the road that led to the sandpit.

"We ought to be near the Sammyadd," said Cyril, "in case we think of anything suddenly."

It is all very well to make up your minds to play

bandits – or chess, or ping-pong, or any other agreeable game – but it is not easy to do it with spirit when all the wonderful wishes you can think of, or can't think of, are waiting for you round the corner. The game was dragging a little, and some of the bandits were beginning to feel that the others were disagreeable things, and were saying so candidly, when the baker's boy came along the road with loaves in a basket. The opportunity was not one to be lost.

"Stand and deliver!" cried Cyril.

"Your money or your life!" said Robert.

And they stood on each side of the baker's boy. Unfortunately, he did not seem to enter into the spirit of the thing at all. He was a baker's boy of an unusually large size. He merely said, "Chuck it now, d'ye hear!" and pushed the bandits aside most disrespectfully.

Then Robert lassoed him with Jane's skipping-rope, and instead of going round his shoulders, as Robert intended, it went round his feet and tripped him up. The basket was upset, the beautiful new loaves went bumping and bouncing all over the dusty chalky road. The girls ran to pick them up, and all in a moment Robert and the baker's boy were fighting it out, man to man, with Cyril to see fair play, and the skipping-rope twisting round their legs like an interested snake that wished to be a peacemaker. It did not succeed; indeed the way the boxwood handles sprang up and hit the fighters on the shins and ankles was not at all peacemaking. I know this is the second fight – or contest – in this chapter, but I can't help it. It was that sort of day. You know yourself there are days when rows seem to keep on happening, quite without your meaning them to. If I were a writer of tales of adventure such as those which used to appear in *The Boys of England* when I was young, of course I should be able to describe the fight, but I cannot do it. I never can see what happens during a fight, even when it is only dogs. Also, if I had been one of these *Boys of England* writers, Robert would have got the best of it. But I am like George Washington – I cannot tell a lie, even about a cherry tree, much less about a fight, and I cannot conceal from you that Robert was badly beaten, for the second time that day. The baker's boy blacked his other eye, and, being ignorant of the first rules of fair play and gentlemanly behaviour, he also pulled Robert's hair, and kicked him on the knee. Robert always used to say he could have licked the baker's boy if it hadn't been for the girls. But I am not sure. Anyway, what happened was this, and very painful it was to self-respecting boys.

Cyril was just tearing off his coat so as to help his brother in proper style when Jane threw her arms round his legs and began to cry and ask him not to go and be beaten too. That "too" was very nice for Robert, as you can imagine – but it was nothing to what he felt when Anthea rushed in between him and the baker's boy, and caught that unfair and degraded fighter round the waist, imploring him not to fight any more.

"Oh, don't hurt my brother any more!" she said in floods of tears. "He didn't mean it – it's only play. And I'm sure he's very sorry."

You see how unfair this was to Robert. Because, if the baker's boy had had any right and chivalrous instincts, and had yielded to Anthea's pleading and accepted her despicable apology, Robert could not, in honour, have done anything to him at a future time. But Robert's fears, if he had any, were soon dispelled. Chivalry was a stranger to the breast of the baker's boy. He pushed Anthea away very roughly, and he chased Robert with kicks and unpleasant conversation right down the road to the sandpit, and there, with one last kick, he landed him in a heap of sand.

"I'll larn you, you young varmint!" he said, and went off to pick up his loaves and go about his business. Cyril, impeded by Jane, could do nothing without hurting her, for she clung round his legs with the strength of despair. The baker's boy went off red and damp about the face; abusive to the last, he called them a pack of silly idiots, and disappeared round the corner. Then Jane's grasp loosened. Cyril turned away in silent dignity to follow Robert, and the girls followed him, weeping without restraint.

It was not a happy party that flung itself down in the sand beside the sobbing Robert. For Robert was sobbing – mostly with rage. Though of course I know that a really heroic boy is always dry-eyed after a fight. But then he always wins, which had not been the case with Robert.

Cyril was angry with Jane; Robert was furious with Anthea; the girls were miserable; and not one of the four was pleased with the baker's boy. There was, as French writers say, "a silence full of emotion".

Then Robert dug his toes and his hands into the sand and wriggled in his rage. "He'd better wait till I'm grown up – the cowardly brute! Beast! – I hate him!

But I'll pay him out. Just because he's bigger than me."

"You began," said Jane incautiously.

"I know I did, silly – but I was only rotting – and he kicked me – look here—"

Robert tore down a stocking and showed a purple bruise touched up with red.

"I only wish I was bigger than him, that's all."

He dug his fingers in the sand, and sprang up, for his hand had touched something furry. It was the Psammead, of course – "On the look-out to make sillies of them as usual," as Cyril remarked later. And of course the next moment Robert's wish was granted, and he was bigger than the baker's boy. Oh, but much, much bigger. He was bigger than the big policeman who used to be at the crossing at the Mansion House years ago – the one who was so kind in helping old ladies over the crossing – and he was the biggest man *I* have ever seen, as well as the kindest. No one had a foot-rule in his pocket, so Robert could not be measured – but he was taller than your father would be if he stood on your mother's head, which I am sure he would never be unkind enough to do. He must have been ten or eleven feet high, and as broad as a boy of that height ought to be. His Norfolk suit had fortunately grown too, and now he stood up in it – with one of his enormous stockings turned down to show the gigantic bruise on his vast leg. Immense tears of fury still stood on his flushed giant face. He looked so surprised, and he was so large to be wearing an Eton collar, that the others could not help laughing.

"The Sammyadd's done us again," said Cyril.

"Not us – *me*," said Robert. "If you'd got any decent

feeling you'd try to make it make you the same size. You've no idea how silly it feels," he added thoughtlessly.

"And I don't want to; I can jolly well see how silly it looks," Cyril began.

But Anthea said, "Oh, *don't*! I don't know what's the matter with you boys today. Look here, Squirrel, let's play fair. It is hateful for poor old Bobs, all alone up there. Let's ask the Sammyadd for another wish, and, if it will, I do really think we ought to be made the same size."

The others agreed, but not gaily; but when they found the Psammead, it wouldn't.

"Not I," it said crossly, rubbing its face with its feet. "He's a rude, violent boy, and it'll do him good to be the wrong size for a bit. What did he want to come digging me out with his nasty wet hands for? He nearly touched me! He's a perfect savage. A boy of the Stone Age would have had more sense."

Robert's hands had indeed been wet – with tears.

"Go away and leave me in peace, do," the Psammead went on. "I can't think why you don't wish for something sensible – something to eat or drink or good manners, or good tempers. Go along with you, do!"

It almost snarled as it shook its whiskers, and turned a sulky brown back on them. The most hopeful felt that further parley was vain.

They turned again to the colossal Robert.

"Whatever shall we do?" they said, and they all said it.

"First," said Robert grimly, "I'm going to reason

with that baker's boy. I shall catch him at the end of the road."

"Don't hit a chap littler than yourself, old man," said Cyril.

"Do I look like hitting him?" said Robert scornfully. "Why, I should *kill* him. But I'll give him something to remember. Wait till I pull up my stocking." He pulled up his stocking, which was as large as a small bolster-case, and strode off. His strides were six or seven feet long, so that it was quite easy for him to be at the bottom of the hill, ready to meet the baker's boy when he came down swinging the empty basket to meet his master's cart, which had been leaving bread at the cottages along the road.

Robert crouched behind a haystack in the farmyard, that is at the corner, and when he heard the boy come whistling along, he jumped out at him and caught him by the collar.

"Now," he said, and his voice was about four times its usual size, just as his body was four times its, "I'm going to teach you to kick boys smaller than you."

He lifted up the baker's boy and set him on top of the haystack, which was about sixteen feet from the ground, and then he sat down on the roof of the cowshed and told the baker's boy exactly what he thought of him. I don't think the boy heard it all – he was in a sort of trance of terror. When Robert had said everything he could think of, and some things twice over, he shook the boy and said, "And now get down the best way you can," and left him.

I don't know how the baker's boy got down, but I do know that he missed the cart, and got into the very hottest of hot water when he turned up at last at the bakehouse. I am sorry for him, but, after all, it was quite right that he should be taught that English boys mustn't use their feet when they fight, but their fists. Of course the water he got into only became hotter when he tried to tell his master about the boy he had licked and the giant as high as a church, because no one could possibly believe such a tale as that. Next day the tale was believed – but that was too late to be of any use to the baker's boy.

When Robert rejoined the others he found them in the garden. Anthea had thoughtfully asked Martha to let them have dinner out there – because the dining-room was rather small and it would have been so awkward to have a brother the size of Robert in there. The Lamb, who had slept peacefully during the whole stormy morning, was now found to be sneezing, and Martha said he had a cold and would be better indoors.

"And really it's just as well," said Cyril, "for I don't believe he'd ever have stopped screaming if he'd once seen you the awful size you are!"

Robert was indeed what a draper would call an "out-size" in boys. He found himself able to step right over the iron gate in the front garden.

Martha brought out the dinner – it was cold veal and baked potatoes, with sago pudding and stewed plums to follow.

She of course did not notice that Robert was anything but the usual size, and she gave him as much meat and potatoes as usual and no more. You have no idea how small your usual helping of dinner looks when you are many times your proper size. Robert groaned, and asked for more bread. But Martha would not go on giving more bread for ever. She was in a hurry, because the keeper intended to call on his way to Benenhurst Fair, and she wished to be dressed smartly before he came.

"I wish *we* were going to the fair," said Robert.

"You can't go anywhere that size," said Cyril.

"Why not?" said Robert. "They have giants at fairs, much bigger ones than me."

"Not much, they don't," Cyril was beginning, when Jane screamed, "Oh!" with such loud suddenness that they all thumped her on the back and asked whether she had swallowed a plum stone.

"No," she said, breathless from being thumped, "it's – it's not a plum stone. It's an idea. Let's take Robert to the fair, and get them to give us money for showing him! Then we really *shall* get something out of the old Sammyadd at last!"

"Take me, indeed!" said Robert indignantly. "Much more likely me take you!"

And so it turned out. The idea appealed irresistibly to everyone but Robert, and even he was brought round by Anthea's suggestion that he should have a double share of any money they might make. There was a little old pony trap in the coach-house – the kind that is called a governess-cart. It seemed desirable to get to the fair as quickly as possible, so Robert – who could now take enormous steps and so go very fast indeed – consented to wheel the others in this. It was as easy to him now as wheeling the Lamb in the mail-cart had been in the morning. The Lamb's cold prevented his being of the party.

It was a strange sensation being wheeled in a pony carriage by a giant. Everyone enjoyed the journey except Robert and a few people they passed on the way. These mostly went into what looked like some kind of standing-up fits by the roadside, as Anthea said. Just outside Benenhurst, Robert hid in a barn, and the others went on to the fair.

There were some swings, and a hooting, tooting blaring merry-go-round, and a shooting gallery and coconut shies. Resisting an impulse to win a coconut – or at least to attempt the enterprise – Cyril went up to the woman who was loading little guns before the array of glass bottles on strings against a sheet of canvas.

"Here you are, little gentleman!" she said. "Penny a shot!"

"No, thank you," said Cyril, "we are here on business, not pleasure. Who's the master?"

"The what?"

"The master – the head – the boss of the show."

"Over there," she said, pointing to a stout man in a dirty linen jacket who was sleeping in the sun, "but I don't advise you to wake him sudden. His temper's contrary, especially these hot days. Better have a shot while you're waiting."

"It's rather important," said Cyril. "It'll be very profitable to him. I think he'll be sorry if we take it away."

"Oh, if it's money in his pocket," said the woman. "No kid now? What is it?"

"It's a *giant*."

"You *are* kidding?"

"Come along and see," said Anthea.

The woman looked doubtfully at them, then she called to a ragged little girl in striped stockings and a dingy white petticoat that came below her brown frock, and leaving her in charge of the "shooting gallery" she turned to Anthea and said, "Well, hurry up! But if you *are* kidding you'd best say so. I'm as mild as milk myself, but my Bill, he's a fair terror and—"

Anthea led the way to the barn. "It really *is* a giant," she said. "He's a giant little boy – in Norfolks like my brother's there. And we didn't bring him up to the fair because people do stare so, and they seem to go into kind of standing-up fits when they see him. And we thought perhaps you'd like to show him and get pennies; and if you like to pay us something, you can – only it'll have to be rather a lot, because we promised him he should have a double share of whatever we made."

The woman murmured something indistinct, of which the children could only hear the words, "Swelp me!", "balmy", and "crumpet", which conveyed no definite idea to their minds.

She had taken Anthea's hand, and was holding it very firmly, and Anthea could not help wondering what would happen if Robert should have wandered off or turned his proper size during the interval. But she knew that the Psammead's gifts really did last till sunset, however inconvenient their lasting might be; and she did not think, somehow, that Robert would care to go out alone while he was that size.

When they reached the barn and Cyril called, "Robert!" there was a stir among the loose hay, and

Robert began to come out. His hand and arm came first – then a foot and leg. When the woman saw the hand she said "My!" but when she saw the foot she said "Upon my civvy!" and when, by slow and heavy degrees, the whole of Robert's enormous bulk was at last completely disclosed, she drew a long breath and began to say many things, compared with which "balmy" and "crumpet" seemed quite ordinary. She dropped into understandable English at last.

"What'll you take for him?" she said excitedly. "Anything in reason. We'd have a special van built – leastways, I know where there's a second-hand one would do up handsome – what a baby elephant had, as died. What'll you take? He's soft, ain't he? Them giants mostly is – but I never see – no, never! What'll you take? Down on the nail. We'll treat him like a king, and give him first-rate grub and a doss fit for a bloomin' dook. He must be dotty or he wouldn't need you kids to cart him about. What'll you take for him?"

"They won't take anything," said Robert sternly. "I'm no more soft than you are – not so much, I shouldn't wonder. I'll come and be a show for today if you'll give me" – he hesitated at the enormous price he was about to ask – "if you'll give me fifteen shillings."

"Done," said the woman, so quickly that Robert felt he had been unfair to himself, and wished he had asked thirty. "Come on now – and see my Bill – and we'll fix a price for the season. I dessay you might get as much as two quid a week reg'lar. Come on – and make yourself as small as you can, for gracious' sake!"

This was not very small, and a crowd gathered

quickly, so that it was at the head of an enthusiastic procession that Robert entered the trampled meadow where the fair was held, and passed over the stubbly yellow dusty grass to the door of the biggest tent. He crept in, and the woman went to call her Bill. He was the big sleeping man, and he did not seem at all pleased at being awakened. Cyril, watching through a slit in the tent, saw him scowl and shake a heavy fist and a sleepy head. Then the woman went on speaking very fast. Cyril heard "strewth," and "biggest draw you ever, so help me!" and he began to share Robert's feeling that fifteen shillings was indeed far too little. Bill slouched up to the tent and entered. When he beheld the magnificent proportions of Robert he said but little – "Strike me pink!" were the only words the children could afterwards remember – but he produced fifteen shillings, mainly in sixpences and coppers, and handed it to Robert.

"We'll fix up about what you're to draw when the show's over tonight," he said with hoarse heartiness. "Lor' love a duck! You'll be that happy with us you'll never want to leave us. Can you do a song now – or a bit of a breakdown?"

"Not today," said Robert, rejecting the idea of trying to sing 'As Once in May', a favourite of his mother's, and the only song he could think of at the moment.

"Get Levi and clear them bloomin' photos out. Clear the tent. Stick up a curtain or suthink," the man went on. "Lor', what a pity we ain't got no tights his size! But we'll have 'em before the week's out. Young man, your fortune's made. It's a good thing you came to me, and not to some chaps as I could tell you on. I've known blokes as beat their giants, and starved 'em too; so I'll tell you straight, you're in luck this day if you never was afore. 'Cos I'm a lamb, I am – and I don't deceive you."

"I'm not afraid of anyone's beating *me*," said Robert, looking down on the "lamb". Robert was crouched on his knee, because the tent was not big enough for him to stand upright in, but even in that position he could still look down on most people. "But I'm awfully hungry – I wish you'd get me something to eat."

"Here, 'Becca," said the hoarse Bill. "Get him some grub – the best you've got, mind!" Another whisper followed, of which the children only heard, "Down in black and white – first thing tomorrow."

Then the woman went to get the food – it was only bread and cheese when it came, but it was delightful to the large and empty Robert; and the man went to post sentinels round the tent, to give the alarm if Robert should attempt to escape with his fifteen shillings. "As if we weren't honest," said Anthea indignantly when the meaning of the sentinels dawned on her.

Then began a very strange and wonderful afternoon.

Bill was a man who knew his business. In a very little while, the photographic views, the spyglasses you look at them through, so that they really seem rather real, and the lights you see them by, were all packed away. A curtain – it was an old red-and-black carpet really – was run across the tent. Robert was concealed behind, and Bill was standing on a trestle-table outside the tent making a speech. It was rather a good speech.

It began by saying that the giant it was his privilege to introduce to the public that day was the eldest son of the emperor of San Francisco, compelled through an unfortunate love affair with the duchess of the Fiji Islands to leave his own country and take refuge in England – the land of liberty – where freedom was the right of every man, no matter how big he was. It ended by the announcement that the first twenty who came to the tent door should see the giant for threepence apiece. "After that," said Bill, "the price is riz, and I don't undertake to say what it won't be riz to. So now's yer time."

A young man squiring his sweetheart on her afternoon out was the first to come forward. For that occasion his was the princely attitude – no expense spared – money no object. His girl wished to see the giant? Well, she should see the giant, even though seeing the giant cost threepence each and the other entertainments were all penny ones.

The flap of the tent was raised – the couple entered. Next moment a wild shriek from the girl thrilled through all present. Bill slapped his leg. "That's done the trick!" he whispered to 'Becca. It was indeed a splendid advertisement of the charms of Robert. When the girl came out she was pale and trembling, and a crowd was round the tent.

"What was it like?" asked a bailiff.

"Oh! – horrid! – you wouldn't believe," she said. "It's big as a barn, and that fierce. It froze the blood in my bones. I wouldn't ha' missed seeing it for anything."

The fierceness was only caused by Robert's trying not to laugh. But the desire to do that soon left him, and before sunset he was more inclined to cry than to laugh, and more inclined to sleep than either. For, by ones and twos and threes, people kept coming in all the afternoon, and Robert had to shake hands with those who wished it, and allow himself to be punched and pulled and patted and thumped, so that people might make sure he was really real.

The other children sat on a bench and watched and waited, and were very bored indeed. It seemed to them that this was the hardest way of earning money that could have been invented. And only fifteen shillings! Bill had taken four times that already, for the news of the giant had spread, and tradespeople in carts, and gentlepeople in carriages, came from far and near. One gentleman with an eyeglass, and a very large yellow rose in his buttonhole, offered Robert, in an obliging whisper, ten pounds a week to appear in the Crystal Palace. Robert had to say, "No".

"I can't," he said regretfully. "It's no use promising what you can't do."

"Ah, poor fellow, bound for a term of years, I suppose! Well, here's my card. When your time's up come to me."

"I will – if I'm the same size then," said Robert truthfully.

"If you grow a bit, so much the better," said the gentleman.

When he had gone, Robert beckoned Cyril and said, "Tell them I must and will have an easy. And I want my tea."

Tea was provided, and a paper hastily pinned on the tent. It said:

CLOSED FOR HALF AN HOUR
WHILE THE GIANT GETS HIS TEA

Then there was a hurried council.

"How am I to get away?" said Robert. "I've been thinking about it all the afternoon."

"Why, walk out when the sun sets and you're your right size. They can't do anything to us."

Robert opened his eyes. "Why, they'd nearly kill us," he said, "when they saw me get my right size. No, we must think of some other way. We *must* be alone when the sun sets."

"I know," said Cyril briskly, and he went to the door, outside which Bill was smoking a clay pipe and talking in a low voice to 'Becca. Cyril heard him say – "Good as havin' a fortune left you."

"Look here," said Cyril, "you can let people come in again in a minute. He's nearly finished his tea. But he *must* be left alone when the sun sets. He's very queer at that time of day, and if he's worried I won't answer for the consequences."

"Why – what comes over him?" asked Bill.

"I don't know; it's – it's a sort of a *change*," said Cyril candidly. "He isn't at all like himself – you'd hardly know him. He's very queer indeed. Someone'll get hurt if he's not alone about sunset." This was true.

"He'll pull round for the evening, I s'pose?"

"Oh, yes – half an hour after sunset he'll be quite himself again."

"Best humour him," said the woman.

And so, at what Cyril judged was about half an hour

before sunset, the tent was again closed, "whilst the giant gets his supper".

The crowd was very merry about the giant's meals and their coming so close together. "Well, he can pick a bit," Bill owned. "You see he has to eat hearty, being the size he is."

Inside the tent the four children breathlessly arranged a plan of retreat.

"You go *now*," said Cyril to the girls, "and get along home as fast as you can. Oh, never mind the beastly pony cart; we'll get that tomorrow. Robert and I are dressed the same. We'll manage somehow, like Sydney Carton did. Only, you girls *must* get out, or it's all no go. We can run, but you can't – whatever you may think. No, Jane, it's no good Robert going out and knocking people down. The police would follow him till he turned his proper size, and then arrest him like a shot. Go you must! If you don't, I'll never speak to you again. It was you got us into this mess really, hanging round people's legs the way you did this morning. *Go*, I tell you!"

And Jane and Anthea went.

"We're going home," they said to Bill. "We're leaving the giant with you. Be kind to him," and that, as Anthea said afterwards, was very deceitful, but what were they to do?

When they had gone, Cyril went to Bill.

"Look here," he said, "he wants some ears of corn – there's some in the next field but one. I'll just run and get it. Oh, and he says can't you loop up the tent at the back a bit? He says he's stifling for a breath of air. I'll see no one peeps in at him. I'll cover him up, and he can take a nap while I go for the corn. He *will* have it – there's no holding him when he gets like this."

The giant was made comfortable with a heap of sacks and an old tarpaulin. The curtain was looped up, and the brothers were left alone. They matured their plan in whispers. Outside, the merry-go-round blared out its comic tunes, screaming now and then to attract public notice.

Half a minute after the sun had set, a boy in a Norfolk suit came out past Bill.

"I'm off for the corn," he said, and mingled quickly with the crowd.

At the same instant a boy came out of the back of the tent past 'Becca, posted there as sentinel.

"I'm off after the corn," said this boy also. And he, too, moved away quietly and was lost in the crowd. The front-door boy was Cyril; the back-door was Robert – now, since sunset, once more his proper size. They walked quickly through the field, and along the road, where Robert caught Cyril up. Then they ran. They were home as soon as the girls were, for it was a long way, and they ran most of it. It was indeed a *very* long way, as they found when they had to go and drag the pony trap home next morning, with no enormous Robert to wheel them in it as if it were a mail-cart, and they were babies and he was their gigantic nursemaid.

I cannot possibly tell you what Bill and 'Becca said when they found that the giant had gone. For one thing, I do not know.

JERMAIN AND THE SORCERESS

PATRICIA C. WREDE
from The Seven Towers

I know it is annoying to be given only the start of a story, but it is a long book and I did want to introduce you to my favourite sorceress. Here she is at her most typical.

JERMAIN CROUCHED LOW on his horse's neck as he urged the animal to greater speed. Small branches stung his face as they whipped past, but he barely felt them. He could hear the sounds of his pursuers crashing through the brush behind him. Too close, they were much too close; he didn't know this forest well enough to lose them. He shut the thought out of his mind and concentrated on escape.

The trees were becoming larger; good. He might be able to gain some ground once his horse was clear of this little bushy stuff. He dug his heels into Blackflame's sides. The horse responded at once. Jermain felt the lengthening stride and knew a moment's hope. No one in the border guard had a horse to match Blackflame. Perhaps he could get away from them before blood loss forced him to stop.

Expertly he guided his mount through the trees. He could feel himself weakening, but he could not spare a hand to staunch the blood. Desperately he spurred the horse once more. His eyes searched the forest for a shelf of rock, a stream, something he could use to hide his trail. He found nothing.

His vision blurred, he did not dare to stop. He clamped his right arm against his side, clenching his teeth against the pain. The pressure might slow down the bleeding, or it might not, but the pain would keep him conscious a little longer. He could make it yet. The shouts and horns were fainter; he had gained a little ground.

The forest seemed to be thinning ahead; perhaps he could gain a little more time. He guided Blackflame towards the place where the trees grew furthest apart. A moment later, they broke into a large clearing. Jermain had just time to see the slight, startled figure standing in Blackflame's path; then the horse planted its forefeet and stopped, so abruptly that it was forced back almost on its haunches. Jermain was flung forward out of the saddle and fell heavily to the ground.

Darkness and pain surged over him. Jermain forced them back. He couldn't pass out now; he would lose too much time. "Dear me," a voice said somewhere above him. "That was a rough stop. Are you hurt?"

Jermain opened his eyes and blinked in disbelief. A woman stood a few feet away, her back towards him. A heavy mass of steel-coloured hair fell to the waist of her pale blue gown. Blackflame stood in front of her, trembling from exertion. The woman had one hand out, stroking Blackflame's nose. She was talking to the horse.

To the *horse*? Jermain blinked again. He tried to roll on to his side so he could see more clearly, and a fresh wave of pain made him gasp. Apparently he had broken a rib or two in that fall. The noise attracted the woman's attention; she turned and looked at Jermain. She was young; not a damsel of sixteen, certainly, but no more than thirty, and obviously a lady.

"It's quite all right," she said vaguely, "I will be there in a minute. Of course, you're here, so it really doesn't matter, but most people seem to feel better if I explain about these things." She turned back to the horse, and her head tilted to one side in critical examination.

For a moment, Jermain lay motionless. He would have cursed, but he had no energy for it. He tried again to get to his feet; he made it to his knees. The woman turned around again.

"You really shouldn't do that, especially if you're not feeling well, which I can see you aren't, what with that hole in your side and so on. I assume you realize that, though one can never tell. People can be so very odd. There was a man I used to know, who always wore his boots on the wrong feet for one day out of every month. So I thought I'd mention it, in case you didn't."

"I have to get out of here," Jermain croaked, ignoring her jumbled speech. She had to help him, or he was finished for certain.

"No, you'll be much better off staying here," the woman said. "Well, not here precisely, at least not for very long. No, certainly not long; you would be very uncomfortable, I am sure, and the damp would get into your wound, which would probably give you a fever, though sometimes it doesn't."

Jermain ignored her completely this time. He was having trouble balancing on his knees, and he knew that if he fell over now he wouldn't be able to get up again. He thought about it for a minute and decided to crawl. That, he could manage. He dropped to his hands and knees, and began working his way slowly towards Blackflame, trying not to think about the pain in his chest. The woman made no move to help or hinder him. "Really, you are being very silly," she said kindly.

The sound of shouts and hoofbeats came clearly to Jermain, growing quickly louder. With the last of his strength, Jermain lunged for Blackflame's stirrup. He missed and sprawled painfully on the ground, fighting to remain conscious. The woman walked over and knelt beside him; he felt gentle fingers on his injured side. "If you stop jumping about like that, you probably won't bleed to death," the woman said, and six horsemen broke into the clearing.

For a brief, nightmarish moment, Jermain was certain he would be trampled. He did not even have enough strength left to try to roll aside; somehow the horses missed him anyway. The border guards pulled their mounts to a halt, forming a circle around Jermain and the woman who knelt at his side. The woman blinked at them.

"Dear me," she murmured. "Such a lot of people."

The leader of the group, a burly man with a captain's braid on the front of his faded jacket, looked at the woman in surprise. Evidently he came to the same conclusion Jermain had, for he bowed respectfully before he said briskly, "Lady, I am Captain Morenar of the King's border guard. This man is a dangerous criminal. You will, of course, oblige us by retiring at once. I would not wish to distress you by executing him in your presence, and we can't risk letting him escape."

The woman looked critically down at Jermain, then back at the captain. "Not at all," she said firmly. "He does not look in the least dangerous. I'm quite willing to believe he is extremely foolish, but a great many people are, and I have never heard of anyone being executed for it, though I couldn't say for sure that it's never happened. Of course, if he continues to run about with that wound bleeding all over everything and making such a mess you won't have to."

Morenar frowned and tried again. "Lady, we have been chasing this man for four hours; I assure you there is no mistake."

"Well, it is certainly rude of you to contradict me, and I don't believe you at all," the woman said flatly. "At least, I believe you have been chasing him, but not for four hours, and certainly he's not a criminal. Though I can understand why you say so; it would probably be very awkward for you to explain. So many things are; awkward, I mean. Large kettles, for instance, and carrying three brooms at once, and those fat brown birds with the red wings whose name I can't remember just at present. They waddle."

"Lady," Morenar said, "we have not made a mistake."

"I didn't say you had. You obviously weren't paying

attention. Why are you chasing him?" the woman said.

"We are under orders direct from Leshiya," Morenar replied, obviously relieved that the woman seemed to be making sense at last.

"But Leshiya is the capital of Sevairn," the woman said gently. "And, of course, you're not in Sevairn just now, and neither am I; but then, there are a great many places that aren't – in Sevairn, I mean – so perhaps you hadn't noticed. The border is back that way." She pointed.

The captain stared at her for a moment. "We have wasted enough time," he said abruptly. "Alver, Rusalk, escort the lady elsewhere, at once."

Two of the soldiers swung down from their horses and started forward. Jermain tensed, wondering whether he was strong enough to get away while they were attending to the woman. He didn't think so; he seriously doubted whether he could even get himself upright again, much less stay there. Beside him, the woman rose to her feet. She looked at the two soldiers, then at Morenar. "This is not wise of you," she said softly. "Not wise at all."

"Take her," Morenar said, and the men reached out.

"Well, if you won't listen," the woman said, and made a swift throwing motion with both hands.

The two soldiers went stumbling backward into a brownish-grey fog that Jermain was certain had not been there a moment ago. One of them screamed; then the brown cloud billowed upward, hiding them, and the rest of the border guards, from Jermain. Only a small area around Jermain was free of the fog; Blackflame and the woman and a little grass were the only things he could see. Even they were whirling; Jermain felt a stab of fear. A face bent over him, framed in steel-coloured hair.

"Don't worry," the woman said as he slipped into unconsciousness. "I will see to things."

That, thought Jermain with the last of his awareness, *is what I am afraid of.*

UNA AND THE RED CROSS KNIGHT

ANDREW LANG

from The Red Book of Romance

ONCE UPON A TIME there lived a king and queen who had only one child, a little girl, whom they named Una, and they all lived happily at home for many years till Una had grown into a woman.

It seemed as if they were some of the fortunate people to whom nothing ever happens, when suddenly, just as everything appeared going well and peacefully with them, a fearful dragon, larger and more horrible than any dragon which had yet been heard of, arrived one night, seized the king and queen as they were walking in the garden after the heat of the day, and carried them prisoners to a strong castle. Luckily, Una was at that moment sitting among her maidens on the top of a high tower embroidering a kirtle, or she would have shared the same fate.

When the princess learnt what had befallen her parents, she was struck dumb with grief, but she had been taught that no misfortune was ever mended by tears, so she soon dried her eyes, and began to think what was best to do, and to whom she could turn for help. She ran quickly over in her mind the knights who thronged her father's court, but there was not one amongst them to whose hands their rescue could be entrusted. One spent his days in writing pretty verses to the ladies who were about the queen, another passed his time in putting on suits more brilliant than any worn by his friends, a third loved hawking, but did not welcome the rough life and hard living of real warfare; no, she must seek a champion out of her own country if her parents were to be delivered out of the power of the dragon. Then all at once she remembered a certain Red Cross Knight whose fame had spread even to her distant land, and, ordering her white ass to be saddled, she set forth in quest of him.

It were long to tell the adventures Una met with on the way, but at last she found the knight resting after a hard-won fight, and told him her tale.

"Right willingly will I help you, princess," said he, "only you must ride with me and guide me to the castle, for I know nothing of the countries that lie beyond the sea." And Una heard his words with joy, and called softly to her ass, who was cropping the short green grass beside her.

"Let us go forth at once," she cried gaily, and sprang into her saddle. The knight hastily fastened on his armour, and, placing a blood-red cross upon his breast, swung himself onto his horse's back. And so they rode over the plain, a trusty dwarf following far behind, and a snow-white lamb, held by a golden cord, trotting by Una's side.

After some hours they left the plain and entered a

forest, where the trees and bushes grew so thick that no path could they see. At first, in their eagerness to escape the storm which was sweeping up the plain behind them, they hardly took heed where they were going; and besides, the beauty of the flowers and the sweet scent of the fruit caused them to forget the trouble they would have to find the road again. But when the sound of the thunder ceased, and the lightning no longer darted through the leaves, they were startled to perceive they had wandered they knew not whither. No sun could they see to show them which was east and which west, neither was there any man to tell them what they fain would know. At length they stopped, for before them lay a cave stretching far away into the darkness.

"We can rest there this night," said the Red Cross Knight, leaping to the ground, and handing his spear to the dwarf, "and first, you, lady, shall remain here, while I enter and make sure that no fierce or loathsome beasts lurk in the corners." But Una turned pale as she listened.

"The perils of this place I better know than you," she answered gravely. "In this den dwells a vile monster, hated by God and man." And the voice of the dwarf cried also, "Fly, fly! This is no place for living men." They might have spared their warnings; when did youth ever heed them? The knight looked into the cave, and:

Forth into the darksome hole he went.
His glistering armour made a little glooming light,
By which he saw the ugly monster plain,
Half like a serpent horribly displayed,

The other half did woman's shape retain.

It was too late to turn back, even had he wished it; but indeed it was the monster who looked round, as if to find a way to flee. Before her stood the knight, his sword drawn, waiting for a fair chance to plunge it into her throat. Escape there was none, and she prepared for battle.

The knight fought valiantly, but never had he met a foe like this. The monster was so large and so scaly that he could not get round her, while his sword glanced, blunted, from off her skin. Blow after blow he struck, but they only served to increase her fury, till, gathering all her strength together, she wound her great tail about his body, pressing him close against her horny bosom.

"Strangle her, else she sure will strangle thee," cried Una, who had been watching the combat as well as the darkness would let her; and the knight heard, and seized the monster by the throat, till she was forced to let go her hold on him. Then, grasping his sword, he cut her head clean from her body.

Fain would they now leave the dreadful wood which had been the nurse of such an evil creature, and by following a track where the leaves grew less thickly, they at last found themselves on the other side of the plain, just as the sun was sinking to rest. They pushed on fast, hoping to find a shelter for the night, but none could they spy. The plain seemed bare, save for one old man in the guise of a hermit who was approaching them.

Him the Red Cross Knight stopped and asked if he knew of any adventures which might await him in that place. The old man, who was in truth the magician Archimago, the professor of lore which could read the secrets of men's hearts, answered that the hour was late for the undertaking of such things, and bade them rest for the night in his cell hard by. So saying, he led them into a little dell amidst a group of trees, in which stood a chapel and the dwelling of the hermit.

It was but a short space before both knight and lady were sleeping soundly on the beds of fern which the hermit told them he had always at hand for the entertainment of guests. But, for himself, he crept unseen to a little cave inside a rock, and taking out his magic books he sought therein for mighty charms to trouble sleepy minds!

He soon found what he wanted, and repeated some strange words aloud. In an instant there fluttered round him a crowd of little sprites awaiting his bidding, but he motioned all aside except two – one of whom he kept with him, and the other he sent on a message to the house of Morpheus, the god of sleep.

"I come from Archimago the wizard," said the sprite when he reached his journey's end. "Give me, I pray you, as swiftly as may be, a bad dream, that I may carry it back to him."

Slowly the god rose up, and, going to his storehouse, where lay dreams of all sorts – dreams to make people happy, dreams to make people miserable, dreams to stir people to good, and dreams to move them to every kind of wickedness – he took from the shelf a small but very black little dream, which the sprite tied round his neck, and hurried to the cave of Archimago.

The wizard took the dream in silence, and, going

into the den where the knight was sleeping, laid it softly on his forehead. In a moment his face clouded over; evil thoughts of Una sprang into his mind, till at length, unable to bear any longer the grief of mistrusting her he so loved and honoured, the knight called to the dwarf to bring him his horse, and together they rode away. But when Una woke and found both of her companions departed she wept sorely. Then, mounting her milk-white ass, she set out to follow them.

Meanwhile the Red Cross Knight was wandering he knew not whither, so deep were the wounds in his heart. He rode on with his bridle hanging loosely on his horse's neck, till a bend in the path brought him face to face with a mighty Saracen, bearing on his arm a shield with the words "Sans foy" written across it. By his side, mounted on a palfrey hung with golden bells, was a lady clad in scarlet robes embroidered with jewels, who chattered merrily as they passed along.

It was she who first perceived the approach of an enemy, and turning to Sansfoy, bade him begin the attack. He, nothing loth, dashed forward to meet the knight, who had barely time to steady himself to receive the blow, which caused him to reel in his saddle. The blow was indeed so hard that it would have pierced the knight's armour had it not been for the cross upon his breast; which, when the Saracen saw, he cursed the power of the holy emblem, and prepared himself for a fresh attack.

But either the Christian knight was the more skilful swordsman, or the cross lent new strength to his arm, for the fight was not a long one. Only a few strokes had passed between them, when the boastful Sansfoy fell from his horse, and rolled heavily to the ground. The lady hardly waited for the issue of the combat, and galloped off lest she too should be in danger. But the knight did not wage war on ladies, and, calling to the dwarf to bring the Saracen's shield as a trophy, he spurred quickly after her.

He did not take long to come up with her for, in truth, she intended to be overtaken, and turned a woeful countenance to the young knight, who listened, believing, to the false tale she told. Pitying her from his heart, he assured her of his care and protection, and while they are faring through the woods together, let us see what had become of Una.

The maiden was herself wandering distraught, seated on her "unhastie beast", when with a fearful roar a lion rushed out from a thicket with eyes glaring and teeth gleaming, seeking to devour his prey. But at the sight of Una's tender beauty he stopped suddenly, and, stooping down, he kissed her feet and licked her hands.

At this kindness on the part of the great creature, Una bent her head and wept grievously. "He, my lion and my noble lord, how does he find it in his cruel heart to hate her that him loved?" she moaned sadly, and the lion again looked pityingly at her, and at last the maiden checked her sobs and bade her ass go on, the lion walking by her side during the day, and sleeping at her feet by night.

They had travelled far and for many days, through a wilderness untrodden by either man or beast, when at the foot of a mountain they spied a damsel bearing on her shoulder a pot of water. At sight of the lion she flung down the pitcher, and ran to the hut where she dwelt, without once looking behind her. In the cottage sat her blind mother, not knowing what could be the meaning of the shrieks and cries uttered by her daughter, who shut the door quickly after her, and caught trembling hold of her mother's hands.

It was the first lion the girl had ever seen, or she would have known that if he was determined to enter, it was not a wicket-gate that would prevent him. As neither mother nor daughter replied to Una's gentle prayer for a night's lodging, her "unruly page" put his paw on the little door, which opened with a crash. The maiden then stepped softly over the threshold, begging afresh that she might pass the night in one corner, and receiving no answer – for the women were still too terrified to speak – she curled herself up on the earthen floor with the lion beside her.

About midnight there arrived at the door, which Una had refastened, a thief laden with spoils of churches, and whatever else he had managed to pick up by stealth. To spend the night in thieving was his custom, and hither he brought his spoils, as he thought none would suspect a blind woman and her daughter of harbouring stolen goods.

Many times he called, but the two women were in grievous dread of the lion, and durst not move from the corner where they were crouching; at last the man grew angry, and burst the door asunder, as the lion had done before him. He entered the hut, and straightway beheld the dreadful beast, with glaring eyes and gleaming teeth, as Una had first beheld him. But Kirkrapine (such was his name) had neither beauty nor goodness to still the lion's rage, and in another moment his body was rent in a thousand pieces.

The sun had scarce sent his first beams above the horizon when Una left the hut, mounted on her ass, and, followed by the lion, again began her quest of the Red Cross Knight. But, alas! Though she found him not, she met her ancient foe, the magician Archimago, who had taken on himself the form of him whom she sought. Too true and unsuspecting was she, to dream of guile in others, and the welcome she gave him was from her whole heart. In the guise of the knight, Archimago greeted her fondly, and bade her tell him the story of her woes, and how came she to take the lion for her companion. And so they journeyed, the flowers seeming sweeter and the skies brighter to Una, as they went, when suddenly they beheld:

One pricking towards them with hasty heat;
Full strongly armed, and on a courser free.

On his shield the words "Sans loy" could be read, written in letters of blood.

Now, though Archimago had clad himself in the outward shape of the Red Cross Knight, he lacked his courage and his skill in war, and his heart was faint from fear, when the Saracen reined back his horse and prepared for battle. In the shock of the rush the wizard was borne backwards, and the blood from his side dyed the ground.

"The life that from Sansfoy thou tookest, Sansloy shall from thee take," cried the Paynim, and was unlacing the vizor of the fallen man to deal him his death-stroke when a cry from Una stayed his hand for a moment, though it was not her prayers for mercy that would have kept him from drawing his sword, but the sight of the hoary head beneath the helmet, which startled him.

"Archimago!" he stammered, "what mishap is this?" And still Archimago lay on the ground stunned, and answered nothing.

For a moment Una gazed in amazement at the strange sight before her, and wondered what was the meaning of these things. Then she turned to fly, but, quick as thought, the Saracen plucked at her robe to stop her.

Now when the lion, her fierce servant, saw that Paynim knight lay hands on his sovereign lady, he sprang on him with gaping jaws, and almost tore the shield from his arm. But the knight leapt swiftly back, and swinging his sword plunged it into the heart of the faithful creature, who rolled over and died amidst the tears of his mistress.

After which the knight set Una on his steed before him and bore her away.

While Una was riding through forest and over plains, with her faithful lion for her guard, the knight whom she sought had given himself over into the care of Duessa (for such was the name of Sansfoy's companion), by whom he was led to the gates of a splendid palace. The broad road up to it was worn by the feet of hosts of travellers; but though many peeped through the doors few returned. As the knight stood aside and watched, all manner of strange people passed before him, though none spoke. At length a man, but newly issued from the palace, and bearing a shield with the words "Sans joy" written across it, stopped suddenly in front of the knight's page, then snatched from his arm a shield like his own, bearing the name "Sansfoy". The page, overcome by the quickness of the action, did not resist, but a blow on the helmet from the Red Cross Knight made Sansjoy stagger where he stood.

The fight was fierce, and no one could tell with whom the victory lay till the queen of that place came by, and bade them cease their brawling, for on the morrow they should meet in the lists.

But the battle next day went against the Paynim, in spite of the presence of the queen and the counsel of the false Duessa. Short would have been his shrift had not thick darkness fallen about him, and when the Red Cross Knight cried to him to begin the fray afresh, only silence answered him.

Then the false Duessa, ever wont to take the side of him who wins, hurried up to him, and whispered, as she had whispered to Sansjoy, "The conquest yours, I yours, the shield and glory yours," but the knight did not heed her, for his eye was ever bent on the wall of thick darkness which shut in his foe. Indeed, so busy were his thoughts that he never knew that blood was streaming from his wounds, till the queen ordered him to be carried into the palace, and ointments to be laid on his body.

As was her custom, Duessa talked much and loudly of the care she would give him, and of his speedy cure under her hands; but when night fell she stole forth and came to the spot where Sansjoy lay, still covered with the enchanted cloud. Then, in an iron chariot, borrowed from the Queen of Darkness, she drove him down to the underworld, and across the river which divides the kingdom of the living from that of the dead. Here giving him into the hands of the oldest and greatest of physicians, she went her way to the bedside of the Red Cross Knight.

But for all that concerned that knight she might well have stayed in the kingdom of darkness; for in her absence the dwarf, wandering through the palace, had come upon a dungeon full of wretched captives, who filled the air with their wailings.

Filled with fear, the dwarf hastened back to his master and prayed him to flee that place before the sun rose. Which the young knight gladly did, creeping away through a secret postern, though it was hard to find a footing amidst the corpses piled up on all sides, which had come to a bad end by reason of their own folly.

And what had become of Una when she had fallen into the power of Sansloy? Well, trembling she had followed him into the midst of a forest, where, to her wonder, from every bush sprang a host of fauns and people of the wood, and ran towards her. When the Saracen beheld them, he was so distraught with fear that he galloped right away, leaving Una behind him. But she, not knowing what to fear the most, stood shaking with dread, till the wood folk pressed around her, and, kneeling on the ground stroked lovingly her hands and feet. Then she understood that she was safe amongst them, and let them lead her where they would, and smiled at their songs and merry dances. If she could not be with the Red Cross Knight, then it mattered little where she was, and it gave her a feeling of rest and safety to lie hidden among the woods, with a people who would let nothing harmful come near her.

So she stayed with them long, and taught them many things, while they in their turn showed her how to play on their pipes and to dance the prettiest and most graceful of their dances.

Time passed in this wise, when one day it chanced that a noble knight, Satyrane by name, came to seek his kindred among the wood folk. He wondered greatly to find so lovely a maid among them, and still more to see how eagerly they listened to her teachings, and henceforth he formed part of the throng that sat at her feet when the heat of the day was over.

In this manner Una and the knight Satyrane soon became friends, and at length one day she poured out all her sad tale, and besought his help in her search for the Red Cross Knight. It was not easy to escape from the kind people who always thronged about her, and her heart was sore at the thought of leaving them, but she felt that for her captive parents' sake, as well as for the knight's, she could delay no longer.

Therefore one morning, when the wood folk had gone to hold a feast in the forest, she rode away in company with Satyrane, and issuing from the forest soon reached the open plain. Towards evening they met a weary pilgrim, whose clothes were worn and soiled, and so true a pilgrim did he look, that Una did not know him to be the wizard Archimago. The knight instantly drew rein, and asked what tidings he could impart, and Una begged with faltering voice that he would tell her aught concerning a knight whose armour bore a red cross.

"Alas! dear dame," answered he slowly, "these eyes did see that knight, both living and eke dead," and with that he told her all his story.

When he had finished, it was Satyrane who spoke.

"Where is that Paynim's son, that him of life, and us of joy hath reft?" And the pilgrim made answer that he was hard by, washing his wounds at a fountain.

Satyrane wasted no more words, but went right straight to the fountain, where he found Sansloy, whom he challenged instantly to fight. Sansloy hastily buckled on his armour, and cried that, though he had not slain the Red Cross Knight, he hoped to lay his champion in the dust. Then, both combatants being ready, the battle began.

The sight was too dreadful for Una to bear, and she galloped away, not knowing that her deadliest foe, the wizard Archimago, was following her.

Meanwhile Duessa had left the splendid palace, and was riding over the country in pursuit of the Red Cross Knight, for it was bitter to her to see any escape, who had ever been under her thrall. Her good fortune, which never seemed to forsake her, before long led her to his side, where he lay resting on the banks of a stream, and he greeted her gladly.

The sun was hot, and the water rippling clear over the stones seemed inviting. The knight was tired, and leaned down to drink, never knowing that the stream was enchanted. But in a moment his strength seemed to fail, and his arms grew weak as a child's, though he felt nothing till a horrible bellowing sounded in the wood. At the dreadful sound he started up and looked around for his armour, but before he could reach it a hideous giant was upon him.

The fight did not take long, and in a short while the Red Cross Knight was a prisoner in the hands of the giant, who, accompanied by the false Duessa, carried his captive to a dungeon of his castle. After the door was safely locked and barred, the two then retired into the large hall, where they ate and made merry.

From that day the giant brought forth his choicest treasures with which to deck Duessa. Her robes were purple, and a triple crown of gold was on her head, and, what she liked not so well, he gave her a seven-headed serpent to ride on.

Now the faithful dwarf had watched the fate of his master, and when he saw him borne away senseless by the giant, he took up the armour which had been lain aside in the hour of need, and set out he knew not whither.

He had gone but a little distance when he met Una, who read at a glance the evil tidings he had brought. She fell off her ass in a deadly swoon, and the dwarf, whose heart was nigh as sore, rubbed her temples with water and strove to bring her back to life. But when she heard the tale of all that had befallen the Red Cross Knight since last she had parted from him, she would fain have died, till the thought sprang suddenly into her mind that perhaps she might still rescue him. So with fresh hope she took the road to the giant's castle, but the way was far, and she was woefully tired before even its towers were in sight. Brave though she was, the maiden's courage failed her at last, and she began to weep afresh, when her eyes happened to light upon a good knight riding to meet her. He was clad in armour that shone more than any man's, and well it might, as it had been welded by the great enchanter Merlin. On the crest of his helmet a golden dragon spread his wings: and in the centre of his breast-plate a precious stone shone forth amidst a circle of smaller ones, "like Hesperus among the lesser lights."

As he drew near, and saw before him a lady in distress, he reined in his horse, and with gentle words drew from her all her trouble.

"Be of good cheer," he said, when the tale was ended, "and take comfort; for never will I forsake you till I have freed your captive knight."

And, though she knew him not, at his promise Una took heart of grace, and bade the dwarf lead them to the giant's castle.

Conducted by the dwarf and followed by the squire, the knight and lady soon reached the castle. Bidding Una to await him outside, and calling to his squire to come with him, they both walked up to the gates, which were fast shut, though no man was guarding them.

"Blow your horn," said the knight, and the squire blew a blast. At the sound, the gates flew open, and the giant came foaming from his chamber to see what insolent thief had dared disturb his peace.

And the giant did not come alone. Close after him rode Duessa, "high mounted on her many-headed beast," and at this sight the knight raised his shield and eagerly began the attack.

But, horrible though the serpent was, he was not the sole foe that the knight had to fight with. The giant's only weapon was his club, but that was as thick as a man's body, and studded with iron points besides. Luckily for the knight, this was not the first giant to whom he had given battle, and ere the mighty blow could fall he sprang lightly to one side, and the club lay buried so deep in the ground that before the giant could draw it out again, his left arm was smitten off by the knight's sword.

The giant's roars of pain might have been heard in the uttermost parts of the kingdom, and Duessa quickly guided her baleful beast to the help of her wounded friend. But her way was barred by the squire, who, sword in hand, "stood like a bulwark" between his lord and the serpent. Duessa, full of wrath at being foiled, turned the serpent on him, but not one foot would the squire move till, beside herself with anger, the witch drew out her cup and sprinkled him with the poisonous water. Then the strength went out of his arms and the courage from his heart, and he sank helpless on the ground before the snake, who fain would have trampled the life out of him, and it would have fared ill with him had not the knight rushed swiftly to his rescue, and dealt the snake such a wound that the garments of Duessa were all soaked in blood. She shrieked to the giant that she would be lost if he did not come to her aid, and the giant, whose one arm seemed to have gained the strength of two, struck the knight such a blow on the helmet that he sank heavily on the ground.

The giant raised a shout of joy, but he triumphed too soon. The knight, in falling, caught the covering of his shield upon his spear, and rent it from top to toe. The brilliance that flowed from it burnt into the eyes of the giant, so that he was "blinded by excess of light", and sank sightless on the ground. At a fresh cry from Duessa he struggled to his feet, but all in vain. He had no power to hurt nor to defend, and fell back so heavily that the very earth shook beneath him, and was an easy prey for his foe, who smote his head from his body.

Duessa, as we know, never stayed with those with whom the world went ill, and she was stealing away quietly, when once more the squire stopped her.

"You are captive to my lord," he said, and, holding her firmly, led her back.

Then Una came running full of grateful words, but when she saw Duessa a cloud of fierce wrath passed over her face.

"Beware lest that wicked woman escape," cried she, "for she it is who has worked all this ill, and thrown my dearest lord into the dungeon. Oh, hear how piteously he calls to you for aid!"

"I give her into your keeping," answered the knight, turning to the squire, "and beware of her wiles, for they are many." And, leaving the rest behind him, he strode into the castle, meeting no man as he went.

At last there crept forth from one corner an old, old man with a huge bunch of rusty keys hanging from his arm. The knight asked him in gentle speech whence had gone all the people who dwelt in the castle, but he answered only that he could not tell, till the knight waxed impatient, and took the keys from him.

The doors of all the rooms opened easily enough, and inside he found the strangest medley. Everywhere blood lay thick upon the floors, while the walls were covered with cloth of gold and splendid tapestry. No signs were there of any living creature, yet he knew that in some hiding-place in the castle the captive lay concealed.

The knight had come to the last door of all. It was of iron, and no key on the bunch would open it. On one side was a little grating, and through it he called loudly, lest perchance any man might hear his voice.

At that there answered him a hollow empty sound, and for a while he could not make out any words. Then from out the wailing in the darkness something spoke, "Oh, who is that which brings me happy choice of death? Three moons have waxed and waned since I beheld the face of heaven. Oh, welcome, welcome art thou who hast come to end my weary life!"

The moaning sound of the voice thrilled the brave champion with horror. Putting his shoulder to the iron door, he gave a mighty heave, and the hinges gave way. Nothing could he see, for the darkness was terrible, and his foot, which he stretched cautiously inward, touched no floor. And, besides, the foul smells rushed out, poisoning him with their fumes.

But when he had grown in some measure used to the darkness and the odours, he began to think how he could best deliver the Red Cross Knight from the pit into which he had fallen. To this end he sought through the castle till he found some lengths of rope, which he carried back with him, as he did not know how deep the pit might be. He knotted three or four together and let the rope down, but even when a faint cry from the captive told him that it had reached the bottom, his labours were not ended yet. Twice the knots gave way, by good fortune, before the man was more than a foot or two from the ground, and other pieces of rope had to be fetched. Then, when all was made fast, the prisoner had grown so weak that he could scarce draw himself up; and again the knight feared greatly lest he himself should not have strength to hold fast the rope. But at length his courage and patience prevailed, and the Red Cross Knight, hollow-eyed, and thin as a skeleton, looked once more upon the sun.

His parents might have gazed on him and not known him for their child, but Una's heart leapt when the unknown knight brought him to her.

"Welcome," she said, "welcome in weal or woe. Your presence I have lacked for many a day," and fain would she have heard the tale of his sufferings, had not the knight, who knew that men love not to speak of their sorrows, begged her to tend the captive carefully, so that his forces might come to him again. Further, he bade them remember that they had in their power the woman who had been the cause of all their grief, and the time had come to give sentence on her.

"I cannot slay her, now she is mine to slay," answered Una, "but strip her robe of scarlet from off her, and let her go whither she will."

With her robes and her jewels went all the magic arts that gave her youth and beauty. Instead of the dazzling maiden who had wrought so much havoc in the world, there stood before them an old bald-headed shaking crone, that seemed as ancient as the earth itself. Silently they gazed, then turned away in horror, while Duessa wandered into paths of which she alone knew the ending.

It was not until they had rested themselves awhile in the castle that the stranger knight told who he was and why he came there. He was, he said, Arthur, the ward of Merlin, and had ridden far and long in quest of the Faerie Queen. And having fulfilled his vow to Una, in delivering the Red Cross Knight out of the power of the giant, he bade both farewell, leaving behind him, as a remembrance of their friendship, a diamond box containing a precious ointment, which would cure any wound, however deep or poisonous.

So they parted, but not yet was the Red Cross Knight able to face the monstrous dragon who held captive Una's royal parents. Luckily she knew of a house not far off where they would be made welcome for as long as they chose to stay. Hither they fared, and for many weeks the knight's armour was laid away, and the ladies who dwelt in that place gave him all the strength and counsel that they could think of. Then, when at last he had become what he had been of yore, Una bade farewell to her hosts with great thanks, and set out for the royal castle. After three days the walls of a high tower might be seen dimly across the plain.

"It is there that my parents are kept imprisoned by the dragon," said Una, pointing to it with her hand, "and I see the watchman watching for good tidings, if happily such there be. Ah, he has waited long!"

As she spoke, a roaring hideous sound was heard that seemed to shake the ground and to fill all the air with terror. Turning their heads, they beheld on their right a huge dragon, lying stretched upon the sunny side of a great hill, himself like a great hill. But no sooner did he see the shining armour of the knight than he roused himself and made ready for battle.

Hastily the Red Cross Knight bade Una withdraw herself to another hill, from which she could see the fight without herself being in danger. Crouching behind a rock, she watched the dreadful beast approaching, half flying and half walking as he went. Run he could not, his size was too vast.

Her heart sank as she looked, for how could mortal man get the better of such a creature! Besides the brazen scales which thickly covered his body, his wings were like two sails, and at the tip of each huge feather was a many-pronged claw; while his back was hidden with the folds of his tail, which lay doubled in a hundred coils, and in his mouth were three rows of sharp-pointed teeth. Una could look no more; she shut her eyes and waited.

The knight felt that if he was to win the victory at all it must be by means of his lightness of foot, as the monster was so large he could not turn himself about quickly. So, getting a little behind his head, he tried to pierce his neck between the scaly plates, but the spear glanced off harmlessly, and a stroke from the tip of the tail laid both him and his horse on the ground.

They rose again instantly, and returned to the charge, but a second blow met with no better fate. Then the dragon in wrath spread wide his sails and rose heavily above the earth, till, suddenly and swiftly darting down his head, he snatched both horse and man off the ground. But here the knight had the advantage, for with his spear he stung the beast so sore that the monster speedily set his captives again on the earth.

Not giving the dragon time to gather himself up, the knight dealt him a blow under the left wing. With a roar of agony, the beast snapped the spear asunder with his claws and pulled out the head. At that a sea of blood gushed from the wound which would have turned a water-mill, and in his pain and rage flames of fire gushed from his mouth.

Unwinding his tail from his back, he coiled it like lightning about the legs of the horse, which fell to the ground with his rider. But in an instant the knight was on his feet, and by the mere force of his blows forced his enemy to reel, though the brazen scales were still unpierced. Though his courage was as great as ever, the young man began to lose patience, when of a sudden he noticed that the monster could no longer rise into the air by reason of his wounded wing. That sight gave him heart, and he drew near once more, only to be scorched by the deadly fire from the dragon's jaws. Half blinded and suffocated, he staggered, which the dragon seeing, he dealt the knight such a blow that he fell backwards into a well that lay behind.

"So that is the end of him," said the dragon to himself; but, if he had only known, it was the beginning, for the well into which the knight had fallen was the well of life, which could cure all hurts and heal all wounds.

All night Una watched at her post, for darkness had come before the knight received his final blow. In the morning, before the sun had risen above the plain, she was looking for the knight, who was lying she knew not where. Her eyes dropping by chance on the well, she was sore amazed to see him rise out of it fairer and mightier than before. With a rush he fell upon the dragon, who had gone to sleep, safe in the knowledge of his victory, and, taking his sword in both hands, he drove right through the brazen scales, and wounded him deep in his skull. In vain did the monster roar and struggle; the blows rained thick and fast, and most of his tail was cut from his body.

Again and again the knight was overthrown, and again and again he rose to his feet, and laid about him as valiantly as ever. But while the fight was still hanging in the balance, the dragon thrust his head forward with wide-open jaws, thinking to swallow his enemy and make an end of him. Quick as thought the knight sprang aside, and, thrusting his sword in the yawning gulf up to the hilt, gave the dragon his death-blow.

Down he fell, fire and smoke gushing from his nostrils – down he fell, and men thought some mighty mountain must have cast up rocks on the earth.

The victor himself trembled, and it was long ere Una dared draw near, dreading lest the direful fiend should stir. But when as last she knew him dead, she came joyfully forth, and, bursting into happy tears, faltered her gratitude for the good he had wrought her.

There is little more to be told of Una and the Red Cross Knight.

The watchman on the wall, who had seen the dreadful battle, was the first to tell the king and queen that the dragon was dead and that they were free. Then the king commanded the trumpets to sound and the people to assemble, so that fitting rejoicings might be made at the destruction of their foe.

This being done, a mighty procession came down, headed by the king and queen, to lay laurel boughs at the feet of the victor, and to set a garland of bay on the head of the maiden. Once more Duessa and Archimago sought to prevent the betrothal of the Red Cross Knight and Una by a plot to send the wizard in the guise of a messenger, proclaiming the knight to have been already bound to the daughter of the emperor, but the false tale was easily seen through, and Archimago thrown into a dungeon.

After that the king himself performed the marriage rite, and a solemn feast was held through the land, but the wedded pair were not long left together. A vow the knight had made when he received his spurs to do the Faerie Queen six years of service called him from Una's side, and, sad though the parting might be, both held their word too high ever to break it.

Based on The Faerie Queene *by Edmund Spenser and adapted by Mrs Andrew Lang.*

WHAT THE CAT TOLD ME

DIANA WYNNE JONES

I AM A CAT. I am a cat like anything. Keep stroking me. I came in here because I knew you were good at stroking. But put your knees together so I can sit properly, front paws under. That's better. Now keep stroking, don't forget to rub my ears, and I will purr and tell.

I am going to tell you how I came to be so very old. When I was a kitten, humans dressed differently and they had great stamping horses to pull their cars and buses. The old man in the house where I lived used to light a hissing gas on the wall when it got dark. He wore a long black coat. The Boy who was nice to me wore shabby breeches that only came to his knees, and he mostly went without shoes, just like me. We slept in a cupboard under the stairs, Boy and I. We kept one another warm. We kept one another fed, too, later on. The old man did not like cats or boys. He only kept us because we were useful.

I was more useful than Boy. I had to sit in a five-pointed star. Then Boy would help old man mix things that smoked and made me sneeze. I had to sneeze three times. After that things happened. Sometimes big purple cloud things came and sat beside me in the star. Fur stood up on me and I spat, but the things only went away when Old Man hit the star with his stick and told them "*Begone*!" in a loud voice. At other times the things that came were small, real things you could hit with your paw: boxes, or strings of shiny stones no one could eat, or bright rings that fell *tink* beside me out of nowhere. I did not mind those things. The things I really hated were the third kind. Those came inside me and used my mouth to speak. They were nasty things with hateful thoughts, and they made *me* hateful. And my mouth does not like to speak. It ached afterwards and my tongue and throat were so sore that I could not wash the hatefulness off me for hours.

I so hated those inside-speaking things that I used to run away and hide when I saw Old Man drawing the star on the cellar floor. I am good at hiding. Sometimes it took Boy half the day to find me. Then Old Man would shout and curse and hit Boy and call him a fool. Boy cried at night in the cupboard afterwards. I did not like that, so after a while I scratched Old Man instead. I knew none of it was Boy's fault. Boy made Old Man give me nice things to eat after I had sat in the star. He said it was the only way to get me to sit there.

Boy was clever, you see. Old Man thought he was a fool, but Boy told me – at night in the cupboard – that he only pretended to be stupid. Boy was an orphan like me. Old Man had bought him for a shilling from a baby-farmer ages before I was even a kitten, because his hair was orange, like the ginger patches on me, and that is supposed to be a good colour for magic. Old

Man paid a whole farthing for me, for much the same reason, because I am brindled. And Boy had been with Old Man ever since, learning things. It was not only magic that Boy learnt. Old Man was away quite a lot when Boy was small. Boy used to read Old Man's books in the room upstairs, and the newspapers, and anything else he could find. He told me he wanted to learn magic in order to escape from Old Man, and he learnt the other things so that he could manage in the wide world when he did escape; but he had been a prisoner in the house for years now and, although he knew a great deal, he still could not break the spell Old Man had put on him to keep him inside the house. "And I really hate him," Boy said to me, "because of the cat before you. I want to stop him doing any more magic before I leave."

And I said—

What was that? How could Boy and I talk together? Do you think I am a stupid cat, or something? I am nearly as clever as Boy. How do you think I am telling you all this? Let me roll over. My stomach needs rubbing. Oh, you rub well! I really like you. Well – no, let me sit up again now – I think the talking must be something to do with those inside-speaking things. When I was a kitten, I could understand what people said of course, but I couldn't do it back, not at first, until I had been lived in and spoken through by quite a lot of Things. Boy thought they stretched my mind. And I was clever to start with, not like the cat before me.

Old Man killed the cat before me somehow. Boy would not tell me how. It was a stupid cat, he said, but he loved it. After he told me that, I would not go near Boy for a whole day. It was not just that I was nervous about being killed too. How *could* he love any cat that wasn't *me*? Boy caught me a pigeon off the roof, but I still wouldn't speak to him. So he stole me a saucer of milk and swore he would make sure Old Man didn't kill me too. He liked me a lot better than the other cat, he said, because I was clever. Anyway, Old Man killed the other cat doing magic he would not be able to work again without a certain special powder. Besides, the other cat was black and did not look as interesting as me.

After Boy had told me of a lot of things like this, I put my nose to his nose and we were friends again. We made a conspiracy – that was what Boy called it – and swore to defeat Old Man and escape somehow. But we could not find out how to do it. We thought and thought. In the end I stopped growing because of the strain and worry. Boy said no, it was because I was full grown. I said, "Why, in that case, are *you* still growing? You're already more than ten times my size. You're nearly as big as Old Man!"

"I know," said Boy. "You're an elegant little cat. I don't think I shall be elegant until I'm six feet tall, and maybe not even then. I'm so clumsy. And *so* hungry!"

Poor Boy. He did grow so, around then. He did not seem to know his own size from one day to the next. When he rolled over in the cupboard he either squashed me or he burst out into the hallway. I had to scratch him quite hard, several nights, or he would have smothered me. And he kept knocking things over when he was awake. He spilt the milk jug – which I didn't mind at all – and he kicked Old Man's magic tripod by accident and smashed six jars of smelly stuff. Old Man cursed and called Boy a fool, worse than ever. And I think Boy really was stupid then, because he was so hungry. Old Man was too mean to give him more to eat. Boy ate my food, so I was hungry too. He said he couldn't help it.

I went on the roof and caught pigeons. Boy roasted them over the gaslight at night when Old Man was asleep. Delicious. But the bones made me sick in the corner. We hid the feathers in the cupboard and, after I had caught a great many pigeons, night after night, the cupboard began to get warm. Boy began to get his mind back. But he still grew and he was still hungry. By the time I had stopped growing for a year, Boy was so big his breeches went right up his legs and his legs went all hairy. Old Man couldn't hit him any more then, because Boy just put out a long, long arm and held Old Man off.

"I need more clothes," he told Old Man.

Old Man grumbled and protested, but at last said, "Oh, all right, you damn scarecrow. I'll see what I can do." He went unwillingly down into the cellar and heaved up one of the flagstones there. He wouldn't let me look in the hole, but I know that what was under that flagstone was Old Man's collection of all the rings and shiny stones that came from nowhere when I sat in the five-pointed star. I saw Old Man take some chinking things out. Then he slammed down the stone and went away upstairs, not noticing that one shiny thing had spilled out and gone rolling across the floor.

It was a little golden ball. It was fun. I chased it for hours. I patted it and it rolled, and I pounced, and it ran away all round the cellar. Then it spoiled the fun by rolling down a crack between two flagstones and getting lost. Then I found I was shut in the cellar and had to make a great noise to be let out.

That reminds me – does your house have balls in it? Then buy me one tomorrow. Until then, a piece of paper on some string will do.

Where was I? Oh yes. Someone came and let me out, smelling of mildew. I nearly didn't know Boy at first. He had a red coat and white breeches and long black boots on, all rather too big for him. He said it was an old soldier's uniform Old Man had picked up cheap, and how did I get shut in the cellar?

I sat round his neck and told him about the flagstone where Old Man kept his shinies. Boy was *very* interested. "That would buy an awful lot of food," he said. He was still hungry. "We'll take it with us when we escape. Let's try escaping next time he works magic."

So that night we made a proper plan at last. We decided to summon a Good Spirit, instead of the hateful things Old Man always fetched. "There must be *some* good ones," Boy said. But since we didn't know enough to summon a good one on our own, we had to make Old Man do it for us somehow.

We did it the very next day. I played up wonderfully. As soon as Old Man started to draw on the cellar floor, I ran away, so that Old Man would not suspect us. I dug my claws hard into Boy's coat when he caught me, so that Old Man could hardly pull me loose. And I scratched Old Man, very badly, so that there was blood, when he put me inside the pointed star. Then I sat there, humped and sulky, and it was Boy's turn.

Boy did rather well too. At first he was just the usual kind of clumsy, and kicked some black powder into some red powder while they were putting it out in heaps, and the cellar filled with white soot. It was hard not to sneeze too soon, but I managed not to. I managed to hold the sneeze off until Old Man had done swearing at Boy and begun on the next bit, the mumbling. Then I sneezed – once. Boy promptly fell against the tripod, which dripped hot stuff on the spilt powder. The cellar filled with big purple bubbles. They drifted and shone and bobbed most enticingly. I would have loved to chase them, but I knew I mustn't, or we would spoil what we were doing. Old Man couldn't leave off his mumbling, because that would spoil the spell, but he glared at Boy through the bubbles. I sneezed again – two – to distract him. Old Man raised his stick and began on the chanting bit. And Boy pretended to trip and, as he did, he threw a fistful of powder he had ready into the gaslight.

Whup! it went.

Old Man jumped and glared, and went on grimly chanting – he had to, you see, because you can't stop magic once you have started – and all the bubbles drifted to the floor and burst. *Smicker, smicker*, very softly. As each one burst, there was a little tiny pink animal on the floor, running about and calling "Oink, oink, oink!" in small squeaky voices. That nearly distracted me, as well as Old Man. I stared out at them with longing. I would have given *worlds* to jump out of the star and chase those beasties. They looked so beautifully *eatable*! But I knew I mustn't try to come out of the star yet, so I shut my eyes and yawned to hold in the third sneeze and thought hard, hard, hard of a Good Thing. *Let a Good Thing come!* I thought. I thought as hard as you do when you see a saucer of milk held in the air above you, and you want them to put it on the floor – quick. Then I gave my third sneeze.

That reminds me. Milk? Yes, please, or I won't be able to tell you any more.

Thank you. Keep your knee steady. You may stroke me if you wish. Where was I?

Right. When I opened my eyes all the delicious beauties had vanished and the light burnt sort of dingily. Old Man was beating Boy over the head with his stick. He could do that for once, because Boy was crouched by the wall laughing until his face ran tears. "Pigs!" he said. "Tiny little pigs! Oh, oh, oh!"

"I'll pig *you!*" Old Man screamed. "You spoilt my spell! Look at the pentangle – there's nothing there at all!"

But there was. I could feel the new Thing inside me. It wasn't hateful at all, but it felt lost, and a bit feeble. It was too scared to say or do anything, or even let me move, until Old Man crossly broke the pentangle and stumped away upstairs.

Boy stood rubbing his head. "Pity it didn't work, Brindle," he said. "But wasn't it worth it, just for those pigs!"

"Master," the Good Thing said with my mouth. "Master, how can I serve you, bound as I am?"

Boy stared, and his face went odd colours. I always wonder how you humans manage that. "Good Lord!" he said. "Did we do it after all? Or is it a demon?"

"I don't think I'm a demon," Good Thing said doubtfully. "I may be some kind of spirit. I'm not sure."

"Can't you get out of me?" I said to it in my head.

"No. Our master would not be able to hear me if I did," it told me.

"Bother you then!" I said, and started to wash.

"You can serve me anyway, whatever you are," Boy said to Good Thing. "Get me some food."

"Yes, Master," it made me say, and obeyed at once. I had just reached that stage of washing where you have one foot high in the air. I fell over. It was most annoying. Next minute, I was rolling about in a huge room full of people cooking things. A kitchen, Boy said it was later. It smelt marvellous. I hardly minded at all when Good Thing made me leap up and snatch a roast leg of mutton from the nearest table. But I did mind – a lot – when two men in white hats rushed at me shouting, "*Damn cat!*"

Good Thing didn't know what to do about that at all, and it nearly got us caught. "Let *me* handle this!" I spat at it, and it did. I told you, it was a bit feeble. I dived under a big dresser where people couldn't reach me and crouched there right at the back by the wall. It was a pity I had to leave the meat behind. It smelt wonderful. But I had to leave it, or they'd have gone on chasing me. "Now," I said, when my coat had settled flat again, "you tell me what you want me to take and I'll take it properly this time."

Good Thing agreed that might work better. We

waited until they'd all gone back to cooking and then slunk softly out into the room again. And Good Thing had been thinking all this time. It made me a sort of invisible sack. It was most peculiar. No one could see the sack, not even me, and it didn't get in my way at all. I just knew it was behind me, filling up with the food I stole. Good Thing made me take stuff I'd never have dreamed of eating myself, like cinnamon jelly and – yuk! – cucumber, as well as good honest meat and venison pie and other reasonable things.

Then we were suddenly back in the cellar, where Boy was glumly clearing up. When he saw the food spilling out on to the floor, his face lit up. Good Thing had been right. He loved the jelly and even ate cucumber. For once in his life he really had enough to eat. I helped him eat the venison pie and we both had strawberries and cream to finish with. I love those.

Which reminds me – Oh, strawberries are out of season? Never mind. I'll stay with you until they come back in. Rub my stomach again.

I was heavy and kind of round after that meal. Good Thing complained rather. "Well, get out of me then and it won't bother you," I said. I wanted to sleep.

"In a minute," it said. "Master, the cat tells me you want to escape, but I'm afraid I can't help you there."

Boy woke up in dismay. He was dropping off to sleep on the floor, being so full. "Why *not?*"

"Two reasons," Good Thing said apologetically. "First, there is a very strong spell on you, which confines you to this house, and it is beyond my power to break it. Second, there is an equally strong spell on me. You and the cat broke part of it, the part which confined me to a small golden ball, but I am still forced to stay in the house where the golden ball is. The only other place I can go is the house I – came from."

"Damn!" said Boy. "I did hope—"

"The spell that confines the cat is nothing like so strong," Good Thing said. "I could raise that for you."

"That's something at least! Do that," said Boy. He was a generous Boy. "And if you two could keep on fetching food, so that I can put my mind to something besides how hungry I am, then I might think of a way to break the spell on you and me." I was a little annoyed. It seemed that we had got Good Thing just because the golden ball had escaped from Old Man, and not because of Boy's cleverness or my powers of thought. But though I knew the ball was down a crack just inside the place where Old Man usually drew his pentangle, I didn't mention it to Boy in case his feelings were hurt too.

We had great good times for quite a long while after that, Boy, Good Thing and I, and Old Man never suspected at all. He was away a lot round then anyway. While he was away, there were always a jug of milk and a loaf that appeared magically every four days, but Boy and I would have half-starved on that without Good Thing. Good Thing took me to the kitchen-place every day at supper time and we came back with every kind of food in the invisible sack. When Good Thing was not around – it quite often went away in the night and left me in peace – I went out across the roofs. I led a lovely extra life on top of the town. I met other cats by moonlight, but they were never as clever as me. I found out all sorts of things and came and told them to Boy. He was always very wistful about not being able to go out himself, but he listened to everything. He was like that. He was my friend. And he was a great comfort to me when I had my first kittens. I didn't know what was happening to me. Boy guessed and he told me. Then he told me that we must hide the kittens or Old Man would know I had been able to get out. We were very secret and hid them in our cupboard in a nest of pigeon feathers.

I am good at having kittens. I'll show you presently. I always have three, one tabby, one ginger, and one mixed like me. I had three kittens then, and Old Man never knew, even though they were quite noisy sometimes, especially after I taught them how to play with Good Thing.

When Good Thing came out of me, I could see it quite well, though Boy never could. It was quite big outside me, up to Boy's shoulder, and frail and wafty, and it could float about at great speed. It enjoyed playing. I used to hunt it all round the house and leap on it, pretending to tear it to bits – and of course it would waft away between my paws. Boy used to guess where Good Thing was from my behaviour and laugh at me hunting it. He laughed even more when my kittens were old enough to play hunting Good Thing too.

By this time, Boy was a fine strong boy, full of thoughts, and his soldier clothes were getting too short and tight. He asked Good Thing to get him some more clothes next time Old Man was away. So Good Thing and I went to another part of the mansion where the kitchen was. Boy said "house" was the wrong word for that place. He was right. It was big and grand. This time when we got there, we went sneaking at a run up a great stair covered with red carpet – or I went sneaking with Good Thing inside me – and along more carpet to a large room with curtains all round the walls. The curtains had pictures that Good Thing said were lords and ladies hunting animals with birds and horses. I never knew that *birds* were any help to people.

There was a space between the curtains and the walls, and Good Thing sent me sneaking through that space, around the room. There were people in the room. I peeped at them through a crack in the curtains.

There was a very fine Man there, almost as tall and fine as my Boy, but much older. With him were two of the ones in white hats from the kitchen. They held their hats in their hands, sorrowfully. With them was a Woman in long clothes, looking cross as Old Man.

"Yes indeed, sir, I saw this cat for myself, sir," the Woman said. "It stole a cake under my very eyes, sir."

"I swear to you, sir," one of the white hats said, "it appears every evening and vanishes like magic with every kind of food."

"It *is* magic, that's why," said the other white hat.

"Then we had better take steps to see where it comes from," the fine Man said. "If I give you this—"

Good Thing wouldn't let me stay to hear more. We ran on. "Oh dear!" Good Thing said in my head as we ran. "We'll have to be very careful after this!" We came to a room that was white and gold, with mirrors. Good Thing wouldn't let me watch myself in the mirrors. The white and gold walls were all cupboards filled with clothes hanging or lying inside. We stuffed the invisible sack as full as it would hold with clothes from the cupboards, so that we would not need to go back. For once it felt heavy. I was glad to get back to Boy waiting in Old Man's room.

"Great Scott!" said Boy as the fine coats, good boots, silk shirts, cravats and smooth trousers tumbled out on to the floor. "I can't wear these. These are fit for a king! The Old Man would be bound to notice." But he could not resist trying some of them on, all the same. Good Thing told me he looked good. I thought Boy looked far finer than the Man they belonged to.

After this, Boy became very curious about the mansion where the clothes and the food came from. He made me describe everything. Then he asked Good Thing, "Are there books in this mansion too?"

"And pictures and jewels," Good Thing said through me. "What does Master wish me to fetch? There is a golden harp, a musical box like a bird, a—"

"Just books," said Boy. "I need to learn. I'm still so ignorant."

Good Thing always obeyed Boy. The next night, instead of going to the kitchen, Good Thing took me to a vast room with a round ceiling held up by freckled pillars, where the walls were lined with books in shelves. Good Thing had one of its helpless turns there. "Which do you think our Master wants?" it asked me feebly.

"*I* don't know," I said. "I'm only a cat. Let's just take all we can carry. I want to get back to my kittens."

So we took everything out of one shelf, and it was not right. Boy said he did not need twenty-four copies of the Bible: one was enough. The same went for Shakespeare. And he could not read Greek, he said. I spat. But we gathered up all the books except two and went back.

We had just spilt all the books on the floor of the room with the freckled pillars, when the big door burst open. The Man came striding in, with a crowd of others. "There's the cat now!" they all cried out.

Good Thing had me snatch another book at random and we went.

"And I daren't go back for a while, Master," Good Thing said to Boy.

I saw to my kittens, then I went out hunting. I fed Boy for the next few days – when he remembered to eat, that was. I stole a leg of lamb from an inn, a string of sausages from the butcher down the road, and a loaf and some buns from the baker. The kittens ate most of it. Boy was reading. He sat in his fine clothes and he read, the Bible first, then Shakespeare, and then the book of history Good Thing had made me snatch. He said he was educating himself. It was as if he were asleep. When Old Man suddenly came back, I had to dig all my claws into Boy to make him notice.

Old Man looked grumpily round everywhere to make sure everything was in order. He was always suspicious. I was scared. I made Good Thing stay with the kittens in the cupboard and hid the remains of the sausages in there with them. Boy was all dreamy, but he sat on the book of history to hide it. Old Man looked at him, hard. I was scared again. Surely Old Man would notice that Boy's red coat was of fine warm cloth and that there was a silk shirt underneath. But Old Man said, "Stupid as ever, I see," and grumped out of the house again.

Talking of sausages, when do you eat? Soon? Good. No, go on stroking.

The next day, Old Man was still away. Boy said, "Those were wonderful books. I must have *more*. I wish I didn't have to trust a cat and a spirit to steal them. Isn't there *any* way I can go and choose books for myself?"

Good Thing drifted about the house, thinking. At last it got into me and said, "There is no way I can take you to the mansion bodily, Master. But if you can go into a trance, I can take you there in spirit. Would that do?"

"Perfectly!" said Boy.

"Oh no," I said. "If you do, I'm coming too. I don't trust you on your own with my Boy, Good Thing. You might go feeble and lose him."

"I will *not!*" said Good Thing. "But you may come if you wish. And we will wait till the middle of the night, please. We don't want you to be seen again."

Around midnight Boy cheerfully went into a trance. Usually he hated it when Old Man made him do it. And we went to the mansion again, all three of us. It was very odd. I could see Boy there the way I could see Good Thing, like a big, flimsy cloud. As soon as we were there, Boy was so astonished by the grandeur of it that he insisted on drifting all round it, upstairs and down, to see as much as he could. I was scared. Not everyone was asleep. There were gaslights or candles burning in most of the corridors, and someone could easily have seen me. But I stuck close to Boy because I was afraid Good Thing would lose him.

It was not easy to stay close. They could go through doors without opening them. When they went through one door upstairs, I had to jump up and work the handle in order to follow Boy inside. It was a pretty room. The quilt on the bed was a cat's dream of comfort. I jumped up and padded on it, while Boy and Good Thing hovered to look at the person asleep there. She was lit up by the nightlight beside the bed.

What a lovely girl! I felt Boy think. *She must be a princess.*

She sat up at that. I think it was because of me treading on her stomach. I went tumbling away backwards, which annoyed me a good deal. She stared. I glowered and wondered whether to spit. "Oh!" she said. "You're that magic cat my father wants to catch. Come here, puss. I promise I won't let him hurt you." She held out her hand. She was nice. She knew how to stroke a cat, just like you do. I let her stroke me and talk to me, and I was just curling up to enjoy a rest on her beautiful quilt, when a huge Woman sprang up from a bed on the other side of the room.

"Were you calling, my Lady?" she asked. Then she saw me. She screamed. She ran to a rope hanging in one corner and heaved at it, screaming, "*That cat's back!*"

"Run!" Good Thing said to me. "I'll look after Boy."

So I ran. I have never run like that in my life, before or since. It felt as if everyone in the mansion was after me. Luckily for me, I knew my way round quite well by then. I ran upstairs and I ran down, and people clattered after me, shouting. I dived under someone's hands and dodged through a crooked cupboard place, and at last I found myself behind the curtains in the Man's room. He ran in and out. Other people ran in and out, but the Princess really had done something to help me somehow and not one of them thought of looking behind those curtains.

After a bit I heard the Princess in that room too. "But it's a *nice* cat, Father – really sweet. I can't think why you're making all this fuss about it!" Then there was a sort of grating sound. I smelt the smallest whiff of fresh air. Bless her, she had opened the Man's window for me.

I got out of it as soon as the room was empty. I climbed down on to grass. I ran again. I knew just the way I should go. Cats do, you know, particularly when they have kittens waiting for them. I was dead tired when I got to Old Man's house. It was right on the other side of town. As I scrambled through the skylight in the roof, I was almost too tired to move. But I was dead worried about my kittens and about Boy too. It was morning by then.

My kittens were fine, but Boy was still lying on the floor of the bookroom in a trance, cold as ice. And, as if that were not enough, keys grated in the locks and Old Man came back. All I could think to do was to lie round Boy's neck to warm him.

Old Man came back and kicked Boy. "Lazy lump!" he said. "Anyone would think you were in a trance!" I couldn't think what to do. I got up and hurried about, mewing for milk, to distract Old Man. He wasn't distracted. Looking gleefully at Boy, he carefully put a jar of black powder away in his cupboard and locked it. Then he sat down and looked at one of his books, not bothering with me at all. He kept looking across at Boy.

My kittens distracted Old Man by having a fight in the cupboard about the last of the sausages. Old Man heard it and leapt up. "Scrambling and squeaking!" he said. "Mice! Could even be rats by the noise. Damn cat! Don't you ever do your job?" He hit at me with his stick.

I tried to run. Oh, I was tired! I made for the stairs, to take us both away from Boy and my kittens, and Old Man caught me by my tail halfway up. I was that tired. I was forced to bite him quite hard and scratch his face. He dropped me with a thump, so he probably did not hear the even louder thump from the bookroom. I did. I ran back there.

Boy was sitting up, shivering. There was a pile of books beside him.

"Good Thing!" I said. "That was stupid!"

"Sorry," said Good Thing. "He would insist on bringing them." The books vanished into the invisible sack just as Old Man stormed in.

He ranted and grumbled at Boy for laziness and for feeding me so that I didn't catch mice, and he made Boy set mouse-traps. Then he stormed off to the cellar.

"Why didn't you come back sooner?" I said to Boy.

"It was too marvellous being somewhere that wasn't this house," Boy said. He was all dreamy with it. He didn't even read his new books. He paced about. So did I. I realized that my kittens were not safe from Old Man. And if he found them, he would realize that I could get out of the house. Maybe he would kill me like the cat before. I was scared. I wished Boy would be scared too. I wished Good Thing would show some sense. But Good Thing was only thinking of pleasing Boy.

"Don't let him go into a trance again," I said. "Old Man will know."

"But I *have* to!" Boy shouted. "I'm *sick* of this house!" Then he calmed down and thought. "I know," he said to Good Thing. "Fetch the princess here."

Good Thing got into me and bleated that this wasn't wise, now Old Man was back. I said so, too. But Boy wouldn't listen. He had to have Princess. Or else he would go into a trance and see her that way. I understood then. Boy wanted kittens. Very little will stop boys or cats when they do.

So we gave in. When Old Man was asleep and snoring, Boy dressed himself in the middle of the night in the Man's finest clothes and looked fine as fine. He even washed in horrible cold water, in spite of all I said. Then Good Thing went to the mansion.

Instants later, Princess was lying asleep on the floor of the bookroom. "Oh," Boy said sorrowfully. "What a shame to wake her!" But he woke her up all the same.

She rubbed her eyes and stared at him. "Who are you, sir?"

Boy said, "Oh, Princess—"

She said, "I think you've made a mistake, sir. I'm not a princess. Are you a prince?"

Boy explained who he was and all about himself, and she explained that her father was a rich magician. She was a disappointment to him, she said, because she could hardly do any magic and was not very clever. But Boy still called her Princess. She said she would call him Orange because of his hair. She may not have been clever, but she was nice. I sat on her knee and purred. She stroked me and talked to Boy for the whole night, until it began to get light. They did nothing but talk. I said to Good Thing that it was a funny way to have kittens. Good Thing was not happy. Princess did not understand about Good Thing. Boy gave up trying to explain. Good Thing drifted about sulking.

When it was really light, Princess said she must go back. Boy agreed, but they put it off and kept talking. That was when I had my good idea. I went to the cupboard and fetched out my kittens, one by one, and put them into Princess's lap.

"Oh!" she said. "What beauties!"

"Tell her she's to keep them and look after them," I said to Boy.

He told her, and she said, "Brindle can't *mean* it! It seems such a sacrifice. Tell her it's *sweet* of her, but I *can't*."

"Make her take them," I said. "Tell her they're a present from you, if it makes her happier. Tell her they're a sign that she'll see you again. Tell her anything, but make her take them!"

So Boy told her and Princess agreed. She gathered the tabby and the ginger and the mixed kitten into her hands and Good Thing took her and the kittens away. We stood staring at the place where she had been, Boy and I. Things felt empty, but I was pleased. My kittens were safe from Old Man now, and Princess had kittens now, which ought to have pleased Boy, even if they were mine and not his. I did not understand why he looked so sad.

Old Man was standing in the doorway behind us. We had not heard him getting up. He glared at the fine way Boy was dressed. "How did you come by those clothes?"

"I did a spell," Boy said airily. Well, it was true in a way. Boy's mood changed when he realized how clever we had been. He said, "And Brindle got rid of the mice," and laughed.

Old Man was always annoyed when Boy laughed. "Funny, is it?" he snarled. "For that, you can go down to the cellar, you and your finery, and stay there till I tell you to come out." And he put one of his spells on Boy, so that Boy had to go. Old Man locked the cellar door on him. Then he turned back, rubbing his hands and laughing too. "Last laugh's mine!" he said. "I *thought* he knew more than he let on, but there's no harm done. I've still got him!" He went and looked in almanacs and horoscopes and chuckled more. Boy was eighteen that day. Old Man began looking up spells, lots of them, from the bad black books that even he rarely touched.

"Brindle," said Good Thing, "I am afraid. Do one thing for me."

"Leave a cat in peace!" I said. "I need to sleep."

Good Thing said, "Boy will soon be dead and I will be shut out for ever unless you help."

"But my kittens are safe," I said, and I curled up in the cupboard.

"They will not be safe," said Good Thing, "unless you do this for me."

"Do what for you?" I said. I was scared again, but I stretched as if I didn't care. I do *not* like to be bullied. You should remember that.

"Go to the cellar in my invisible sack and tell Boy where the golden ball is," Good Thing said. "Tell him to fetch it out of the floor and give it to you."

I stretched again and strolled past Old Man. His face was scratched all over, I was glad to see, but he was collecting things to work spells with now. I strolled quite fast to the cellar door. There Good Thing scooped me up, and we went inside, in near-dark. Boy was sitting against the wall.

"Nice of you to come," he said. "Will Good Thing fetch Princess again tonight?" He did not think there was any danger. He was used to Old Man behaving like this. But I thought of my kittens. I showed him the place where the golden ball had got lost down the crack. I could see it shining down there. It took me ages to persuade Boy to dig it out, and even then he only worked at it idly, thinking of Princess. He could only get at it with one little finger, which made it almost too difficult for him to bother.

I heard Old Man coming downstairs. I am ashamed to say that I bit Boy, quite hard, on the thumb of the hand he was digging with. He went "*Ow!*" and jerked, and the ball flew rolling into a corner. I raced after it.

"Put it in your mouth. Hide it!" said Good Thing.

I did. It was hard not to swallow it. Then when I didn't swallow, it was hard not to spit it out. Cats are made to do one or the other. I had to pretend it was a piece of meat I was taking to my kittens. I sat in the corner, in the dark, while Old Man came in and locked the door and lit the tripod lamp.

"If you need Brindle," Boy said, sulkily sucking his hand, "*you* can look for her. She bit me."

"This doesn't need a cat," Old Man said. Boy and I were both astonished. "It just needs *you*," he told Boy. "This is the life-transfer spell I was trying on the black cat. This time, I know how to get it right."

"But you said you couldn't do it without a special powder!" Boy said.

Old Man giggled. "What do you think I've been away looking for all this year?" he asked. "I've got a whole jar of it! With it, I shall put myself into your body and you into my body, and then I shall kill this old body off. I won't need it or you after that. I shall be young and handsome and I shall live for years. Stand up. Get into the pentangle."

"Blowed if I shall!" said Boy.

But Old Man did spells and made him. It took a long time, because Boy resisted even harder than I usually did, and shouted spells back. In the end, Old Man cast a spell that made Boy stand still and drew the five-pointed star round him, not in the usual place.

"I shall kill my old body with you inside it rather slowly for that," he said to Boy. Then he drew another star, a short way off. "This is for my bride," he said, giggling again. "I took her into my power ten years ago, and by now she'll be a lovely young woman." Then he drew a third star, overlapping Boy's, for himself, and stood in it, chuckling. "Let it start!" he cried out, and threw the strong, smelly black powder on the tripod. Everything went green-dark. When the green went, Princess was standing in the empty star.

"Oh, it's *you!*" she and Boy both said. "Ahah!" said Old Man. "He-hee! So you and she know one another, do you? How you did it, boy, I won't inquire, but it makes things much easier for me." He began on his chanting.

"Give the golden ball to Princess," Good Thing said to me. "Hurry. Make Boy tell her to swallow it."

I ran across to Princess and spat the golden ball into her star. She pulled her skirt back from it.

"Brindle wants you to swallow it," Boy said. "I think it's important."

People are peculiar. Princess must have known it was very important, but she said faintly, "I can't! Not something that's been in a cat's *mouth!*"

Old Man saw the golden ball. He glared, still chanting, and raised his stick. The ball floated up and came towards him. Princess gave a last despairing snatch and caught it, just in time. She put it in her mouth.

"Ah! Back again!" said Good Thing.

Princess swallowed. She changed. She had been nice before, but sort of stupid. Now she was nice and clever as Boy. "You toad!" she said to Old Man. "That was part of my soul! You took it, didn't you?"

Old Man raised his stick again. Princess held up both hands. Magic raged, strong enough to make my fur stand up, and Old Man did not seem to be able to do much at first. It was interesting. Princess had magic too, only I think it had all gone into Good Thing. But not quite enough. She started to lose. "Help me!" she said to Boy.

Boy started to say a spell, but, at that moment, the

door of the cellar burst open, and half the wall fell in with it. The Man rushed in with a crowd of others.

"Father!" said Princess. "Thank goodness!"

"Are you all right?" said the Man. "We traced you through those kittens. What are you trying to do here, Old Man? The life-transfer, is it? Well, that's enough of *that!*" The Man made signs that stood my coat up on end again.

Old Man screamed. I could tell he was dying. The spell had somehow turned back on him. He was withering and shrinking and getting older and older. Boy jumped out of his star and ran to Princess. They both looked very happy. Old Man snarled at them, but he could do nothing but round on me. Everyone does that. They all kick the cat when they can't kick a person. "So you had *kittens!*" he screamed. "This is all your fault, cat! For that, you shall have kittens to drown for the next thousand years!"

"I soften that curse!" the Man shouted.

Then everything went away and I was not in the town I knew any more. I have been wandering about, all these years, ever since. Old Man's curse means that I am good at having kittens. It is not a bad curse, because the Man has softened it. Old Man meant my kittens to be drowned every time. But instead, if I can find an understanding person – like you – who will listen to my story, then my kittens will have a good home, and so will I for a time. You won't mind. They'll be beautiful kittens. They always are. You'll see very soon now. After supper.

ACKNOWLEDGEMENTS

The publisher would like to thank the copyright holders for permission to reproduce the following copyright material:

Joan Aiken: Victor Gollancz for "'Who Goes Down This Dark Road?" from *A Touch of Chill* by Joan Aiken (Gollancz 1979). Copyright © Joan Aiken Enterprises Ltd 1979. **K. M. Briggs:** A. P. Watt Ltd on behalf of Katharine Law for the extract from *Hobberdy Dick* by K. M. Briggs (Puffin 1972). Copyright © K. M. Briggs 1955. **Elizabeth Goudge:** David Higham Associates for the extract from *Henrietta's House* by Elizabeth Goudge (Duckworth & Co. Ltd 1968). Copyright © Elizabeth Goudge 1968. **Brothers Grimm:** Random House UK Ltd and Verlag Carl Ueberreuter GmbH for "The Peasant and the Devil" from *Grimms' Fairy Tales* (Jonathan Cape 1962). **Eva Ibbotson:** Pan Macmillan Children's Books, a division of Pan Macmillan Ltd, for the extract from *Which Witch?* by Eva Ibbotson (Macmillan 1979). Copyright © Eva Ibbotson 1979. **Tove Jansson:** A. & C. Black (Publishers) Ltd for the extract from *Finn Family Moomintroll* by Tove Jansson (Ernest Benn Ltd 1950). Copyright © Tove Jansson. **Norton Juster:** HarperCollins Publishers Ltd and Random House Inc. for the extract from *The Phantom Tollbooth* by Norton Juster (Collins 1962). Copyright © Norton Juster 1961. **Noel Langley:** David Higham Associates Ltd for the extract from *The Land of Green Ginger* by Noel Langley, published in Puffin Books 1966. Copyright © Noel Langley 1966, 1975. **C. S. Lewis:** HarperCollins Publishers Ltd for the extract from *The Silver Chair* by C. S. Lewis (HarperCollins). Copyright © C. S. Lewis 1953. **John Masefield:** The Society of Authors as the literary representative of the Estate of John Masefield for the extract from *The Box of Delights* (Heinemann 1935). Copyright © John Masefield 1935. **Andre Norton:** Putnam Berkeley Group, Inc. for "Ully the Piper" from *High Sorcery* by Andre Norton (Ace Books). Copyright © Andre Norton 1970. **Patricia C. Wrede:** Valerie Smith Literary Agent for the extract from *The Seven Towers* by Patricia C. Wrede (Ace Fantasy Books). Copyright © Patricia C. Wrede 1984. **Diana Wynne Jones:** Diana Wynne Jones and Laura Cecil Literary Agency for "What the Cat Told Me" by Diana Wynne Jones. Copyright © Diana Wynne Jones 1993. **Jane Yolen:** Curtis Brown Ltd, New York, for "Boris Chernevsky's Hands" from *Hecate's Cauldron* by Jane Yolen (DAW Books). Copyright © Jane Yolen 1982.

Every effort has been made to obtain permission to reproduce copyright material but there may be cases where we have been unable to trace a copyright holder. The publisher will be happy to correct any omissions in future printings.